"Stop it," Gina hissed at Josh

"Stop what?" Josh asked, putting on an expression that was pure fake.

"There are no cameras here the way there were on the show. You don't have to pretend." Thank goodness the aspirin was kicking in. The throbbing in her head had subsided to a dull ache.

"Pretend? Me?"

"Yes, you."

"And what am I pretending?" His eyes took on a devilish gleam as he treated himself to a long, languorous lick of ice cream. A runnel of it dripped down his wrist and Gina imagined licking it off. She made herself look away.

"That you—that you…" Words failed her. She averted her eyes, no longer angry. She was exhausted, though. Anger could do that to a person.

"That I'm fascinated by you," he said simply….

Dear Reader,

Most of us, at one time or another, have been dumped by a guy we cared about. Me, too. It wasn't in front of millions of people, as happened to Gina Angelini, the heroine of this book. But it still hurt.

Oh, you say. I remember what that's like. It was awful.

I know, my friend. I know.

So there I was, after my own personal experience, watching one of those television reality shows where a handsome bachelor chooses one out of many fabulous women to continue a relationship. The choice was down to two. One was in love with him; the other didn't seem to be. But guess who he chose? Not the one who loved him.

Afterward I felt so sorry for the one whose heart was broken, because I knew exactly how she felt. I started thinking, what if? What if this guy lives to regret his choice?

Thus the idea for *Heard It Through the Grapevine* was conceived. I wanted that girl to get the guy eventually, so that's what happens to Gina. She goes home, gets on with her life and then…the man who dumped her turns up and wants to make amends.

In fiction we can right past wrongs. We can make things turn out happily ever after. That's not always true of real life, but guess what? It happens sometimes.

You know the guy who broke up with me? I eventually married him. Yes, really. And when I watched the TV show that gave me the idea for this book, he was right there beside me. He said, "You could write a book about this."

And I did.

With love and best wishes,

Pamela Browning

HEARD IT THROUGH THE GRAPEVINE

Pamela Browning

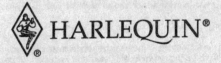

HARLEQUIN®

TORONTO • NEW YORK • LONDON
AMSTERDAM • PARIS • SYDNEY • HAMBURG
STOCKHOLM • ATHENS • TOKYO • MILAN • MADRID
PRAGUE • WARSAW • BUDAPEST • AUCKLAND

For Alix, the never-to-be-forgotten frog princess,
with wishes for her present and future happiness;
and for Bethany, with thanks for her technical advice.

ISBN 0-373-75043-9

HEARD IT THROUGH THE GRAPEVINE

Copyright © 2004 by Pamela Browning.

ABOUT THE AUTHOR

Unlike her heroine in *Heard It Through the Grapevine*, Pamela Browning has never been on a reality-TV show, but she once was a contestant on *Jeopardy!*

She divides her time between homes in Florida and the North Carolina mountains, but enjoys visiting her relatives in California's Napa Valley once or twice a year.

Pam invites you to visit her Web site at www.pamelabrowning.com.

Books by Pamela Browning

HARLEQUIN AMERICAN ROMANCE
854—BABY CHRISTMAS
874—COWBOY WITH A SECRET
907—PREGNANT AND INCOGNITO
922—RANCHER'S DOUBLE DILEMMA
982—COWBOY ENCHANTMENT
994—BABY ENCHANTMENT
1039—HEARD IT THROUGH THE GRAPEVINE

Don't miss any of our special offers. Write to us at the following address for information on our newest releases.

Harlequin Reader Service
U.S.: 3010 Walden Ave., P.O. Box 1325, Buffalo, NY 14269
Canadian: P.O. Box 609, Fort Erie, Ont. L2A 5X3

Chapter One

The last tourist bus had lumbered out of the Good Thymes parking lot, and Gina Angelini narrowed her eyes at the broad-shouldered guy lurking behind the display of dried sunflowers. At first she thought that maybe he'd missed the bus, but a glance out the window revealed a snazzy BMW parked under the olive tree. It shouldn't be there. That morning she had posted a neatly lettered sign on the front door notifying customers that her herb shop was closing early today.

"Ah-choo!"

The man's sneeze startled her so that she almost dropped the tray of dried rosemary that she was removing from the sales floor. "Bless you," she said distractedly before carefully setting the tray down beside the cash register.

"Thank you," said her last customer. He emerged slowly from behind the sunflowers and favored her with a brilliant smile. Gina felt her jaw drop, and she grasped the edge of the counter for support. She knew this man. She knew him only too well. But what was he doing in Good Thymes? And two years after he'd dumped her?

"Get out," she said as soon as she regained her voice. Unfortunately, this wasn't before she registered that broad chest, those wide shoulders, the blue eyes that sparkled in pleasure as he gave her a quick and appreciative once-over.

He cocked a skeptical eyebrow and stuck his hands deep

in his pockets as he leaned against a table holding vases of lavender. "So, Gina, I guess you still love me," he said.

She charged toward him past the goldenseal, the chamomile, the valerian. A pot of chives sat close at hand, and she could have thrown it at him. Instead she showed remarkable restraint, considering that he'd humiliated her in front of millions of people on national TV.

"Wrong," she said. "It's not the first misjudgment you've made, either."

"I had my reasons for choosing Tahoma," he said. "Maybe you'd like to hear them." It didn't help that he looked as if he'd stepped right out of *Gentleman's Quarterly.* The blazer was Armani, Gina was sure, and his Italian leather loafers were polished to a high gloss.

She turned her back on him with all the determination she could muster, considering that she didn't trust him not to pounce. There was a certain tigerish quality contained in Joshua Corbett's well-groomed, well-mannered personage, which was probably why he'd been chosen to be Mr. Moneybags on the reality-TV show. That's where Gina had met him, thanks to her overzealous cousin Rocco, who had submitted her name to a contestant search unbeknownst to her.

"I don't want to hear anything you have to say," she said, stalking back to the cash register and taking refuge behind the counter. She'd never thought she'd set eyes on him again, and though she never let him know it, she was seriously rattled, so much so that she was trembling.

"Maybe you should," he said mildly. "It might be a good idea to have this conversation outside, if you don't mind." He sneezed again.

"I don't love you, I don't like you, and what are you doing here in the Napa Valley, anyway?" It seemed like a logical question, since he used to live in Boston.

"I happened to be in the neighborhood and came to see if you're married and have a couple of kids," he said, moving closer and hitching himself onto a stool nearby.

"She isn't married, and that's why she doesn't have children," said a little voice from beneath the counter. A curly red head popped up. The moppet to whom it belonged stared at him curiously for a moment before breaking into a wide gap-toothed grin.

Gina wondered if it was too late to clap a hand over her niece's mouth. Probably it was, and anyhow, she'd done her own share of talking.

"Who are you?" Josh asked.

"Mia Suzanne Sorise. My favorite color is purple, I love lasagna, and I live next door. Who are you?" she asked, abandoning the hidey hole under the counter where she had staked out the cat's old bed as a good place to read the latest Harry Potter book.

"I'm Josh Corbett," he said, smiling as Gina rolled her eyes in disbelief. She'd watched as he'd charmed twenty contestants vying for his affection on *Mr. Moneybags,* and now he was charming her own nine-year-old niece.

Mia's eyes grew even rounder. "Ooh, you're the guy who dumped my aunt Gina," she said.

"I wish you wouldn't put it that way," Josh said, a pained expression flitting across his features.

Mia leaned her elbows on the counter and studied Josh. "Why didn't you pick her?" she asked. "My aunt Gina is really a very nice person."

"No argument there," Josh said with a faint smile.

"Ha!" Gina replied, reflecting that it was sometimes possible to be *too* nice. She pretended to stack papers and clip them together. She needed something to do if Josh insisted on eyeing her in that coolly appraising way of his. She wished she'd run a comb through her hair after picking up Mia from soccer practice. She wished she had worn something other than her old peasant blouse and a skirt that fell short of her knees.

Josh had the good grace to look uncomfortable. "Actually, there was a lot more to the situation than that."

"And less. Mia, you'd better finish that chapter you're reading. We need to go soon," Gina said. She sounded more confident than she felt.

"I already read it. I'm playing ticktacktoe now, but it's not much fun to play against yourself."

"I'm a great ticktacktoe player," Josh said.

"Good! You can play with me." Mia laboriously spread a grubby piece of notebook paper on the counter and handed Josh a pencil.

"How about a chance to explain," Josh asked Gina.

"When you play, do you like *X*s or *O*s?" Mia asked.

"*X*s will be fine," he said, but he was watching Gina expectantly. "Well?"

Despite the impending game, Gina decided against her better judgment to continue the conversation. "How about telling me why you were so insistent on showing me the heather back at Dunsmoor Castle? How about explaining what that—that procedure behind the pantry door meant?" She slapped the papers into a drawer beneath the cash register and slammed it, summoning up her recollection of the heather, which had been rippling gently in the breeze, and of Josh's eyes, which had been blue and sincere. They were still blue; it was his sincerity that was in doubt here.

"The heather was a planned date. The producers of the show set it up. I had a great time, though, didn't you? And the procedure behind the pantry door—it was a way to proceed, if you know what I mean." He nonchalantly entered an *X* in one of the ticktacktoe squares.

The procedure had been a kiss; only, Gina didn't want to say it in front of her niece, who could be counted upon to ask too many questions. In fact, on that night before his final choice of the twenty contestants, Josh had sought her, Gina, out and kissed her so tenderly and then so thoroughly that she'd known for sure that she would be the winner the next day. Wrong-o. He'd chosen the other semifinalist, a schemer named Tahoma. Gina found no consolation in the fact that according to one poll, seventy-eight percent of the viewing audience believed that Mr. Moneybags had made the wrong choice.

"The procedure was something you threw in to confuse people, including me," Gina said.

"Not exactly," Josh said seriously. "The only person I confused was myself. If you'd let me—"

"I'm not letting you do anything," Gina said pointedly.

"I won! I won!" Mia crowed. She grinned up at Josh. "Hey, you know what? I really like you."

"In that case, isn't there a consolation prize? Like dinner with your aunt?"

"No," said Mia. "But you could come to crush if you like."

"Crush?"

"You know, it's what we do after harvest. There's this really funny *I Love Lucy* show where Lucy and Ethel are in a big barrel stomping on grapes. It's like that."

Gina glanced at Josh to see how he was taking this.

"That's one of my favorite *I Love Lucy* episodes, but I thought they had machinery for squeezing the juice out of the grapes these days," he said to Mia.

"The stomping is just matrimonial," Mia replied.

Gina hastened to correct her. "*Ceremonial,* Mia. Wrong word."

"Ceremonial, then. Ooh, that's a good one to tell Frankie." Mia prided herself in collecting words to impress her eleven-year-old cousin. "Anyway, at our family's winery we have a grape-stomping contest. They don't use any of the stomped juice to make wine, though, because we stomp barefoot and that wouldn't be sanitary. They have crushers to get the juice out of the grapes for the wine that we make, and after that there's a whole lot of things they do to the grapes to make them into wine. My dad's the winemaker, so that's how I know all this. It's cool. Would you like to come to crush with us?" She gazed disingenuously up at Josh.

"I—" Josh began, but Gina had heard enough.

"He would *not* like," she said pointedly. "He has other things to do, I'm sure." To Josh, she added, "Did Tahoma come with you?"

"Tahoma?" he replied, wrinkling his forehead. "Why would she?"

"I thought you were in love with her. Why else would you toss me aside like yesterday's old salami?" Gina walked to the far end of the counter.

"Maybe because I really cared about you," Josh said with a determined air.

Gina indulged in a ladylike snort. "How could I not have known? Who would have thought?"

"Listen, Gina, I'd like a chance to talk it over."

Gina treated this statement with the stony silence it deserved.

Josh turned to Mia. "Crush sounds like so much fun that I'd like to go."

"Oh, it is." Mia's eyes sparkled up at him. She ducked under the counter and bobbed back up with the Harry Potter book, careful to mark her place with the ticktacktoe paper. "You can explain everything to Aunt Gina when we're at crush. You can't miss it. It's bad luck if someone doesn't go."

Gina set her straight. "That only applies to family members, Mia. It doesn't apply to people you've invited for no reason at all."

"But, Aunt Gina, I invited Josh because he likes *I Love Lucy*," Mia said, frowning. "My mom says that we can invite anyone to crush. She says it's hospital."

"I think you mean *hospitable*, Mia. It means making people welcome. And we don't have to show that kind of courtesy to Mr. Corbett."

"But, Gina, we're old friends," said Josh. "Doesn't that count for something?" He beamed the full wattage of his smile on Gina, who immediately steeled herself against his charm.

"We *were* friends," Gina corrected him. Turning her back on Josh, she said, "Mia, I have to run upstairs and get my jacket." The October day was cool, and the night might become chilly.

"Please hurry," Mia said. "We don't want to be late."

With one last scalding look over her shoulder at Josh, Gina ran up the stairs of the rustic stone cottage that served as both shop and living quarters. When she returned, Mia was pulling on her own sweater, a cable knit in bright purple.

"Now we can leave," Gina said.

"When you have a customer?" Josh asked plaintively.

"That's not what I would call you." For emphasis, she went to the door and flipped the Open sign so that it read Closed.

"I was going to buy—" he cast his gaze around wildly "—some sachets for my landlady."

"At this moment, nothing in here is for sale. We officially closed at noon. Are you ready to go, Mia?"

"Yes, and I can't wait to get there. Josh, you can ride in the front seat with Aunt Gina. We have to pick up Frankie 'cause his dad's helping to cook the barbecue."

"Oh, I forgot about Frankie," Gina said. Frankie was at his accordion lesson about a half mile away. She had no idea what to do about Josh short of a knock-down, drag-out argument, which didn't seem fair to Mia.

Shooting a go-eat-roadkill look in Josh's direction, Gina grabbed her keys and ushered Mia out of the shop in front of her, with Josh following along behind. She had probably no more than a minute to think of some tactic that would send Josh on his way. So far, nothing had occurred to her. Nothing legal, anyway. Murder was not an option, and neither was assault. She could only hope that he would take the hint and back off.

Her red-and-white 1966 Ford Galaxie convertible was

parked with its top down in its customary spot under the olive tree, and Mia climbed into the back seat.

"We could ride in my car," Josh said.

"There is no 'we' as far as you're concerned," Gina retorted. She started the car.

"I invited Josh," Mia piped in her clarion voice. "It would be rude to tell him he can't go."

Mia was into defining the differences between rude and polite these days, mostly because her parents emphasized good manners at their house. Gina, knowing this, wavered under the power of Mia's righteous and expectant gaze.

"I invited him," Mia repeated. Her voice was beginning to take on the aggrieved tone that preceded a bunch of difficult questions.

Gina exhaled and rolled her eyes. "Get in," she said to Josh, who beamed.

He opened the door and slid in beside her with the air of someone who expected to be included all along. "Nice car," he said.

She edged a glance toward the BMW parked near the door of the shop. "So is yours," she pointed out as she backed out and turned.

"It's rented," he said. "I flew in a couple of days ago and had to have wheels."

So he'd been here for a while and was only now getting around to saying hello? She could have taken offense at the delay if she cared anything about him. Which she most emphatically did not.

"Aunt Gina loves this car," Mia said, squeezing her head through the gap between the front seats and sending a whiff of Juicy Fruit their way. She chomped on the gum enthusiastically.

"Mia, dear, would you mind leaning back?" Gina said, trying not to sound as annoyed with her niece as she felt.

"It is a fine car," Josh said, taking in the restored upholstery, the gleaming knobs on the radio.

"My father bought it used when I was a kid," she said. She didn't add that she'd fallen in love with the Galaxie's style and elegance from the first moment that her father wheeled it into their driveway. "He always meant to restore it and give it to me, and after he died, I discovered that he'd put money aside for years for the restoration. My cousin Rocco volunteered to do the work." For a moment she had forgotten that she was talking to the man who'd broken her heart two years ago, and she fell silent as she headed down the bumpy road toward Vineyard Oaks, the winery that the Angelini family had owned ever since her grandfather, Gino, his brother and two sisters had bought it shortly after arriving in the United States sixty-seven years ago.

The vineyard, planted with merlot, sangiovese, petite syrah and zinfandel vines now stripped of their grapes, stretched out toward the distant mountain ranges on either side of the fertile valley. After a few minutes, Gina pulled the car over in front of a small house set back from the road, where Leo Buscani, retired Vineyard Oaks winemaker now accordion teacher, lived. A boy of eleven emerged, lugging an accordion case.

Mia bounced up and down. "That's Frankie. He's okay most of the time—for a boy, I mean. Get in back with me, Frankie. I'm being hos-*spit*-able."

Frankie balked. "You're going to *spit* on me?" he asked skeptically.

Mia dissolved into giggles. "That's my new word. It means making someone welcome."

Frankie chucked his accordion case in the back seat and climbed in after it. He was a captivating, curly-haired boy whose dark eyes snapped with merriment.

"Aunt Gina, Mr. Buscani says I'm the best student he's ever had," Frankie announced. "He wants me to join his accordion band."

Everyone in the family was pleased that Frankie, who possessed an aptitude for getting into trouble, had taken so well to the accordion. Gina glanced over her shoulder and smiled at him. "That's wonderful," she said.

"Do you think Pop will let me?"

"Oh, Rocco will probably go for it." Rocco and his son were closer than most, possibly because Frankie's mother had died when he was only six.

When Frankie and Mia settled into a spirited discussion about whether or not she should give him her last stick of gum, which Frankie argued was only hospitable, Josh turned to Gina. "You're more beautiful than ever," he said in a low tone.

The compliment discombobulated her more than she liked to let on. "Yeah, right," she said.

"I mean it, Gina."

"You shouldn't say things like that."

"Why shouldn't I? It's true."

Thanks to her Norwegian mother, Gina had grown up blond in a family of dark-haired, olive-skinned Italian-Americans, convinced that her light coloring wasn't attractive. She'd longed to resemble the rest of the family for most of her life, but the only features she seemed to owe to the Italian side of her family were dark eyes and tawny skin. These days, she could finally accept that men found her beautiful, but she wasn't in the mood to hear compliments from Joshua Corbett.

She kept her eyes focused forward. "You act as if nothing happened between us."

Josh slid a cagey look in her direction. "More should happen, don't you agree?"

She shook her head in disbelief. "Not if I can help it."

"Would it change things if I told you that I wasn't smart in the way I handled the *Mr. Moneybags* choice? That I realize it now? That I want to make amends?"

Gina bit back an exasperated retort. "Didn't it work out with Tahoma?"

Josh kept his eyes focused on the road ahead. "The woman

happened to be living with a boyfriend she never mentioned. After she walked away with the million dollars, I never heard from her again.''

"Bummer," Gina said, trying unsuccessfully to keep the sarcasm out of her voice. She'd never liked Tahoma much, though she'd been cordial to her for the sake of the show. The woman had pranced around the chilly Scottish castle where the show was filmed thrusting her silicone-enhanced chest in front of the ever-present video cameras while stuffed into dresses the size of cocktail napkins. It was a wonder she hadn't caught pneumonia.

"You live and you learn," Josh said philosophically.

"Did it ever occur to you that I might be angry about losing the million dollars I would have won if you'd chosen me?" Of course it hadn't; he was independently wealthy. The show's publicity had touted him as being the scion of a prominent Boston family. Gina seemed to recall pictures of a huge mansion and a family of bluebloods with ties to the *Mayflower*.

He appeared disconcerted. "If you'll recall, no one told me that the woman I chose would win that much money. I thought—"

"They told the contestants right at the start. You mean you didn't figure it out?" He had a Yale education, for Pete's sake.

"The million dollars for the winner was a total surprise to me. The first I knew about it was when the butler marched into the room carrying a check on a silver platter and handed it to Tahoma. If I'd caught onto that little secret, I'd have realized early in the game I couldn't trust anything the contestants told me."

"Did you trust what I told you?"

He took his time answering, and when he did it was with an air of thoughtfulness. "Whenever the conversation touched on the Napa Valley and your family, your eyes shone. You didn't promote yourself like some of the other contestants. You seemed sincere in everything you said. Of course I trusted you.''

She was touched that he'd recognized her sincerity; it was how she had determined to play the *Mr. Moneybags* game in the beginning, and she'd stuck to that decision even when it might not have been in her best interest. And she couldn't believe he recalled how longingly she'd spoken of home, family and her good fortune at having been born and reared in Rio Robles, California, population eight thousand, many of them Angelinis.

"I don't want to talk about it," she said. She'd trusted him, too, but she never would again. Why would she? He'd broken her heart.

"You brought the whole thing up," he reminded her in a mild tone. As she turned down the long driveway that led between the two rows of ancient oaks giving the Angelini winery its name, he changed the subject. It was just as well; she'd wallowed in her own disillusionment and pain for a long time before she'd managed to climb her way out of the miserable funk brought about by Josh's rejection.

"Is that the winery up there?"

They were crossing a narrow stone bridge and had begun the climb up the slope that led through several acres of vineyards. At the top of the hill was a large timber-and-stone barn housing the winery office, the tasting room and wine vats. From this angle, the doors to the wine cave in the hillside beyond were barely visible.

"Yes, this is Vineyard Oaks," she said, schooling her voice to sound dispassionate, trying not to think about how a million dollars would come in handy now that her family was looking for financing so they could buy the equipment they needed to keep the winery competitive. Of course, she'd wanted to use part of the prize money to fund the proposed new teen center, too, but that was another story and one that Joshua Corbett probably had no interest in hearing. Her failure to win that money had contributed more than a little to the anguish of the months immediately following her appearance on the show.

A low stone wall separated the parking area from the expanse of grass where tables were set up. As they got out of the car, Gina smelled the thick, sweet-sour aroma of harvested grapes, a familiar fragrance that would sweep over this valley until crush was over. She remembered that scent from her childhood when her parents would bring her to the annual celebration after the harvest and she and her cousins would run in and out of the wine cave, sit down to enormous meals prepared by the aunts and listen spellbound to tales of the old country told by her grandfather and great-uncles. She hadn't known it then as she knew it now: her family was her strength. They made it possible to bear whatever obstacles life threw in her path.

A group of whooping youngsters ran up to greet them. They grew suddenly silent and wide-eyed at the sight of Josh.

"You're the guy from the TV show, right?" asked Emma, the daughter of Gina's cousin Jennifer.

"Sure am," Josh said easily.

"Why didn't you marry Aunt Gina?" piped a voice that Gina identified as Alexander, her cousin Donna's son.

"Alexander!" Gina said.

"I want to know," the boy said stubbornly.

"Did it occur to you that I might not have wanted him?" Gina said lightly, ruffling Alexander's hair with one hand and squeezing Emma's shoulder as they began to walk toward the tables.

"He *is* rather handsome," said Mia's sister, Stacey, after unabashedly staring at his profile.

"Thank you," Josh told her gravely. "For sticking up for me."

Gina's cousin Rocco, his beefy face flushed from the heat of the barbecue fire, detached himself from a group of men— all uncles, nephews or cousins.

"Hey, Gina. How about introducing me?" He was studying Josh, taking in the highly polished leather shoes and the blazer, now casually slung over one shoulder. Rocco stopped in his tracks. "No, wait a minute. You're the *Mr. Moneybags* guy, right?"

Josh extended his hand. "Otherwise known as Josh Corbett," he said.

Rocco's expression didn't change, but Gina knew what he was thinking. *Got to protect my little cousin from this guy who did her wrong. Got to vet him out. Got to let him know he can't treat her the way he did before.* She suppressed a laugh at the almost imperceptible but defensive change in Rocco's body posture and the cool handshake he offered Josh. Rocco had always been her protector; she couldn't expect him to abandon her now. The Angelini men looked after their women. Never mind that Gina had outgrown her need for their services by the time she was ten and had learned a couple of handy karate chops. And Rocco, like everyone else, had never realized how miserable she'd been after Josh Corbett's rejection.

Rocco raised inquiring brows at Gina, who nodded to let him know that it was all right to admit Josh into the family circle. At least for today, while she tried to come to terms with his reappearance in her life.

At her signal, Rocco's demeanor changed immediately. "Welcome, Josh. Come over and meet the guys. We've got a game of bocce going."

"Bocce?"

"Yeah, we put in regulation courts last year. What's the matter, haven't you played before?"

Josh, for the first time all day, appeared discomfited. "No, I can't say that I have."

"We'll take care of that." Rocco threw a casual arm across Josh's shoulders and led him to the bocce court, where a group of Gina's male relatives were watching his approach. Her cousin Paul shoved an elbow into his brother's ribs, and Gina almost laughed out loud. After a couple of games with those guys, Josh would be running for the hills. They were experts.

Josh aimed a pleading glance over his shoulder at Gina and mouthed "Help!" but all she did was smile and wave as if they had the most friendly relationship in the world. At the same time, she felt grim satisfaction in the thought that Rocco and company would probably accomplish what she hadn't been able to do today—get rid of Josh Corbett for good.

Chapter Two

Rocco was a stocky man, the beginning of a paunch swelling beneath his T-shirt. His quick introductions made Josh's head spin: Gathered around the bocce court was a Tom, a Tim and at least two guys named Tony, all even bigger than Rocco. They eyed him with what seemed like suspicion as he removed his blazer, assessing his muscles. Rocco showed him where to hang his coat over a low-hanging branch and proceeded to explain bocce.

"My grandfather and uncles brought the game over from Italy with them, and we grew up with it," Rocco told him.

Josh opened his mouth to say that he'd never seen a bocce ball, nor had he ever observed any games, but Rocco didn't give him a chance to speak. The game, Rocco said, was played on a long sand court that appeared to be about ten feet wide by sixty feet long. The brightly colored bocce balls seemed slightly larger than those in the old croquet set that Josh had shared with his sister at their summer house in Maine, but no mallets were involved, so Josh assumed that bocce balls were thrown or tossed.

"Now, Josh," Rocco told him. "You don't have to be Italian to learn this game. Right, Collin?"

The other man, standing with a bunch of mostly male onlookers, just grinned. This, Josh decided, was not encouraging.

"Collin married into the family, but that doesn't make him any less an Angelini," Rocco confided. "Even though his last name *is* Beauchamp."

"Of the Virginia Beauchamps," Collin said. "Spelled the French way, pronounced Beecham."

Josh had known some Beauchamps at his posh northeastern prep school, but mentioning that exclusive institution didn't seem like a good idea, considering the good-natured guffaws that greeted Collin's statement.

"The game can be played indoors or outdoors, and there can be two to four players on a team. Four balls are assigned to each team. You'll play on my team," Rocco said.

Tim and Tom were also on Rocco's team. The other team consisted of the two men named Tony, someone called Angelo and an older white-haired guy named Fredo, who was treated deferentially by everyone involved.

"First, the pallino," Fredo said, holding up a ball that was smaller than the others. There was a coin toss, and Fredo's team won the right to throw the pallino. Fredo rolled it onto the court, where it inched to a stop a little more than halfway to the end. At that point, Josh craned his head to search for Gina and discovered that she was surrounded by a bevy of women close to her age, all of them talking and laughing. Gina was holding a baby, patting it on the back and crooning to it, and paying no attention to what was going on over here.

While Josh was looking elsewhere, Fredo rolled one of his team's balls, to the accompaniment of shouts of encouragement from his own team and groans from Josh's team when the second ball rolled close to the pallino.

"Kiss it, kiss it!" cried one of the Tonys, which Josh figured meant that he wanted the two balls to touch. He shot another surreptitious glance toward Gina, remembering with a pang of regret the sweet softness of her lips. He must have been crazy to turn his back on her in Scotland.

"All right," Rocco said, interrupting his reverie by slapping a ball in Josh's hand. "Now you."

Josh, whose mind for the past few moments had been engaged in wistful remembrances of a heather-strewn moor, stared at him blankly.

"Go ahead. We have to bowl until one of our balls is closer to the pallino than the ball that Fredo rolled."

Josh hefted the ball in his hand and summoned enough bravado to convince himself that this game was a piece of cake. Unfortunately, he slipped as he rolled the ball, and it landed about as far away from the others as it could without jumping the sides of the court.

"You'll do better next time," Rocco said before rolling another ball, which edged somewhat closer to the pallino than Josh's.

Rocco's team bowled until all balls had been thrown, but not without a lot of good-natured jesting. After that, it was Fredo's turn again.

"When both sides have bowled all their balls, the side with the ball closest to the pallino gets a point. A point is also awarded for any other ball from that side that is closer to the pallino than any ball rolled by the opponents. Thus, only one team can score in a frame, and that side can get up to four points. The first team to score sixteen points wins," Rocco told him.

Josh didn't need long to figure out that bocce was a game of strategy. The pallino could be moved by a shot, so a player often scored by knocking the pallino closer to balls previously rolled by his team. On the other hand, a player whose team already had balls in scoring position sometimes chose to place a ball in front of the pallino to keep it from being moved.

Whenever it was Josh's turn, he managed to goof up. If he tried to land his ball close to the pallino, it inevitably pushed the pallino the wrong way. If he wanted to keep it from hitting the pallino, it always did. He found that he couldn't estimate how much a ball would roll from where he stood to throw it, and he tended to throw short. If he didn't throw short, he overcorrected.

Rocco, on the other hand, was a virtuoso. "Bocce is as simple or complicated as you want to make it," he told Josh, and then he'd proceed to blow everyone away with a cunning move.

When the game was finally over, Josh realized that he was the one who had virtually lost for Rocco's team. Even though the others tried to gloss over his many errors, he felt bad about letting the team down.

"Don't worry, we're playing two out of three to win," Rocco said by way of reassurance, which was not at all reassuring to Josh. He looked around, wishing an excuse to bail out would come to mind. But Gina had disappeared, and Mia was hanging over a bench, waiting to cheer him on.

Well, maybe this time he'd give Mia something to cheer about. He forced a halfhearted grin and girded himself for the second game.

Unfortunately, he didn't play any better in the second game than he had in the first. The only good thing was that now he knew the rules. The third game was a disaster, though his teammates were generous in not blaming their loss on him. Still, by the time everyone dispersed, Josh felt extremely apologetic, not to mention dejected for letting the team down.

"That's okay," Rocco told him. "A lot of guys wouldn't have even tried to play."

Josh resisted the temptation to invite Rocco and company to play lacrosse. Or hockey. Or water polo, in which he excelled.

Mia jumped down from the bench and ran over. "Don't worry, Josh," Mia consoled him. "You'll get better at bocce."

"I'm not so sure," he said, wiping the perspiration from his face with a handkerchief. He was still bummed out from his disappointing performance. He kept scanning the crowd for Gina, but he didn't see her near the barbecue, the big doors that led to the wine cave or near the group of women she'd been standing with before.

Fredo stumped over, his white hair an aureole standing out around his head. "Come along, my boy," he said to Josh. "I'll show you where to clean up." Josh followed him on a circuitous route along a well-worn grass path past the barbecue, the picnic tables and three or four kids playing with skateboards in front of the winery office.

"You know," Fredo said as they washed up in the men's room inside the small tasting facility, which held a bar and a few tiny tables, "it's not the game that's important, Joshua. It is the family, and that we play together as well as work together."

Josh splashed water on his face. "That's, um, good," he said. He was surprised that Fredo was treating him as an equal, considering how everyone else deferred to him.

"My father, the first Gino Angelini, always held family to be more important than anything. This is the philosophy that we have let govern our family winery since we started it."

"When we were in Scotland, Gina talked about her family a lot," Josh told him. "The other women playing the game never mentioned their parents, brothers, sisters." He hadn't, either.

"Yes, that's our Gina. She is named after my father and her father, too. Gino Junior was my elder brother. He died when Gina was twenty-two." Fredo dried his hands on a paper towel and then handed one to Josh before clapping him on the shoulder. "Come, Josh. We must join the others. It is almost time for the stomping of the grapes."

As they were making their way past the winery office, Fredo was distracted by questions from some of the children playing nearby, and Josh stepped to one side to wait for him. After a few moments, someone walked up behind him and gently put a hand on his arm. "Josh Corbett? I'm Maren, Gina's mother."

When he turned and looked into Maren's face, he saw

Gina's delicate features, the same straight nose and high cheekbones. But where Gina's eyes were dark, almost black, Maren's were sapphire-blue, and her skin was ivory, not golden like Gina's.

"I'm happy to meet you," Josh said.

"And I'm glad to meet *you,*" Maren said, studying his face for a long moment.

"Aunt Maren, they're pouring the grapes in the barrels," Frankie announced as he bounded past.

"Is this the first time you've been to a crush?" Maren asked.

"Yes," Josh said, scanning the group for Gina but trying not to be obvious about it. He spotted her setting food out on one of the tables, her breasts shifting gently against the gathered fabric of her blouse as she leaned over. She looked serenely at home in these surroundings, not at odds and edgy as she had in Scotland. Suddenly, she glanced his way and their eyes locked, stilling her laughter. A breeze stirred the leaves overhead, sending a romantic ripple of sunlight across Gina's lovely face. In that moment his reason for wanting to come to the Napa Valley became perfectly clear: this trip, he admitted to himself for the first time, had little to do with writing an article about the Napa Valley and less to do with Starling Industries' search for a winery; it had everything to do with Gina.

"Come, we should go watch the grape-stomping," Maren said, appropriating his arm and leading him away. Reluctantly, he followed.

On a platform on the far side of the barn, men were dumping grapes into a row of twelve oaken half barrels. Fredo broke away from the children and mounted the stairs, first saying a few words to the group about being glad that everyone could be at crush, and then joining Josh and Maren as an accordion band began to play boisterous music. Josh noticed Frankie standing on the sidelines, tapping his foot in time to the beat and looking for all the world as though he wished he were playing with them.

Josh's attention was distracted when he saw Gina walking toward him, her long hair swinging around her shoulders. "Hello, Uncle Fredo," she said.

Fredo gave Gina an affectionate hug, his weathered face crinkling into a smile. "Not only do we Angelinis know how to grow grapes, Josh, we also understand how to grow beautiful young women, each as individual as a vintage of wine."

"Uncle Fredo," Gina protested with a light laugh, but whatever she might have said was cut off when Mia ran up, dragging Frankie along behind her.

"They're going to start the contest! Whose team are you on, Aunt Gina?" Mia tugged excitedly at her arm.

"I—"

"Hey," said Fredo expansively. "Why don't you show Josh the ropes, Gina? Be a team?"

"But—"

"Oh, I think that's a good idea," Frankie said seriously. "You have very big feet, Josh. That's important because the team that squashes the most juice out of the grapes in two minutes wins."

"Frankie!" Gina protested. "Talking about the size of someone's feet isn't good manners."

"That's okay," Josh said quickly because of the way Frankie's face fell as a result of this rebuke. "I know my feet are big."

"This grape-stomping is a tiring thing," Mia grumbled. "You have to stomp and stomp and stomp."

"It's time for me to be out of here," Maren declared with a half laugh. "I have to help in the kitchen." She hurried off toward the entrance to the wine cave, where people were bringing out food.

Gina was trying to melt into the crowd, but some of her family members pushed her forward. "Go ahead, Gina. Go on," they said.

Rocco dragged Josh along with him to the platform. "You can't fully experience crush unless you stomp the grapes," Rocco insisted, and next thing Josh knew, he was rolling up his pantlegs and his shoes were being collected by one of the Tonys, to put in a secure place where they would not be spattered with grape juice.

"I didn't ask for this," Gina said helplessly as they faced each other in one of the grape-filled barrels, which was barely large enough for two people to stand in. "I tried to get out of it." She was so close that he could smell the heady fragrance of her cologne over the scent of the grapes.

"I'm glad you weren't successful," he murmured so that no one else could hear, and she glared at him.

"Okay, wait for the sound of the bell, and then you have two minutes to demonstrate your stomping skills," instructed the person in charge, who Josh recalled was Gina's brother-in-law and Mia's father, Nick. "The idea is to crush as much juice from the grapes as you can. When I ring the bell at the close of your round, we measure the juice. The team that provides the most juice wins."

"Wins what?" Josh asked Gina in a low tone.

"A bottle of wine, what else?" she said. She had hitched her short skirt even higher so that an expanse of creamy thigh showed.

"I'd like something more than that," Josh muttered, and Gina's eyebrows flew sky high.

Nick, who did not hear Josh's remark, cleared his throat. "All right, contestants. On your mark, get set, *go!*"

The accordions struck up a frenzied melody. Gina said through gritted teeth, "Okay, Corbett. *Move.*" She'd done this before; he hadn't. But he did his best, hating the way the grapes felt as they oozed up between his toes but liking the way Gina couldn't avoid touching him as they jumped and squished and stomped and in general threw all decorum to the wind. Mia was right; this wasn't easy. He grew tired long before the bell rang to signal the contest's close, and when it did, he tried a sagging maneuver in Gina's direction in the hope of bodily contact, but she was already stepping over the side of the barrel.

A hurried consultation ensued while the grape juice from each of the twelve barrels was measured, and then Nick declared, "The winners—Rocco and Jaimie!" Jaimie, who wore a silver tongue stud and had been pointed out earlier by Rocco as one of his cousins, accepted the bottle of wine and acknowledged the applause of her relatives with an exaggerated bow.

"You came in second," Nick said to Josh as Frankie ran up and slapped him an exuberant high-five. "Where's Gina?"

Josh gestured toward the crowd. "She's wandered off, I guess," he said.

"You did okay for your first time," Nick said. "Here are a couple of T-shirts. See that Gina gets hers, will you?"

As a new group of contestants climbed into the barrels, Josh looked down at his feet. They were purple. So were all the other previous contestants', but they didn't seem to care, so why should he? He scrambled down from the platform and took off in pursuit of Gina, whose ash-blond hair was highly visible near the food-laden tables. He caught up with her as she was piling barbecued ribs onto a plate.

"Here," she said, unceremoniously shoving the plate in his direction.

"Nick said to give you this," he said, handing her the T-shirt.

She afforded him a grudging smile as she tossed it over her arm. "Thanks, Josh. Second place isn't bad, you know, for your first grape-stomping experience." Her gesture encompassed the abundance of dishes on the tabletop. "Please help yourself to the food. There's Aunt Dede's special penne-and-artichoke salad. She's a caterer here in the valley and my mother works for her. Also, Claire—she's Uncle Fredo's daughter—made her prize carrot cake, and you might want to try that.''

Josh set the plate of ribs aside momentarily so that he could roll his pantlegs down. Gina caught sight of the purple stains on the fabric.

"Uh-oh," she said with a grimace. "I'm sorry about your pants.''

"Don't be. It's nothing a good dry cleaner can't fix.'' He picked up the plate and helped himself to Aunt Dede's salad.

"Try the bruschetta,'' Gina said as they moved past the layered salad, the marinated mushrooms, the artichoke pie.

"Hey, Gina, did you make your special mussels-and-tomato fettucine?'' Rocco called from a table at the outskirts of the group.

"Not this time. Too busy,'' she called back.

"Aw, that's too bad. I'll let you sit with us, but only if you promise to invite me over for it soon.''

Gina glanced up at Josh. "Do you mind hanging out with Rocco? Or have you had enough?''

Which was how Josh found himself part of another amiable family group. He met Gina's vivacious cousin Bobbi, who said she'd served in the Peace Corps, and her husband, Stan, who owned a chain of fresh markets. He met Albert Aurelio, a salt-of-the-earth type who had married into the Angelini family and was now chief financial officer at Vineyard Oaks. When Josh's plate was empty, he returned to the buffet table for more food and found Maren putting out bread and rolls that she'd baked herself, and later he listened with rapt attention as Gina's cousin Carla, who was unmarried, talked animatedly about her career in public relations with the local winegrowers' association.

"Are you the one who made the carrot cake?'' he asked her. "It's the best I've ever tasted.''

"No, that was Claire. She's over there—the tall one with the long earrings. Don't worry,'' Carla said with a laugh. "No one could get all the Angelinis straight right away. A lot of people have the same name—for instance, Big Tony and Little Tony.''

''I met them playing bocce,'' Josh said, digging into the artichoke pie.

''They're not to be confused with Anthony Ceravolo, Rocco's dad, who married Aunt Gianna and is sometimes called Tony. And of course Aunt Gianna is not to be confused with my cousin Gina, who brought you here, and neither of them should be mistaken for Jennifer Saltieri Thompson, who for some unimaginable reason is sometimes referred to as Jeni, with a long *e*. Oh, and Marcy, who is Little Tony's wife, is expecting a baby girl in a few months, and she and Little Tony say that they intend to name their new daughter, guess what? Toni.

''Of course,'' she went on, ''we have a Timmy and a Jimmy who are brothers. And Jaimie, naturally, doesn't like to be mixed up with Jimmy. There's Sophia, the grandmother of Sophie, and a Ronnie and a Donny, and Victorine, Vicki and Victor.''

''Don't forget Fredo and Fred, Emma and Emily, Suzanne and Susan, and Mia, whose middle name is Suzanne,'' chimed in an older woman, who introduced herself as Audra.

''Maren and Maureen,'' contributed Carla. ''Margo, Marco and Mark.''

''Thank goodness for Teresa and Angelo Bono. They named their kids Zizi and Dodie. They'll never get mixed up with anyone else.''

''I wouldn't bet on that,'' said Gina. ''Zizi and Dodie are only nicknames.''

Audra frowned. ''What *are* their real names?''

''No one remembers, thank goodness,'' Carla said with a laugh.

Josh grinned, and all in all, by the time dinner was over, he thought he had never met more interesting people gathered in one place in his entire life.

Night fell, and the party, with a final tired wheeze of accordions, was declared to be over by Fredo. Barbara, Nick's wife and Gina's sister, came over to their table and presented Josh with a Super Stomper Certificate in honor of his stomping grapes and attending his first crush. People lingered, gathering up their children, their strollers, diaper bags and wraps as they bade one another fond goodbyes. And before her parents came to carry her home to bed, Mia curled up on Josh's lap and almost fell asleep.

"I have to leave," Gina said to Rocco after the Sorises had departed. "I'll need to be up early to work in the herb garden in the morning." Others were wending their way through the big oaks to their cars, and the cleanup detail was stashing containers of food in a van marked Dede's Catering Service.

"I should help fold the chairs," Josh said, but when he offered, Rocco told him that it wasn't necessary.

"We've got things under control, don't we, Frankie?"

"Sure, Pop," Frankie said with a jaunty grin. "Hey, Josh, how did you like crush?"

Amazingly, he didn't even have to think twice; Josh immediately gave it two thumbs-up, much to Frankie's delight.

"Now, Josh," Rocco said in parting. "You get any extra time, drop by the house. I've got a bocce court in my backyard, and I'll give you some pointers."

As painful as the bocce experience had been, Josh thought he never wanted to see another bocce ball or court as long as he lived. But he did want to see Rocco again, so he managed a halfhearted grin. "Will do," he said before hurrying after Gina, who was halfway to the parking lot by this time.

ONCE THEY WERE AWAY FROM everyone else, Gina was self-conscious around Josh, though she certainly felt more favorably disposed toward him since he'd made such an effort to fit in. She hadn't expected Rocco to take to him so well, nor had she counted on her mother's trying to make him feel welcome.

Josh didn't say much as they put up the Galaxie's convertible top and got in the car. He tossed his shoes in the back seat; the night had never grown as cool as expected and he was still in his bare feet. As they headed down the long Vineyard Oaks driveway toward the road, moonlight dappled the car's long hood with shadows and cast a silvery glow ahead. Gina sneaked a glance at his aristocratic profile and suppressed a grin when she saw that he was smiling. She wasn't quite sure why she was glad that he'd enjoyed himself tonight; whatever vengeful feelings she'd nurtured since the *Mr. Moneybags* show seemed to have been crushed out of her as completely as the juice from the grapes.

"Your niece is a charmer," Josh said, apropos of nothing.

"Which one? Stacey or Mia?"

"Mia. I didn't get too well acquainted with Stacey."

Gina smiled. "They're both my sister Barbara's kids. Stacey recently became a teenager, and she likes to congregate with her cousins at family events. Mia is my godchild as well as my niece. She's great."

"Agreed. And Rocco is a character."

"As well as the worst practical joker in all creation."

"He's the one who sent your application in for the *Mr. Moneybags* show, right?"

Gina nodded and braked for a curve in the road, then accelerated. "That was only one of the pranks he's played on me. It almost rivals the occasion when he got a realistic audiotape of a train wreck and called my aunt Linda from the station at about the time that the wine train with all its sightseers was due to arrive. He told Aunt Linda where he was, then played the tape into the phone, and she started yelling for my uncle Tony to come because she was convinced the train had jumped its track and run over Rocco in the phone booth. She was glad to hear his voice reassuring her that he was unharmed."

"Doesn't anyone ever get suspicious that he's playing jokes?" Josh asked between chuckles.

"No, since Rocco's so unfailingly clever about it. None of us will ever forget the time he borrowed the spare key to Aunt Audra and Uncle Charles's house and took about five of our male cousins over there. When Aunt Audra and Uncle Charles came home that night, they heard what sounded like a bunch of guys laughing and showering in their tiny bathroom. They didn't know whether to call the police or what, but they finally recognized some of the voices and started pounding on the bathroom door. They discovered that Rocco and the guys had turned on the shower but were sitting around the bathroom fully clothed, making an unholy racket so that my aunt and uncle would think some strangers had broken in and were partying in their shower. And then there was the time—"

Josh was still smiling. "Okay, okay, I get the picture. It's all pretty funny, by the way."

"Not if you're the butt of it," Gina said emphatically.

By the time she reached the highway, Josh's laughter had abated and he appeared pensive. They were passing the water tower at the edge of the town limits before he spoke.

"You're lucky," he said into the silence. "To have such a large family to care about you."

That he would feel this way surprised her, and she certainly wouldn't have expected him to mention it. "I know," she said. She tried to recall what she knew about Josh's family from the résumé that had been handed out to all contestants on the show. A mother who listed "philanthropist" as her occupation; a father who was a director of a couple of big corporations. One younger brother and a sister whose ages she couldn't recall.

He shifted in his seat, leaning slightly toward her so that his face was more clearly lit in the light from the instrument panel. He looked somber. "My family is great, don't get me wrong, but we're so spread out that we seldom see one another. My father travels a lot, and my mother spends most of her time raising money for charity. My brother Jason's business keeps him in New York. And then there's my sister, Valerie, who married a banker from Brazil. They live in Rio de Janeiro.''

"I wouldn't like living so far away from everyone who is important to me," she said, trying to imagine such a thing. Not being able to drop by her mother's apartment after Maren tried a new cake recipe, then the two of them sitting and gabbing with her sister, Barbara, while Mia and Stacey dashed in and out of the house? Not to run unexpectedly into Rocco at the market and laugh together at Frankie's latest escapade while they waited their turns at the deli counter? Life anywhere else but Rio Robles would be flat and dull, Gina was sure of it.

Josh sighed and faced forward again. "I was afraid I'd be treated like an outsider today, but everyone was so friendly," he said.

"Oh, that's because Rocco took you under his wing. He may be the family clown, but we all respect his judgment."

"If I'm in with Rocco, I'm in with the rest of the family? Including you?"

She ignored the hopeful note in his voice. "Not necessarily."

"Oh. That's too bad."

Was he being sarcastic? She slid a stealthy look at him out of the corners of her eyes. His expression was neutral and revealed what might be a bit of regret. Okay, so it hadn't been sarcasm. But what was it?

"Anyway, thanks for sharing your family with me," Josh said.

The sincerity of his tone left Gina unable to think of any response other than "You're welcome."

"Besides," Josh said wryly as he peered down at his feet. "I now have feet that would be the envy of Mia. Purple toes." He tendered Gina the famously lovable Mr. Moneybags grin.

She slowed the car as they approached the pillars marking

the entrance to the parking area in front of Good Thymes. The unique stone cottage nestled in a hollow in the land and was shaded by a variety of trees. Flowers spilled out of window boxes, and more flowers bordered the path leading to the red-painted and arched front door.

Gina drew the Galaxie slowly to a stop beside Josh's car and, without looking at him, slid out of her seat. "Come on, you can wash your feet off at the garden spigot," she said.

Josh stepped out of the car and followed her along the flagstone path bordering the cottage, looking around with interest. The stones were cool and damp beneath his bare feet, and the plants in the garden rustled in the light breeze. On the other side of the fence, they could hear the low hiss of drip irrigation in the adjoining vineyard.

"You live back here?" He gazed up at the mellow gray stone, its hard edges softened by the moonlight.

She'd bought the shop using her booty of fifty thousand dollars, the consolation prize from the TV show, as a down payment. "One of the main attractions of this building was that I could reside on the premises," she said, gesturing toward the windows above. "My quarters are big enough, and comfortable, as well."

As she spoke, a furry shape crashed through the underbrush and hurtled toward them. Josh yelled, but Gina staggered backward under a sudden weight. "Don't holler so loud," she said as she righted herself. "You'll scare Timothy."

Josh stared at the squirming ball of fur in her arms. A contented rumble emanated from it. A purr? If so, it was the loudest purr he'd ever heard, and it came from the biggest cat he'd ever seen in his life.

A few moments passed before he recovered. "That's a cat?"

"This is my best buddy. He's a Maine Coon cat with an attitude." Timothy's head appeared, and great unblinking yellow eyes focused on Josh with interest.

"I'll say he has an attitude," Josh said as he recovered his composure. He sneezed.

"Allergic?" Gina asked sweetly.

"Yes. Maybe I should leave."

"I was going to let you wash your feet. Or are you becoming fond of purple?"

"I'd appreciate some running water. Will Timothy mind if I pet him?"

"No. He's harmless."

Josh tentatively reached out a hand and stroked Timothy's head. The cat closed his eyes and purred even louder.

"He likes you."

"Yeah. I wish you did."

"I do, sort of. You were a good sport tonight, Josh."

"How many points does that win me?"

She couldn't help laughing. "Enough." She turned away. "The spigot's right over here," she said, leading the way. "I'll get a bar of soap from the potting shed."

Josh dropped his shoes and blazer on a nearby bench and turned on the water. Gina set Timothy down on the back porch steps and picked her way carefully through the shadows to the shed, where she gathered up the bar of soap, a washcloth and a soft old towel.

Josh stood almost ankle deep in a puddle when she returned. She handed him the soap and washcloth and went to observe from the porch so her shoes wouldn't get wet in the runoff.

"That should do it," Josh said as he dried his feet. Crickets chirped in the garden, filling her ears with sound to block out what she was thinking. She recalled a night in the garden in Scotland two years ago when she and Josh had been enjoying an arranged date. She had climbed up on a crumbling moss-covered bench so she could see over the wall separating the castle from the moor, and Josh had smiled up at her in exactly the same way he was doing now. Then he had taken her hand

and helped her down from the bench while she worried about whether he would try to kiss her.

"What should I do with the towel?" he asked, breaking the bubble of her memories.

Silently, she held out her hand, and he put the towel in it. Timothy meowed, impatient because she hadn't fed him before she'd left earlier.

"Gina, how about going out for a drink or something?" Josh had moved closer and was lounging against the wall with his own brand of careless grace.

Her heart did a flip-flop at the eagerness of his tone, and she willed it to start beating normally. She had no business letting Joshua Corbett think that their romance could heat up again.

"Sorry, I have to get up early in the morning," she said curtly, though the words had a hard time moving past her suddenly dry throat.

Josh straightened, a hint of impatience in his stance. "Gina," he began, but she interrupted.

"I really have to go in now," she said on a slightly frantic note. She was beginning to feel light-headed, and she'd hardly drunk any wine at all.

Before she knew it he had cupped a hand around her nape and was pulling her head down toward him. She seemed to have forgotten how to breathe; all the air seemed to have left her lungs. She closed her eyes and an unbidden picture sprang up from somewhere deep inside—two bodies, theirs, tangled amid bedclothes, and his hand sliding slowly up from her waist to cup her breast and bring it to his mouth. The fantasy expanded until she could imagine his warm skin pressed against hers, and the arch of her back as—

She made herself open her eyes. She shouldn't be thinking of Josh that way. As she knew only too well, moonlight and a romantic setting did not a relationship make. She had found that out all too painfully once before.

She took a deliberate step backward, inadvertently treading

on Timothy's tail. The cat yowled and leaped into space, and
Gina nearly lost her balance.

Josh grabbed her before she went flying off the porch, and
she clutched at him in order to stabilize herself. His muscles
were strong beneath the sleeve of his shirt, the fabric soft and
expensive. The sight of the monogram on the pocket reminded her that he was Joshua James Corbett III, Mr. Moneybags. And she was the same person she had always been,
Gina Angelini of Rio Robles, California, which was hardly
in his league. She'd known it from the beginning, and he'd
more than likely known it, too, since he'd chosen Tahoma
and not her.

Flustered, she pulled away. The mood was broken, but at
least he had the good grace to look sheepish. "Sorry," he
said.

Gina made an effort to pull herself together. To cover her
confusion, she peered into the shadows, looking for Timothy.
He was sulking, no doubt, but he'd get over it when he heard
the electric can opener. That sound always made him come
running.

She had barely regained her composure, when Josh spoke.
"Thanks for the evening, Gina," he said, unexpectedly formal and overly polite.

"You're welcome," she said, equally as formal and polite.

He raised his hand in a farewell salute as she opened the
door and backed inside. Timothy poked his head out of his
favorite refuge, the catnip patch, and meowed plaintively.

"Come in, Timothy. I won't step on you this time." The
cat, eyeing her distrustfully, jumped onto the top step and
followed her up the stairs to her apartment.

Through the kitchen window, Gina kept an eye on the back
of Josh's shirt as he disappeared around the corner of the
cottage. She was in trouble, big trouble. And clearly, she'd
be in over her head if she couldn't say no to Josh Corbett
and mean it.

Chapter Three

Josh drove away in his rented BMW, still smarting from Gina's rejection. In the rearview mirror, he saw a light flick on upstairs in the cottage. He slowed the car and leaned his head out the window to glance back. Gina's shapely silhouette was framed in the square of light, showing off her considerable attributes.

Which happened to include what might be the most voluptuous breasts he'd ever seen; not that he'd actually seen them, but give him time. And that long elegant neck of hers, and that thick mane of naturally ash-blond hair, which set off to perfection her tawny complexion and dark, dark eyes. As Gina moved from one side of the room to the other, Josh accelerated quickly so he wouldn't be witness to whatever she did next. He might have the hots for her, but a Peeping Tom he was not.

Business. I'm here on business, he reminded himself. At the moment, however, pleasure seemed a whole lot more important.

When he reached the large two-story house near the river where he'd rented an apartment yesterday, Mrs. Upthegrove, his landlady, was walking her beagle, Sadie, along the path leading to the back of the house. The landlady was as spare and tall as Sadie was short and fat, which disproved the idea that dog owners tended to resemble their dogs.

"Hello, Josh," she said pleasantly, tossing long salt-and-pepper bangs back from her face. "How's your room? You've got a hundred and something TV channels in there because of my new satellite dish."

Josh hadn't turned on the TV since he'd arrived, but he didn't have the heart to tell her. "Everything's great," he said. His apartment had been carved from the bottom floor of the house and consisted of the former library, an enormous bathroom and a bedroom that had once been a large pantry.

"Did you find Gina at her shop, like I said?"

"Yes," he said, figuring that he might as well stop to scratch an adoring Sadie behind her floppy ears.

"Gina's in a position to help you learn more about the wine country for the article you're writing."

He'd said that an article was in the works, which was true. But that wasn't the only reason he was visiting the Napa Valley. He was prepared to remain mum on that topic, however, so as not to blow his cover.

"Thanks for pointing me in the right direction."

"Oh, no problem. Let me know if I can do anything else to help."

He turned to walk away, but Mrs. Upthegrove, who had urged him to call her Judy Rae yesterday when he'd written her a check for a month's rent, followed along.

"Was it wonderful for you and Gina to get reacquainted after two years?" the landlady asked with great interest. "Was she happy to see you?"

"It was great," Josh replied, though he wasn't sure this was true for Gina. He'd skip answering the second question, since the moment she'd recognized him Gina had ordered him out of her shop.

"Good," said his landlady with great satisfaction. "I always thought you chose the wrong woman. That Tahoma was bad news."

He couldn't have agreed more, but he had his key at the ready to unlock the door and didn't want to prolong the conversation any longer than necessary. "Good night, Mrs. Up-thegrove," he said firmly.

"Judy Rae," she reminded him, so he repeated it after her and closed the door before she could say anything more.

His apartment was configured so that he entered it through the bedroom, which was small, but the double bed was comfortable and the window faced the meandering Napa River. The living room, or the former library, was sumptuously paneled in mellow old oak, and three walls of shelves housed books. At one end was a small rudimentary kitchen, and beside it the entrance to the bathroom, which had a tub with claw feet and a floor made of shiny dark green marble.

This apartment, like the smaller one next door, was tastefully furnished with cast-off furniture from the rest of the house, which Judy Rae had confided was too expensive to maintain without tenants to help with the bills. Some of the pieces, like the bed, were antiques. Others were new, such as the gaily patterned rug covering the tile floor.

Josh peeled off his clothes, lay down on the bed and stared up at the ceiling in the dim light from the lamp across the room. For a moment, he wished he were home in Boston. Yet if he were miraculously able to transport himself to his own comfortable town house on Beacon Hill, he wouldn't be plotting how to wangle more time with Gina Angelini, as he was now.

Gina. Her very name made him feel all warm inside. Gina Angelini, Gina the angel, Gina the beautiful. Why had he ever turned her away?

Because, in his judgment at the time, she was too natural and unspoiled, too gentle and sweet, to be subjected to the media attention sure to follow his choice. Throughout the filming of the show, Gina had sent signals that she was uncomfortable with celebrity; she had been noticeably homesick when she first arrived in Scotland. Still, he'd felt an affinity toward her immediately, from the moment their eyes met. There'd been an indefinable spark. An undercurrent of excitement that made their every encounter sizzle. He'd often wanted to spirit her away from the artificial atmosphere of the show, but he'd had obligations. He had a contract with the producers that prohibited him from deviating from a certain script. And in the end, he couldn't imagine anyone as honest and upfront as Gina appearing with him on *Good Morning, America* or *Oprah* to bill and coo on cue for the cameras. So he'd chosen that hussy Tahoma. But he had regrets. Boy, did he ever.

He fell into a fitful sleep, crazy dreams cartwheeling through his mind so that he woke often. Each time he tried to go back to sleep, there was Gina, her unforgettable face lulling him back to dreamland. Gina smiling, Gina frowning, Gina and that come-hither bat of her eyelashes that he suspected was entirely unwitting.

Finally, when the bedside clock read six o'clock, Josh gave up on sleeping. He swung his feet out of bed and padded across the floor to the bathroom, where he shaved in record time. He had business in the Napa Valley that required his attention, but how could he concentrate on it if all he thought about was Gina, Gina, Gina?

As soon as he finished getting dressed, Josh drove over to Good Thymes, less than a mile away, and parked his car in the same spot as yesterday. He couldn't help glancing automatically at the upstairs window where he had seen Gina's lush silhouette last night. The windows were open now, the curtains looped back, and there was no sign of her. In the lemony first light of day, the cottage seemed like an illustration from a fairy tale, with its weathered green shutters and faded red front door. He half expected Cinderella or Snow White to appear and beckon him inside.

Only it was Gina who appeared on the doorstep, carrying a basket over one arm and looking amazed to see him. He didn't know why. Had she thought he'd give up so easily?

Taking advantage of her speechlessness, he walked over

and gestured at the basket. "Going to Grandmother's house, Little Red Riding Hood?"

"No, but if I'm Little Red Riding Hood, what does that make you? The wolf?" She walked down the steps and alongside the flagstone path leading through the rose arbor to the garden.

He was right behind her. "Yes," he said. "The better to harass you, my dear."

"I don't deserve it," she said loftily. "You might as well annoy someone else." She unhooked the gate latch.

"I tried annoying someone. She had a boyfriend already."

"You mean Tahoma? Smart girl."

Josh didn't like the way this conversation was going, but he followed along doggedly even though she let the arbor gate swing back to punch him in the stomach.

"Oof," he said, and she grinned back at him as she made her way past the dew-drenched plants to the back of the garden.

"Next time don't walk so close behind me," she said.

"I'm keeping a decent distance between us," he told her as she bent down among the rosemary bushes.

"Your idea of decent and mine could be quite different," she said. In the misty morning light, she seemed ethereal and more beautiful than he'd ever seen her. There was also more than a hint of determination in the cant of her jaw, and a mote of resolution in her eyes.

He decided to tackle the problem head-on. "What is your main objection to me?" he asked mildly.

She tilted her head to one side, which only increased her desirability. She was wearing a loose chambray smock over her jeans, and it was unbuttoned low enough to show a hint of cleavage. He swallowed, realizing that she wore no bra. The thought of her breasts swinging unfettered beneath the light fabric made concentrating on her answer to his question hard.

"Number one should be obvious," she said, tossing a sprig

of rosemary into her basket. "You dumped me in front of millions of people."

"I thought I expl—"

"Number two, there's no future in it. We're from different worlds, you and me. I'm from a simple farming family. You live in Boston and went to prep school. You graduated from an Ivy League college, while I only managed one year at UC-Sacramento before I had to drop out and work at the winery. Number three..." She stopped talking and regarded him coolly. "I'm still trying to think of reason number three," she said lamely.

"Does there have to be a future in every relationship?" he asked heatedly. "Isn't it enough to renew old acquaintance and see what develops?"

"Maybe for you," Gina said, half rising and settling herself down in a new place.

"As for your simple farming family, between bocce games I met your cousin Greg who has a Ph.D. in chemistry and teaches at a private college in San Francisco. There was nothing simple about Greg."

"It's true, Gregory is very intelligent." Unperturbed, she tossed several more sprigs into the basket.

Josh continued. "Your cousin Carla seems to have a brilliant grasp of how to build a public relations career. When I was on my return trip to the buffet table, your mother treated me to a fascinating discourse on baking bread and rolls for your aunt Dede's catering service. Don't run down your family, Gina. I told you I think they're wonderful."

"Yes, you did, and yes, they are."

It annoyed him that she wouldn't give him something to refute, anything that would help him prove the point that she ought to stop pushing him away.

"We could at least go out to dinner."

She nailed him with an unfathomable look. "Last night all you wanted was drinks. Now it's dinner. I haven't even given you an inch, and you're already trying to take a mile."

"Come on, Gina, I hardly know anyone in town. Be a good sport and keep me company for a couple of hours."

"You're tearing at my heartstrings." His wheedling seemed to have made no difference at all, and here he was slugging away, trying his hardest.

He forced an expression of optimism. "Good. Does that mean you'll go?"

She leaned back, shaded her eyes against the rising sun with her hand and squinted up at him. "Tell you what, Josh. You go back to Boston and I'll let you know if I change my mind. In other words, don't call me, I'll call you."

He let out a long low whistle of appreciation. "You're one tough cookie, Gina Angelini." He couldn't help grinning down at her.

For a moment, he thought she might be wavering, but no. She did grin back at him, though, and there was a flicker of something—communion? camaraderie?—behind her eyes.

"And you're one persistent fellow," she said, almost without missing a beat.

Whatever else he had in mind to say was lost in the shuffle when two pint-size whirlwinds burst through the gate.

"Gina, Gina! Guess what!" Frankie was first, with Mia hot on his heels. Both of them carried backpacks.

"Frankie's dog is gonna have puppies! And Mom said we could have one!"

Gina rose gracefully and smiled at Mia, whose excitement at this good news was written all over her face. "That's wonderful," she said warmly.

Mia noticed Josh for the first time. "It's gonna be a girl and I'm gonna dress it up in doll clothes," she declared.

Frankie grimaced. "Fat chance. You do that and I'm taking the puppy back."

"We always used to dress our dog, Charlie, in doll clothes, and he liked it," Mia said.

"No way," Frankie said. He turned to Josh. "Say, Josh,

would you like a puppy? Last time Beauty had puppies there were seven.''

"No, Frankie. Thank you, but I don't have enough room in my apartment in Boston for a dog.''

Frankie gave Josh a look of incredulity. "You don't? That's awful. You'd better move right away.''

Josh laughed, liking the look of Gina as she smoothed Mia's unruly hair and adjusted Frankie's collar. He'd never thought of Gina as maternal, yet he could imagine how she'd be someday with her own children, by turns solicitous and gently admonitory. They'd be cute kids, too, if they inherited her piquant features.

Gina smiled indulgently at both children. "You'd better get out to the road. It's almost time for the school bus.''

"'Bye, Aunt Gina. See you later. 'Bye, Josh.''

"Let me know if you want a puppy,'' Frankie said before he raced after Mia.

"Mia said she lives next door, but I didn't realize that Frankie and Rocco lived so close,'' Josh said into the silence they left behind.

"They're right down the road. One of the reasons I bought this place was that my sister and Rocco were nearby.'' She knelt and began to pluck weeds from the soil, turning her back toward him.

Josh sat down on a low stone bench nearby. "You mean the cottage wasn't always in the family?''

Gina took note of his occupation of the bench, seemed about to say something, then perhaps thought better of it. She shook her head. "This was a country store that was put out of business by the convenience stores that started springing up around here a few years back. The owner moved away and I bought it for my herb business a year and a half ago. I was lucky that I could live above the shop. I hated to move out of Mother's house, but she was ready to scale down to an apartment by then, she said. She's getting along fine, and so am I.''

"Most of the people I know could hardly wait to move out of their parents' homes," he observed carefully. Gina was how old now—twenty-nine? No, thirty-one. That was a long time to live at home.

She must have noticed his perplexity because she appeared to feel the need for explanation. "Mother needed me after my father died," she said quietly. "They were inseparable, and his final illness exhausted her. Barb had already married, and it was up to me to take care of our mother. She'd always been a stay-at-home mom and was faced with getting a job, which I thought would be a difficult adjustment. Fortunately, she's launched a new career with Aunt Dede's catering service and loves it."

Josh would bet that Maren Angelini was every bit as independent as her daughter. "I like your mother," he said.

"Most people do." Gina stood up. He did, too, following her as she headed back toward the cottage. She stopped at the back door to wipe the mud off her feet. "Now," she said with the utmost patience, "I'd better go in and get ready for the rest of my workday."

"What time does the store open?"

"Nine o'clock."

"I'll be back to buy something."

"Josh, stop it. You're a pest. Go. Now." She wasn't as put out with him as she sounded, if he judged her correctly. Her mouth quirked up at the corners, and she couldn't hide the warm amused light in her eyes.

"Okay, okay, I'm out of here. But remember, Gina, the Big Bad Wolf only pretended to leave. Once he was out of sight, he circled around the woods until he could surprise Little Red at another juncture in the road."

He thought she might burst into laughter at that, but she only lifted her eyebrows. "Well, Josh, you've described your MO very well so far. I suppose I shouldn't be surprised when you show up at Grandmother's house wearing her nightcap and sleeping in her bed."

She'd given him an opening and he delighted in using it. "It's not your grandmother's bed I want to sleep in. Haven't you figured that out by now?"

Again he thought she might laugh. But she only said, "Ooh, Grandma, what big teeth you have." Then she tripped on into the house and shut the door in his face.

Josh laughed to himself and went off to find a place where he could buy a decent cup of coffee. Then he'd make a few phone calls. If all went well he might be able to arrive back here by ten o'clock or so.

He wasn't about to give up on Gina so easily.

JOSH DIDN'T WASTE TIME on any of the trendy tourist hangouts around town. He discovered a real old-fashioned diner called Mom's on the outskirts of Rio Robles, its squatty silver shape boldly contrasting with the hazy mountain peaks in the distance. After quickly sizing up the vehicles in the parking lot, he decided that the large number of pickups boded well for finding a lot of grape growers inside. He'd dressed in jeans and a plain gray sweatshirt so he'd fit in with the locals, and when he sauntered in, hardly a head turned in his direction.

The tantalizing odor of bacon and fried onions assailed his nostrils. The regulars spared glances in his direction before returning to their conversations or newspapers. "Coffee, please," he said to the guy behind the counter as he hoisted himself up on a red-vinyl-and-chrome stool. The guy stood almost seven feet tall and had to stoop to walk into the low-ceilinged area where the coffee was made, and when he returned with Josh's cup, Josh saw that the name written on his uniform was Mom.

"Hey, Mom, I'll have another one of those doughnuts," called a man sitting at the end of the counter. Mom reached into a covered container, withdrew a powdered doughnut and tossed it under his arm to its intended recipient. Whereupon everyone chuckled, including Josh.

"Good old Mom, he keeps it lively in here," said the man next to him. He set a folded copy of *The Juice: A Journal for Growers* down beside Josh and took a long pull from his cup.

"That's his real name?"

"Yeah, 'fraid so. It's Momford or Mumford or some unfortunate name like that. I can sympathize, since my parents named me Maurice. I go by Mike."

Josh extended his hand. "Josh Corbett," he said.

"Oh, you're that Mr. Moneybags guy who came all the way from Boston to get reacquainted with Gina."

Josh was slightly taken aback at the familiarity. "Not exactly. I have business here, and it made sense to look her up."

"I heard that some of the Angelinis were surprised when you showed up at their crush last night." Mike eyed him curiously.

"How do you know?"

"That's the scuttlebutt."

"There's gossip already? I only arrived two days ago."

"I see Devon Vost every morning when I drop my daughter off at day care. She's Gina's cousin."

Josh vaguely remembered Devon, a cheerful young woman with a kind face whom he'd met at crush. He wondered why she would be telling this Mike person what the Angelinis thought about his showing up.

Mike answered his unasked question. "You see, Devon is married to my sister's brother-in-law. Practically everyone you'll meet around here is related to the Angelinis in some way."

Josh sipped his coffee; it was good. He thought about asking Mom for a doughnut but discarded the idea, amusing though it was to watch one flying through the air.

"They seemed friendly," he said to Mike. "The Angelinis, I mean."

"There are no nicer people in the world. You don't want

to get on the wrong side of them, though. About Gina—everyone thinks she's pretty special, and folks in Rio Robles didn't like it that she wasn't picked to win the million dollars.''

"I gathered that," Josh said on a note of regret.

Mike eyed Josh speculatively. "You're not figuring to make a play for her, are you?"

Josh didn't want to tip his cards to someone he'd just met. "You never know," he said.

"You do that and you hurt Gina again, the Angelinis won't let you get away with it."

Great. A threat. That was all he needed.

"What kind of business did you say you have here?" asked Mike.

He hadn't. "I'm writing an article about the valley."

"For some big newspaper or something?"

"No, it's for a company newsletter. The company has an interest in winemaking." A recent interest, and the article would appear in the newsletter after the beverage conglomerate in which his family had a controlling interest bought out a winery or two in the valley. This was all hush-hush so far, and it was going to stay that way, at least as long as Josh had anything to say about it.

"You might like to read *The Juice*," Mike said, pushing it toward Josh. "Being that you write for a newsletter and all."

Josh accepted the folded paper and stood up. "I'd better be going. Thanks for the paper and the warning," he said as he tossed a bill on the counter.

"Sure. Nice meeting you. I'm here every morning about this time, and I hope we'll run into each other again."

When Josh left, Mike was asking Mom for a doughnut. This time Mom ran with it to the kitchen, feinted and tossed it overhand.

"Best play I've seen since the last Super Bowl," hollered one of the customers.

"One of their scouts tried to recruit me last week," Mom said.

This provoked a round of good-natured jeers. But Josh didn't stick around to hear any more. He had business here, all right. He was going to put his phone calls on the back burner and try to talk Gina into having lunch with him. He'd struck out with his invitations to drinks and dinner, but lunch? It was a nonthreatening suggestion, time limited and requiring no special dress.

He was willing to bet that Gina would say yes when he asked her. She'd had that glint in her eye that was the give-away of an interested female, and come to think of it, he seldom met any other kind.

Chapter Four

"No," Gina said firmly. She was standing on a ladder, tacking up bunches of dried flowers over the cash register. Josh sneezed.

"You really should take an allergy pill whenever you decide you're going to stop by and be a nuisance," she said as she climbed down from the ladder. She had discarded this morning's smock and put on a short, sleeveless ribbed top. It fit so snugly that he could see her nipples through her bra.

"You're right," he said, unable to tear his eyes away. When he did, they aimed themselves downward and focused on the strip of skin between the top and her jeans. Her belly button showed, a sweet little dimple that put him in mind of intimacies that the two of them had never shared.

She folded the ladder and shoved it behind a tall screen covered in burlap. Sprigs of various dried herbs were pinned to the screen, all tied up in bright scraps of ribbon. Gina had an artistic bent; he could tell from the way she'd decorated her store. She had draped lace fabric across shelves and scrunched it up to make display places for packages of herbs, and here and there he saw several other original touches.

A customer walked up to the counter and set several small paper and plastic bags of herbs that she'd selected from bins set into old wine casks arrayed along the side wall. "Hello,

Gina. I'm on my monthly run over from St. Helena to stock
up on my favorites.''

''Did your mother try brewing the chamomile tea you took
home last month?'' Gina asked.

''Yes, and she's sleeping much better, thanks.''

''Wow, Tori, that's great. Tell her I said hello.''

''I will.''

Gina rang the transaction up on the cash register and put
all the bags into a larger one with a handle for carrying.
During the few minutes it took, Tori looked him over with
more than a little curiosity. Josh was sure she recognized him
from the TV show—who didn't? He tried to downplay his
presence by wandering off to study a row of cookbooks.

''I'll see you next month, Tori,'' Gina said as she handed
her customer the bag.

''Oh, I wouldn't miss my visit to Good Thymes for the
world,'' Tori said. With a last lingering look at Josh's back,
she left.

''People don't want to let the *Mr. Moneybags* show die,''
Josh observed to Gina as her customer's big SUV jolted out
of the parking lot.

''I certainly do,'' Gina said as she began to tick numbers
off on a list.

''Was the experience so bad?'' he asked. A shaft of sunlight penetrated the filmy curtain on the nearby window,
sparking silvery highlights in Gina's hair. She wore it combed
to one side, and she had braided a small strand and tucked
the braid up with the help of a small daisy. The effect was
enchanting.

''I don't see any need to rehash what happened.'' Her head
remained bowed over her list.

''That's fine. We should pick up where we left off and
forget about the past.''

''Mmm,'' Gina said, clearly not paying attention.

That Gina could ignore his heartfelt friendship and his wish
to let bygones be bygones irked him. At the same time he

realized that this could be the opportunity he'd been waiting for. "And I've heard that polar bears have eaten all the reindeer, so Santa won't be here for the little boys and girls this Christmas."

"Mmm-hmm," Gina replied.

"And as far as stocks are concerned, they've gone through the roof, so how about if we have lunch together today." He was talking nonsense, of course, but it might have the desired effect. He held his breath.

"Mmm...what?" Gina tossed aside the pad of paper and frowned.

"Lunch. You almost agreed to it."

She stood up. "That's it, Josh Corbett! You're not going to trick me into something I don't want to do. Out!"

She pointed a finger at the door, through which two elderly customers happened to be walking.

"Us?" quavered the one in front, a violet-haired woman using a cane.

"Sister and me?" asked the other, wrinkling her powdery brow.

Gina rushed forward to greet them. "Oh, no, of course not, Miss Tess and Miss Dora. Please come in. What can I get for you today? More goldenseal, or perhaps a bit of catnip for dear little Felix?" Over their heads, she glared at Josh.

"We don't need goldenseal, do we, Dora? Catnip would be good. Felix is feeling his age, and it perks him right up." The one with the cane started down the aisle toward the catnip.

"I'd like one of those nice cookbooks, you know, the one that benefits the teen center. We're going to send it to our cousin in Seattle."

"Right over here, Miss Tess." Gina guided her toward the rustic cabinet where the cookbooks were displayed and helped her to pull one down from the shelf.

Josh realized that he was standing beside a wicker basket piled high with lavender sachets. In addition to buying some for his landlady, he supposed he could send packets to his mother and sister. Their scent made his nose itch, though. Lavender always did.

Gina rang up the ladies' order, which took a while because they'd bought a number of items. When she had finished, she turned to Josh. "You'll help Miss Tess and Miss Dora carry these things out to their car, won't you, Josh?"

He stacked the lavender sachets on the counter beside the cash register. "I'd be glad to," he said easily, scooping up their bag.

Neither one of the ladies moved particularly fast, so he was treated to a long and drawn-out account of Felix's last hairball episode, whereupon the two of them became involved in an argument about the best remedies for feline hairballs. By the time he had installed the women in their elderly compact sedan, Josh was eager to get back inside. Then the sedan backed up, heading straight for him. He jumped out of the way barely before being hit.

Miss Tess leaned out the window. "Young man, you look a lot like that Mr. Moneybags fellow. Are you?"

Josh nodded. "Yes, I am."

"You listen to me, sir. Our Gina is a nice girl. Don't you dare hurt her again!"

"I—" Josh began. He didn't get a chance to finish the sentence, since Miss Dora, who was driving, scratched off and left him standing in a cloud of dust.

Did everyone in town dislike him for what he had done to Gina on the show? Didn't they understand it was all a bit of make-believe, conjured up by a couple of producers who were interested in the show's entertainment value and not much else? They hadn't expected him to fall in love with the woman he chose. The most they had hinted should happen was that he and Tahoma might want to keep in touch and give themselves a chance for real romance to develop. He wished there were some way he could let everyone know that

he realized he'd chosen the wrong woman. What was he supposed to do—emblazon a sign across his forehead? He pondered the wording of such a sign. I Should Have Picked Gina.
No, that made her sound like a bunch of grapes. I Was Stupid.
Now, that was more like it. It seemed to fit in with the locals'
opinions of him.

Josh walked slowly back into the cottage. Gina was arranging fresh flowers in a vase on one of the front window-
sills, and he marched up to her.

"Gina, tell me one thing. Do you hate me for the way the
show turned out?"

She was so startled that she dropped a handful of cut ferns,
which scattered around her feet. Josh bent to help her pick
them up.

"Well," Josh demanded, "do you?"

At that moment several other customers came in, and Gina,
after one last annoyed glance in his direction, went to see to
their needs.

She hadn't answered. So perhaps she did hate him. If so,
was any of this pursuing doing any good? Was she so totally
dead set against renewing their friendship that all his efforts
were a waste of time? Would it help if he told her how much
he'd matured since the Mr. Moneybags experience, now that
he'd reflected on what had happened? If he mentioned that,
ultimately, choosing the wrong woman had made him a
wiser, better man?

He hoped that the customers wouldn't linger over their
choices, but two of them seemed inclined to study every bin
and the card next to it in order to learn more about treating
various symptoms with herbs, and another, who was apparently a friend of Gina's, embarked on a long explanation of
a complicated family situation that required patient listening
on Gina's part.

As if that weren't enough, Josh stood too near some dried
goldenrod, began to sneeze and couldn't stop. He fled outside

and sat down on a garden bench beneath an oak tree while he waited for the customers to leave.

The trouble was, they stayed longer than Josh expected, and fast on their heels came three more carloads of people. He peered in the window and saw Gina talking animatedly with one group while the others browsed, and she soon had a line at the cash register.

As soon as everyone left, Josh ambled back inside. Gina, who wore a pencil behind one ear and was adding up receipts, glanced up with a smile of greeting as he entered. It quickly faded when she saw him.

"I thought you'd gone," she said pointedly.

"I was only biding my time. Could you ring up those sachets for me, please?"

"Glad to," she said through tight lips.

"About lunch, Gina."

She tucked his lavender and his cash register receipt into a bag and handed it to him.

"What about it?"

"Let's run downtown and grab a sandwich."

She let out a long sigh. "I can't leave. My relief salesperson won't be in today, so I'm going to make do with peanut butter and crackers."

Disappointment washed over him. "Who's your relief?" The thought occurred to him that he could find whoever it was and beg him or her to show up.

"My sister fills in for me when I need a break. She lives so close that it usually works out well. Today she's at the winery, cleaning up after last night's party. Oh, hello, Shelley. How are things at the Bootery?"

Josh grew glum as he listened to the two women talking about Shelley's business, a shoe store downtown, and soon more customers arrived, some on a tour bus on a day trip to the valley from San Francisco, which was only an hour and a half's drive away. Getting time alone with Gina was almost impossible.

When twelve o'clock came and went, he decided that he might as well leave, but not for good. He'd be back soon, this time with food.

GINA BREATHED AN AUDIBLE sigh of relief as she saw Josh's car exit the parking lot. She and Shelley had business to discuss: the bachelor auction, which was Gina's latest project. Gina had shepherded the auction project through the city council's permit process, had assembled a crackerjack committee and was going to emcee the event. The project would benefit the teen center that was so important to Gina and her family as well as the entire community.

"I'll see you at the next committee meeting," Shelley said after they'd hammered out several decisions concerning the wine to be served, decorations for the stage and recruiting an auctioneer. As soon as Shelley left, Gina recalled that she had promised to phone the other committee members to let them know the time and place of the next meeting. Since this was a lull, she might as well do it now.

She was flipping through the pages of her address book when the door opened and Josh walked in. He carried a paper bag and looked cheerier than he had a right to be.

"Before you tell me to get out, you'd better hear what I have to say," he announced before setting the bag down on the counter in front of her. From it wafted a tantalizing scent of meatballs and marinara sauce, and she recognized it right away as one of Mom's famous sandwiches. Belatedly, she recalled that she'd never eaten lunch.

"You have to eat something," he said.

She stared at him, taking in his determined stance, his sinfully blue eyes and the earnestness that shone from within. What was it about this man that she found so arresting? So fascinating? So all-fired absorbing?

"I suppose you propose to eat what's in that bag," she managed to say, even as her mouth was watering at the thought of sinking her teeth into one of Mom's savory concoctions.

"That's why I brought it," Josh said. He leaned forward on the counter, resting his hands on it and invading her personal space. "What do you say?"

She studied him for a moment, assessing his immovability and his perseverance.

"I think," she said slowly, "that once we eat these sandwiches, they will practically ensure that we won't want to get this close to each other or anyone else until the garlic wears off. Although," she continued distractedly, "we could nibble parsley. It cleanses the breath." She slid down from the stool and went to a cabinet, where she located a stack of paper napkins.

"That's not all I could nibble," Josh said under his breath, and she almost didn't hear him. She decided to let his comment pass, however, considering the uselessness of objecting. Besides, she was hungry.

"We can eat on the bench outside," she told him. "That way I'll see customers slowing on the road before they get here and be back inside by the time they pull into a parking space."

"Must you always be so practical?" Josh said, but there was a note of triumph in his tone.

"Yes, that's the way I am." She sat on one end of the bench and plunked the napkins in the middle. Josh was forced to occupy the other end, but he didn't seem to mind.

"Tell me, Gina. Haven't you ever done anything that you had an urge to do, just for the fun of it?" His mood had changed, and she wasn't sure if this was good or bad.

"I was a contestant on *Mr. Moneybags*. That was totally impractical." She unwrapped her sandwich and appreciatively inhaled its aroma.

"I thought you told me you didn't send in your application yourself, that Rocco did it for you."

"He never expected that I'd actually be chosen to compete.'' She bit into the sandwich, which tasted like pure heaven. She was hungrier than she'd admitted.

"Have you ever done something really risqué? Like taking off your clothes and dancing naked in the moonlight? Like getting a tattoo on a part of your body that isn't usually visible?"

She paused in mid-bite, afraid that she'd choke with indignation if she tried to swallow. "If I had, I wouldn't tell you," she said finally when she could speak.

"Who would you tell?"

"No one."

He looked as if he were digesting this, then dispensed with his jocular mood. "What I really want to know, Gina, is if you hate me."

"No."

"Or if you're seeing someone, or if you're engaged."

She set the sandwich down very carefully and gazed out across the neighboring vineyard. "No on both counts," she said. That she was still unattached was a sore point with her family. Nice Italian girls were supposed to be married before they were thirty—or at least, that was the way it was in her family.

Josh's jubilation was evident in his quick smile. "That's good," he said, and for a moment she suspected that he might try to give her a greasy high-five. She quickly picked up her sandwich again.

"I figured there might be some reason that you don't want to hang out with me," he explained. "Those were the only things I could think of."

"Surely those weren't the *only* things," she said.

"They were, too."

Her first impression of Josh on the night all the contestants had met him was that he was conceited, though charming and handsome. "What is it with men?" she asked. "They tend to think that women should be falling all over them."

"Some women do."

"Not me," Gina said. Rocco sometimes reminded her that this was why she was still unmarried. She usually ignored his jibes, but the words stung more than she cared to admit.

"Why don't you try it? Starting, like, right now."

"You're impossible."

"Could we make that *was?* As in, I *was* impossible? I've changed, Gina, since we first met."

She edged a look in his direction. "What do you mean?" Then, unsure about the conflicted expression flitting across his features, she added quickly, "I don't want to hear anything about you and Tahoma, okay?"

"I wasn't going to talk about her."

"Good."

"I'll be the first to admit that I could have used a comeuppance back there at Dunsmoor Castle. Somebody should have told me off, should have informed me that I was too in love with myself to love anyone else."

"Is that true?" She stared at him openmouthed, then rapidly clamped her mouth shut, considering that she was eating.

"That's why I goofed up. I've learned my lesson, believe me."

"What does that mean?"

"Rejection hurts. I realize that now."

"Mmm," Gina said, bewildered at this unexpected revelation. The silence thickened between them, which was fine with her. They'd be better off to get lunch over with so she could go back to work.

"So, anyway," he said, "I wanted you to know that."

Gina narrowed her eyes, trying to read his expression. He met her gaze unwaveringly, and she decided that he was serious.

"I don't understand why you're telling me this now, Josh."

"Because I've thought about you a lot. Because you haven't let me talk to you in any serious way since I've been here."

"I didn't think you *could* be serious."

"Obviously. Now that you know, maybe we could spend some quality time together."

"Isn't that what we're doing?" she said. "Doesn't this count?"

"Any chance you get to push me away seems to be important to you, so I figure you'll do it again soon. Which only enhances your attraction, by the way."

She didn't know how much more of this conversation she could take. It was time to lighten things up. "Do you mean that if I wasn't pushing you away, you'd lose interest?"

He laughed, a welcome sound. "I doubt it, Gina Angelini. I find you to be a most fascinating human being."

"Why?" She couldn't help asking.

He had finished with his sandwich, and he was folding the wrapper into a neat rectangle. "You're fascinating because you're kind to children and cats. Because I know what you're thinking, at least some of the time. Because you're beautiful and unaware of it. And, oh—because you're sexy as hell, and you do know that, don't you?" His eyes twinkled with amusement at her discomfiture.

"I don't know any such thing," she said faintly, unable to look away from his perfectly arched brows, the dimple that appeared fleetingly when he smiled, the groove in his upper lip.

"I think you do," he said softly, and then, before she could move away, his hand whipped out to capture her chin. His lips brushed hers in a swift kiss.

She jumped up immediately. "That—that will be quite enough," she said primly, walking over and depositing her sandwich wrapper in the nearby trash can.

"Not for me," Josh said, barely suppressed laughter in his voice. A TV fan mag had once described him as "a chunk of hunk, yet a picture of boyish vulnerability." Gina, however, was the one who was feeling vulnerable at this moment.

Leaving Josh sitting right where he was, Gina rushed inside and grabbed a sprig of parsley to cure her of garlic breath before her customers arrived. There wasn't anything she could take, however, to cure her attraction to Josh.

Chapter Five

Josh congratulated himself on a job well done. He'd moved in on Gina so quickly that she hadn't had a chance to run away. And now that they'd kissed, the barriers between them would begin to fall one by one.

He drove back to his apartment, noting when he arrived that Judy Rae's car wasn't in the garage. *Good,* he thought. *I'll have peace and quiet while I make my phone calls.*

A quick perusal of *The Juice* revealed a couple of possibilities. A winery in Sonoma County had fired its winemaker, indicating, perhaps, troubled management. And why would there be a problem with management? Probably because the winery wasn't making money.

Josh called his father first, but his dad's assistant told him that Mr. Corbett was in a meeting, and would Josh like to leave a message? Josh declined, glad that he wouldn't have to talk to Ethan today. His father would want to know if he'd made progress, and he would have to tell him no. He'd had other things on his mind.

Then he called the CEO of Starling Industries, Walter Emsing.

Walter took his call right away, and as always, he sounded hearty and gregarious.

"Josh! About time I heard from you! Any prospects out there in God's country?"

"So far, only God knows," Josh said wryly. "It's going to take me a while, Walter. I told you that."

"I know, I know. At Starling, we're eager to move, so keep me posted. A small to mid-size company would be best, as we've discussed, and we've sold that winery in Australia. Not enough profit, and not enough reason to keep it, considering the risks. We want to hang on to the top management, though, so we can install them in whatever established winery you recommend."

The plan, most of it, was familiar to Josh. "I'm working on it, Walter. I'll check in again when I have news to report." Before he hung up, he gave Walter his number at Mrs. Upthegrove's.

When it was time for dinner, Josh headed for Mom's. It seemed like a good place to pick up news he could use.

He spotted Rocco sitting in a booth as soon as he walked in.

"Hey, Josh! Come sit with us," Rocco said, waving him over.

"Hi, Josh," said Frankie as Josh slid into the booth with them.

Josh rumpled Frankie's hair, and Frankie grinned.

"Dad, can I go play video games in the back room?"

"Sure, son. Hurry back when Edna brings our food." He forked over a fistful of change.

Edna slapped a menu in front of him, and Josh ordered the blue-plate special, which today was meat loaf.

"Are you finding everything you need here in Rio Robles?" Rocco asked.

"I sure am. Everyone is really friendly," Josh replied, taking in the way Rocco was dressed—coveralls over a T-shirt.

Rocco must have seen him looking. "I came straight from my job at my auto repair shop. I didn't feel like cooking today, so I brought Frankie here for dinner. We eat out two or three times a week. This single-father business is no bed of roses, that's for sure."

"I believe that," Josh said.

"Yeah, well, my wife, Cissy, died five years ago. I never thought I'd be able to manage bringing up a kid on my own. Yet here I am." Rocco laughed and shrugged.

"I'm sorry about your wife. Frankie's a great kid."

"Isn't he? I wish I had six more like him. I worry about him growing up an only child. I had a brother and a sister." Rocco took a long drink of water. "I think about marrying again, but after what happened to Cissy, I—well, I don't know if that's what I want." For a moment he seemed lost in memories.

"Anyway," Rocco went on, "I don't think I could ever find a woman as fine as her."

"Still, like you said, it's not easy being a single dad."

"I'd like to have someone to laugh with, you know what I mean? Cissy and I used to laugh all the time. There are women I've gone out with, but none seriously. I even like one of them a lot. Shelley McMahon. She runs the shoe shop downtown."

"I think I saw her in Good Thymes today. Short, with curly brown hair and freckles?"

"That's the one. She was in Gina's place?"

"They seemed like old friends."

"They were in school together. Gina set us up over a year ago, but then Shelley's father got sick and she went to Oregon to take care of him. She's only been back for a few months. You want to hear something interesting? Shelley plays the accordion, just like my Frankie." Rocco grinned and leaned back against the seat. "What do you think, maybe Shelley and me could get married and have a bunch of kids who play the accordion? I'm not sure the world is ready for that." He laughed.

"Maybe some of them would take up the violin or drums out of mercy for your ears."

Rocco slapped his knee. "Now, that would be something. Say, you know what? You're welcome to come to Frankie's accordion recital Thursday night at the elementary school auditorium. He thinks you're the greatest, and he'd probably get a kick out of it if you showed up."

"Thanks, Rocco, I'll keep it in mind."

"It sure surprises me that Frankie turned out to be a musician. He says he wants to get a job with a band when he grows up. I wonder if there are any rock bands that need an accordion player."

"You never can tell what's going to happen next in the music business," Josh said. This was something he knew about; his brother had made a fortune by selling the online music business he'd started in college to a big Hollywood recording studio.

"Same thing in the wine business," Rocco said more seriously.

"You must be one of the few in your family who doesn't work at Vineyard Oaks," Josh observed.

"I had more of a talent for fixing cars. My uncle Fredo believes that you have to have a passion in life, and mine didn't have anything to do with grapes, although my first car was burgundy. It was a cool Mustang. Anyway, Uncle Fredo gave me his blessing to become a mechanic, God bless him."

"I talked with Fredo at crush," Josh said, recalling the likable man with the bushy white hair.

"I guess you could say he's the true patriarch of the family. Everyone listens to Uncle Fredo. Even Gina. Hell, even me." Rocco chuckled.

Edna delivered their food—pot roast in gravy for Rocco and fried chicken for Frankie, who hurried in from the back room when he saw that the food was ready.

"I got over a thousand points in Troll Maze Challenge," he announced proudly. "That's the best I ever done."

"The best I ever did," Rocco corrected as he reached for the salt and pepper.

Frankie punched his father lightly on the biceps. "You

didn't do it, Pop. I did,'' and he laughed uproariously at his own joke.

"How did you manage to get so good at video games?" Josh asked Frankie.

"I've got my ways. I can read minds, did you know that?" Frankie said.

Josh was sure Frankie was teasing. "No!" he said. "How do you do it?"

"That's a secret. I bet I can read *your* mind." Frankie took a bite of chicken.

Josh was willing to play along. "All right, then. What am I thinking?"

"I have to dial you in," Frankie said. "I have to ask you some questions."

Josh shrugged. "Go ahead."

"Don't tell me what it is, but pick a number between one and ten."

"Got it." Josh chose the number eight.

"Now multiply that number by nine."

In his mind, Josh multiplied eight times nine and got seventy-two. "Okay."

"Subtract five from that number."

Josh did. Five subtracted from seventy-two was sixty-seven.

Frankie put his fork down, really getting into this. "Does the number consist of two digits or one?"

"It consists of two."

Josh glanced at Rocco, who went on forking in mashed potatoes.

"Add the two digits together," Frankie said.

The six and seven in the number sixty-seven equaled thirteen when added together. "All right," Josh said, still with no clue where this game was going.

"Is it still a double-digit number?"

"Yes," Josh told him.

"Okay, add the two digits, but don't tell me what the number is, okay?" By this time, Frankie was on the edge of his seat, enjoying Josh's mystification.

"Yeah," Josh said. He added one and three in his head.

"Now, Josh, if the letter *A* is the number one, and *B* is the number two and *C* is three and so on, assign a letter to the number you have in mind, but don't tell me what it is."

Josh's number was four, so that would be the letter *D.* "Got it," he told Frankie.

Frankie made a big show of putting his hands to his temples, closing his eyes and appearing to concentrate. "It's coming through. I'm starting to get vibes," he said.

"Frankie, are you ever going to get to the end of this?" Rocco asked impatiently.

"Sure, Pop. Josh, think of a country that begins with the letter that you're thinking of, and tell me when you've chosen it. Again, don't say what it is," Frankie cautioned.

Josh had been to Denmark on vacation last year, so that was his choice. "I've got a country," he said.

"The second letter of that country is very important," Frankie said. "You need to think of a mammal whose name starts with that second letter."

The second letter in Denmark was *E.* In his mind, Josh immediately pictured an elephant strolling along a country road near Copenhagen.

"Now think of the color of that animal," instructed Frankie.

The elephant in Josh's imagination, like all elephants Josh had ever seen, was gray.

Frankie was pressing his fingers to his temples again. "I'm getting it, I'm really close. I've got it." His eyes flew open. "You're thinking of a gray elephant from Denmark, correct?"

Josh was flabbergasted. "That's it! You're right! How did you do that?"

Frankie laughed. "I told you I could read your mind," he said, picking up a chicken leg.

"Rocco?"

Rocco lifted his shoulders and let them fall in an expressive shrug. "I haven't a clue. I've never seen him do that before. Frankie, what's the secret?"

"I'm smart, I guess," Frankie said.

Josh thought he'd heard every bar trick in the book, but this was a new one. Or maybe Frankie really did know how to read minds.

"If you can read *my* mind," Rocco was saying jovially to his son, "you'll know that I want you to do all your homework tonight."

As he listened to father and son bantering, Josh was amused at Rocco's jokes and Frankie's kid humor. When dinner was over, they all walked to the parking lot together.

"Oh, wow, a Beemer," Frankie said when he spotted Josh's rented BMW. "Maybe we could paint my bike this shade of white, huh, Pop?" The BMW's paint had a pearl finish to it.

"Naw, son, you decided on bright red. I've already bought the paint."

While Frankie was appreciatively running his hand over the car's highly polished finish, Rocco took Josh aside.

"This thing with my cousin Gina," Rocco said. "You seem like a real nice guy. You can't play bocce worth a damn, but I like you."

Josh started to say something, but Rocco held up his hand to silence him. "What I mean to say is, the other guys in the family and me, we look after Gina."

"She's lucky to have such a close family. I told her that."

Rocco's eyes bored into him, suddenly as hard as agate. "I'm glad you realize it. She's a sensitive girl, and we don't like people who aren't good to her."

Josh felt slightly sick in his gut to think that anyone might suggest that he'd harm Gina; it was the last thing he intended to do. He found his voice. "Don't worry, Rocco. I'll treat her right."

Rocco spared him a curt nod, then became congenial again. "You come around the shop, have a few beers with me and the guys some night, okay? Or stop by the house for a game of bocce, like I told you."

"Okay," Josh said.

Rocco and Frankie got into Rocco's pickup truck. "I'll be glad to save a puppy for you," Frankie called as Rocco backed out of the parking space.

"I'll think about it," Josh promised, even though he knew he couldn't take a dog back to Boston with him. That hadn't changed.

But something had. He wasn't viewing the situation with Gina in quite the same way. She was still a challenge, but Rocco's warning had given him pause.

He never started out by planning to hurt a woman's feelings, but certainly it happened more often than not. Usually, the first attraction didn't hold up under the weight of repeated encounters, or he would conveniently plan an out-of-town trip to cool down the romance, or they'd have an argument that couldn't be avoided. His habit after such an experience was to find another willing woman and to give her a whirl until the same thing happened again. This had been his behavior since prep school, woman after woman after woman.

He told himself that he wasn't ready to settle down. He didn't want a house and a family. He couldn't handle the responsibility. All true, at least until recently.

Now, after seeing Gina with her family, after witnessing the give-and-take, her pleasure in living near and being with her kinfolk, he found himself yearning for a place within a similar family circle. Not that it was possible with his far-flung family, all of whom had divergent interests.

What if—but it was a crazy speculation. He had been thinking, what if he fell in love with Gina Angelini?

A good question, but perhaps not the most important one.

The key was whether or not Gina Angelini could fall in love with him. Considering the way things were going, it wasn't even a remote possibility.

THE NEXT DAY AS SHE WORKED, Gina found herself watching the gateposts in the parking lot for Josh's car to come careering through. It didn't appear, which was the irritating way of things. When she didn't want him around, there he was. When she did, he wasn't in sight. It was enough to drive a person to distraction.

Which was why, when Mia arrived to do her homework because her mother was still working in the office at Vineyard Oaks, Gina wasn't any good at helping her with her times tables. After a while, Mia threw her pencil down on the counter. "Aunt Gina, you're not much good at this! Nine times six is fifty-four, not sixty-four!"

Gina blew out a long breath. "Sorry, Mia. I'm failing at anything that requires concentration today." She went to the door and let Timothy in, and he meowed and twined around her ankles.

"Can I feed him?" Mia asked, her math forgotten.

"Of course. Go upstairs and pour some crunchies in his dish. You know where to find the cat food."

Mia went running up the stairs to Gina's apartment, Timothy in hot pursuit.

Gina sighed and stuck a bunch of cash register receipts on a spindle. Business had been slow today, and there was only half an hour to go before closing time. She had a mind to close up early.

"Mia," she called up the stairs. "Want to stay for dinner? I have lasagna."

"Mmm, I'd love it!"

"Okay, I'll phone your mom and ask if it's okay."

Gina dialed Barbara at the winery. "Hi, Barb, it's me. I invited Mia to stay for lasagna tonight. Is that okay with you?"

Her sister sounded harried. "You bet. In fact, it's a god-send. Uncle Fredo had a big meeting here today, and I'm preparing the minutes. He wants them first thing in the morning, and Elizabeth, who was doing some filing for me, is home with the twins, who both have colds. Stacey wants to sleep over with her best friend tonight, and Nick is in Atascadero for a few days. If I didn't have to cook, the minutes would be a piece of cake."

"No problem. Give me a ring when you get home and I'll bring Mia over."

"It might be late, Gina."

"She can always sleep here."

"You're the best sister I've got," Barbara said. She sounded more relaxed now, not as uptight.

"I'm your only sister," Gina reminded her. They were both laughing when they hung up.

"Aunt Gina, did Mom say it was okay for me to stay?" Mia was at the top of the stairs, calling down to her.

"Yes, so would you take the lasagna out of the fridge so it can warm up a bit before I put it in the oven?"

"Sure."

Gina heard Mia's quick footsteps as she traversed the floor over to the refrigerator. Another customer had come in during her conversation with Barbara, and she turned to see who it was.

"Lasagna, huh? Is there enough for me?"

It was Josh. He wore his Vineyard Oaks T-shirt and jeans, which for him was more casual than usual, and his hair fell across his forehead in kempt disarray.

"I—I didn't see you drive up," she stammered.

"I rode a bike."

"A bike?"

"A mountain bike, to be exact. I rented it downtown."

Mia bounced down the stairs. She smiled in delight when she saw Josh.

"Josh! Did you ask if there was enough lasagna for you? Well, there is. Isn't there, Aunt Gina?"

"I'm not sure," Gina said, wishing Josh would stop looking her over from top to toe.

"It's a whole panful. Do you like lasagna, Josh?"

"Love it," Josh said, his eyes never straying from Gina's figure. Today she was wearing navy pants and a snug red-and-white-striped jersey. Josh Corbett was studying her as if he could see straight through the layers of fabric to her bare skin.

"Then you should stay. Shouldn't he, Aunt Gina?"

If only there were a way to silence her irrepressible niece. "I'm sure Josh has better things to do," she said faintly.

"Oh, I don't know," Josh said, lifting a brow in her direction.

"You're staying, you're staying," Mia crowed as she hopped down the rest of the stairs.

"That sounds good to me." Josh's grin was infuriating, but things had already gone too far. Now Mia was taking Josh's hand and leading him outside.

"I want to show Josh the new bird bath," she said. "I helped pick it out from the truck that brought it," she explained in an aside to Josh. He was glancing back over his shoulder, a glint of amusement in his eyes.

Gina let out an exasperated breath. Being outsmarted by a nine-year-old was galling, to say the least, although she couldn't help admiring the way Mia had finessed the situation.

She'd give Mia a piece of her mind when she got a chance. There was no way she could allow her niece to go on running her life, no matter how much she loved her.

Chapter Six

While Josh and Mia were still outside, Gina smoothed her hair back and ran upstairs. Usually, she wasn't particular about her housekeeping, but having Josh as a guest made her look at her home in a whole new light. The first thing she encountered in the living room was the jacket she'd taken to crush slung over a chair, and she picked it up and hung it in a closet. She grabbed a handful of magazines off the coffee table and stuffed them in a drawer, glancing around to see if anything else was out of place.

She loved her small space, with its handhewn oak beams overhead, its smooth wood floors underfoot and the attic at the rear that was kept fragrant by drying herbs. She had furnished the tiny bedroom with an old brass bedstead that had belonged to her grandparents, and the fabrics she'd used for curtains and bedspread were creamy shades of yellow. The kitchen was a marvel. How her cousin Jimmy, who was a renovator and builder, had managed to squeeze all the requisite appliances in while leaving space for a dining nook was beyond her. It was her favorite room, with its strings of drying garlic and peppers and its marble pedestal table that just managed to seat four if at least three of them were skinny.

"Gina, Gina! Josh and I saw an owl in the big oak tree!" Mia called as the door slammed downstairs.

"I'm up here," she replied.

Mia clattered upstairs. "Josh saw the owl first. It was awesome! Do you think it'll use the bird bath?"

"Maybe," Gina said distractedly as she began to wash sprigs of freshly picked marjoram under the faucet. She wouldn't have fussed over dinner if Josh weren't there. His presence made everything different, made her more critical of her cooking as well as her home.

As he jogged up the stairs, she hastily wiped her hands on her apron. "Come in," she said, although by the time she said it, he was already in.

His gaze roamed the room, but he set her mind at ease immediately. "I really like what you've done to this place," he said, his attention captured by the stained-glass piece that she had hung in the kitchen window before his eyes moved on to the pot holders that she'd embroidered with pictures of herbs.

"Thanks," she said. She paused, awkward now that he was actually standing in the middle of her kitchen. "Would you like a glass of wine?"

"Sure," he said.

The kitchen was so small that her sleeve touched his as she brushed past him on the way to the pantry.

Mia plopped herself on the floor between the living room and kitchen and began to dig through her school backpack. "Aunt Gina, is it okay if I go in your bedroom to work on my social studies assignment?"

"Of course," Gina told her. Mia liked to sit at her small vanity table and do her homework.

"Want me to set the table first?"

"No, I'll take care of it. But thanks."

Mia zipped her backpack and heaved it onto her shoulder. "Call me when you're ready," she said before she left.

Gina wished that Josh would stop staring at her. Had he done that in round one, the *Mr. Moneybags* show? If he had, he hadn't been so obvious about it.

"Where was I?" she said to herself.

"Getting me a glass of wine," Josh reminded her.

"Oh, of course." She took a bottle of wine off the shelf.

Josh studied the label. "It's not a Vineyard Oaks wine?"

"Nope, but it's excellent. Made by friends of our family's, and it tastes great with pasta." She'd chosen a zinfandel with a high acid content, the perfect complement to lasagna.

"I'll do the honors," Josh said.

She handed him a corkscrew, and he proficiently uncorked the wine while she cut several large slices of bread from a fresh-baked loaf.

"Looks good," Josh said when she began to sprinkle the bread with chopped marjoram and parmesan cheese.

"Most people like garlic bread with pasta. I prefer this," she said.

"Did you grow that herb in your garden?"

"Yes, it's marjoram." She arranged the bread on a cookie sheet and put it in the toaster oven.

By this time, Josh had uncorked the bottle. He held it out to her. "Want to sniff?"

She sniffed, but her nose was distracted by a whiff of Josh's after-shave. She couldn't identify the brand, but it was surely something expensive.

"It's fine," she said, though she wasn't referring solely to the wine.

"Glasses?"

"In there." She pointed to a cabinet to Josh's right.

He poured each of them a glass and saluted her with his. "Cheers," he said.

"Cheers," Gina replied automatically. She sipped her wine.

They drifted into the living room, where Gina perched on a chair and Josh sat down across from her on the couch.

"Assuming that you didn't come here merely to annoy me, why are you in Rio Robles?" she asked.

Did she catch a moment's hesitation, or was it her imagination? "I'm writing an article," he said. "About the wine industry."

In response to her questioning look, he said, "It's not my usual. It's an assignment from my family business that gave me an opportunity to travel to the West Coast."

"Which made it possible for you to show up in my shop?"

"Yes, and to visit an old college buddy who lives in San Francisco. I haven't caught up with him yet, unfortunately. He's out of the country on business, and I'm not sure when he'll be back."

"And that's why you have all this extra time on your hands," Gina supplied.

"You might say that. You might also say that I would have wanted to spend time with you even if I'd connected with Brian. He might like to meet you."

"Not interested," she said, much too quickly. "Although my cousin Emily is available. She broke up with her boyfriend a few weeks ago. If Brian isn't married, I mean."

"Brian's a bachelor, like me."

"In that case, bring him around. I'll sign him up to participate in our annual bachelor auction." She could have bitten her tongue when Josh's eyes lit up.

"Bachelor auction? You mean you have so many eligible guys around here that you have to auction them off?"

"Not exactly. The auction benefits the proposed teen center in town, and it's my pet project." She couldn't imagine Josh Corbett being auctioned off to the highest bidder, but she would never discourage him. The teen center was too close to her heart.

"What happens?"

"It's a big fancy affair that we have every year. Everyone dresses up, and women bid for a date with the most eligible bachelors we can find. The auction is carried on the town's public service cable TV channel, and volunteers answer phones to take the bids." She glanced at her watch. "I'd better check the lasagna," she said.

She stood and hurried into the kitchen, where she looked in through the glass in the oven door and saw that the lasagna was bubbly around the edges.

"This is done," she said. She slipped her hand into an oven mitt and removed it from the oven.

"Is dinner ready?" Mia asked, popping out of the bedroom.

"It will be as soon as you toss the salad."

"Can I make the dressing?"

"If you're careful not to spill," Gina said. She had taught Mia how to make a simple oil-and-vinegar dressing a couple of months ago.

"Oh, goody!"

Gina took the oil and vinegar out of the kitchen cabinet. "Don't put too much vinegar in," she cautioned.

Mia wrinkled her nose. "Last time I put too much in and we both became sourpusses," she said to Josh, who laughed.

Gina set the lasagna on the table. "We're ready to eat," she said. "Gather around."

Josh made her nervous in her small kitchen, watching her as she arranged the parmesan-marjoram toast on a small platter.

"Josh, you sit there," Mia said as she sat down across from Gina. "That's the company chair. When Frankie or Stacey come, they sit there." She pointed to the chair across from her.

"Mia, you may say grace," Gina said as she sat down.

They bowed their heads, and Mia offered a brief blessing. When Gina raised her head again, Josh was studying her.

"Do you have much company?" Josh asked, and Gina slanted a keen look at him. He was clearly fishing.

"Once Craig Altman came," Mia said. "He and Aunt Gina had a date."

"Is that so?" Josh said, shooting a speculative glance in Gina's direction.

"Mia, pass Josh the salad," Gina said, flustered to see how

Josh took this information. Craig Altman had been the deejay at the local radio station, and she'd gone out with him a few times before he'd accepted a job in Arizona.

Josh spooned salad into his bowl. "I don't suppose I could be considered one of your dates," he said, causing her to almost drop her fork.

"You were her date in Scotland," Mia said seriously. "You could be her date again if you like."

"Do you like?" Josh asked impishly, turning to Gina.

"No," she said. "You're here due to Mia's perseverance."

"What's perseverance?" asked Mia.

"I'll let Josh explain."

Josh rolled his eyes. "Thanks, Gina."

"You're welcome."

"Well, what is it?" Mia piped, apparently intrigued by this conversation, though it was unclear whether she was more fascinated by the byplay between Gina and Josh or the possibility of learning a new word to impress Frankie.

"Perseverance is persistence," Josh said, but Mia only seemed confused. "It's keeping on and keeping on, trying to get your way."

"Oh, like Frankie when he wanted me to give him my last stick of gum. He kept on talking about it until I gave in."

"Exactly," Josh said. "It can be a good thing, this persistence."

"Like when?" asked Mia.

"Like when you really, really want something." He eyed Gina. "And you don't give up."

Gina had heard enough. "New topic," she said. "Miss Tess and Miss Dora stopped by the shop, Mia. Miss Tess said to say hello to you. She wants you to come over and play with Felix sometime."

"He's a good cat," Mia said. "He doesn't play much anymore, only with me."

"They bought a fresh supply of catnip today," Gina said. "That should pep him up."

"It's too bad they don't have catnip for people," Josh said. "There are some of us who need to play more." He skewered Gina with a meaningful look.

Mia dissolved in giggles. "Catnip for people! That's funny."

"It depends what you consider 'play,'" Gina said, doing her best to ignore Mia.

"Play for grown-ups is anything that allows them to have a good time. I could suggest some things if you don't have any ideas of your own." The roguish tilt of Josh's eyebrows didn't leave room to doubt his meaning.

"I have plenty of ideas of my own," she retorted. "It's just that I prefer to choose my playmates. And I usually don't select those that haven't chosen me."

"Touché," muttered Josh.

Mia, oblivious to the undercurrent of meaning, spoke up. "I think wine makes people play more. I noticed it at crush. All the grown-ups who normally look so-o-o serious were dancing around in the grape barrels. Like you and Aunt Gina."

"Would you care for more lasagna, Josh?" Gina asked, wanting to head the conversation in a different direction.

"Yes, it's wonderful. Absolutely the best lasagna I've ever had, and that's saying something. I like to go to the Italian restaurants in the north end of Boston, and their lasagna can't match yours, trust me."

"That is the problem," Gina said. "I can't trust you." She got up and began to fill their water glasses from the pitcher.

She felt Josh's gaze boring into her back. "Truth in jest, right?"

"You might infer that." Trouncing him didn't give her any feeling of superiority, however. It only made her sad, because at one time, she'd thought he was totally trustworthy.

"The trouble with grown-ups is that half the time you don't understand what they're talking about," Mia observed. "Like now."

"That's true," Josh said soberly. "If it's any consolation, Mia, when you're an adult, you may not understand it, either. Also like now."

Mia slid to the edge of her chair. "May I be excused? I'd like to go watch TV now."

"Of course, but take off your shoes before you climb up on the bed, okay?"

"Okay." Mia left the table and went into the bedroom, where they heard her turn on the television.

"Do you make all your visitors take off their shoes before they get in your bed?"

"That is a really nosy question," she told him.

"If I were invited into your bed, I'd be glad to comply," he answered quickly. "In case you were wondering."

"I wasn't." Gina started to clear the table. There weren't many dishes, and Josh immediately began to help.

"You don't have to do that," she said.

"I want to."

Gina began to stack dishes in the dishwasher. Josh was whistling between his teeth annoyingly as he brought dishes over from the table, ignoring the fact that she had to scrunch into a corner to keep from brushing against him as she loaded the dishwasher.

For his part, he seemed maddeningly unaware of any problem. "Anything wrong?" he asked when she'd slammed the dishwasher door closed and was trying to figure out how to slide past him into the living room.

She decided the time had come to tell him what she really thought. "I'm not sure I appreciate how you weaseled your way in here tonight," she said, feeling two spots of color beginning to burgeon on her cheeks.

"Weaseled? Please! I merely accepted the invitation that was offered."

"That's exactly what you did for crush. Do you think it's fair to manipulate a nine-year-old to help you get what you want?"

He looked doubtful. "That's not how I see it. Mia is a charming child, and I enjoy her company almost as much as yours. Certainly, she's easier to get along with."

"Which brings me to a question. If I'm so difficult, why do you want to hang out with me?" Gina took off her apron and slung it across a chair back.

"Let's just say that I like a challenge, plus there's not much else to do in this little town."

"Oh, but there is. There are wine-tasting tours, and riding bikes, and gondola rides on the river, and—" Too late, she realized that she'd stepped into a trap of her own making. "And lots of things," she finished lamely.

"Why don't you show me how much fun those things can be?" Josh said, his eyes sparkling. "Why don't we go wine-tasting someday?"

To cover her confusion, she called to Mia. "Mia, you'd better phone your house and see if your mom's home from the winery."

"All right," Mia said.

She turned to Josh. "I'm really very busy with the bachelor auction and my shop. I don't have time for frivolous pursuits." He leaned toward her, one arm braced on the countertop behind her. He was so close that she could smell the sunshine in the cotton of his shirt, could sense the hair on her arms rising with the shiver of anticipation that swept through her.

"I should participate in whatever the Napa Valley offers for entertainment," he said. "For the article I'm writing."

She stood stiff and unmoving, her breathing suddenly labored and tense. "I could have my aunt Donna show you around. She works for the chamber of commerce." Josh shifted his weight from one foot to the other, and she took advantage of the opportunity to edge away toward the blessedly fresh air at the window. Her face was hot, and not just because the kitchen was warm from the oven's being on.

"I don't want to see the Napa Valley with your aunt. She's probably seventy years old and—"

"She's only about forty. You'd like her a lot." Beads of perspiration began to break out on her forehead, and with great difficulty, she managed to swallow.

"No doubt she's charming, like all your relatives. Not as charming as you, however. I'm pretty certain of that."

"She's only five years older than you. I'm five years younger than you. You might have much more in common with her than with me. She's been to Italy. She's vacationed in Hawaii twice. She was married to my uncle Richard, who died. You could—"

"I couldn't. Gina, I wish you'd look at me. And stop talking." He reached for one of her hands and drew her closer. "Remember what it was like? On the moor that day?"

She'd been wishing for the past two years that she didn't remember. "It was cold, and I nearly froze." She yanked her hand away, but he only recaptured it.

"We weren't aware of how cold it was. We were all warm and snug in that abandoned stone croft where we sheltered from the wind. Our eyes met and my mind went blank. The only thing I could think of was you—the way your eyes light up from inside when you like something, your pleasure in simple things, like the birds winging overhead into the blue, blue sky."

She gazed at him, spellbound. She remembered that day and those feelings with a stunning clarity. The shimmer of the heather on the hillside, the glassy silver surface of the pond in the distance. The sunlight warm upon her face. The easy companionship of walking hand in hand with Josh.

"We sheltered in the croft from a sudden shower. I saw raindrops glistening on your cheek, and I touched it. I brushed away the rain, like this," and he demonstrated. "Your skin was so silky. I slid my arms around you, just this way, and pulled you closer."

Lost in the memory, she let herself be drawn into the comfortable circle of his arms, oblivious to Mia chatting on the phone in the bedroom, to the insistent meowing of Timothy below in the garden.

"And I kissed you, Gina. Like I'm going to kiss you now."

His words had taken her back to that magic place on the moor where she had first felt the stirrings of love for him. Her head tilted back, and she was holding her breath, as if doing so could freeze that special and very tender moment in time so that she could revisit it whenever she wanted.

"Like this," Josh breathed, the words soft against her cheek, and he touched his lips to hers.

She knew she should have pushed him away, should have made him leave. Instead, she parted her lips and her eyes closed so she could experience the sensation even more deeply. His lips on hers were gentle, then demanding, testing, demanding even more. It was like that day in the abandoned croft, a time that she had replayed over and over again during many lonely nights, only this was better. It was real. She was kissing Josh Corbett himself, not a slowly fading memory of someone she'd been trying desperately to forget.

She was crushed so close against him that she felt his heart beating against hers, and she could taste his hunger for her on his lips. She'd never forgotten the intensity of her feelings when she'd kissed him on that remote Scottish moor so far away from all that she held dear, but she had forgotten the sheer physicality of her response. The racing of her heart, the desire flooding her veins. The passion, and the surrender.

But she could not and would not surrender now. When at last he released her lips, she shakily pushed him away. "That's enough, Josh."

"I don't think so," he said. He started to pull her toward him again, but she sidestepped his grasp.

"Mia, did you talk to your mother?"

Mia came bouncing out of the bedroom, and Gina was

thankful that she had managed to put a decent distance between her and Josh.

"Mom says she won't be home until late, and is it okay for me to spend the night here? She says she talked to you about it earlier."

"Yes, that's fine," she said, hoping that Mia couldn't detect how aroused she still was. "I'll call your mother and tell her."

"Good," Mia said. She turned to Josh. "Are you spending the night, too?"

"I wish," Josh said ruefully, which earned him a warning look from Gina.

"I'd better go now," Josh said.

"I'll walk you downstairs," Mia said.

Gina cleared her throat. "No, Mia, I'll do it. I have to lock up. Why don't you get your mother on the phone again so I can talk to her when I come back."

Mia ran off to do her aunt's bidding, and Gina turned to Josh, keeping her tone low. "I wanted to speak to you privately. That's why I told her I'm going to walk down with you."

"I'd like to speak to you, too. Privately." He glanced toward the bedroom where they could see Mia sitting on the edge of the bed, punching numbers into the phone.

Before Gina could object, he had taken her hand and she was following him down the stairs. At the bottom, Josh pulled her roughly around to face him. When he spoke, his voice rasped with emotion, the same emotion that she read in his eyes. "Gina, that kiss we shared up there should prove to you that the two of us have unfinished business. I want to see you as often as possible. I want to get to know you without the intrusion of the television cameras and a bunch of other people."

She stared into his face, experiencing a sense of déjà vu. This was the face that she'd fallen in love with, after all. More than anything, she needed him to be that person again, the man she'd thought she could trust. But at the same time, it was clear that he wasn't that man, and perhaps he never had been. Perhaps she had expected too much of him from the very beginning.

"Josh, whatever business we had with each other was over and done with two years ago. You can't expect to show up here in Rio Robles and force your way into my life. It's not fair." The words tumbled out in a torrent, and when their eyes caught and held, she realized that he certainly did expect to pick up where they'd left off.

"Do you realize what you're saying?" he demanded.

"I'm saying I don't want you to come around anymore." She would hold firm. She wouldn't give in.

"I don't think you mean that," Josh said, tipping her chin up.

She steeled herself against his charm, his good looks, the flare of disappointment in his eyes. "Go home to Boston, where you belong, Josh." But her thoughts became a jumble inside her head, ricocheted inside her skull and collided with one another in confusion when he allowed his lips to graze her temple in a sweet and gentle kiss.

"I'm not going anywhere," he said close to her ear, in a voice that churned up a thousand forbidden thoughts.

"I can't make you leave Rio Robles; but please, don't come here," she whispered, stricken to know that they would never do any of the things she was thinking about. *Never, never, never,* the words echoed in her heartbeat, in her pulse.

"We'll see," Josh said. Then he was gone, the door slamming behind him, and everything became ordinary again. Timothy was weaving insistently through her ankles, and Mia was calling from upstairs, "Aunt Gina, didn't you want to talk to Mom on the phone?" All was back to normal, yet it was not. She wondered if it would ever be.

She watched through the open door as Josh strapped on a bike helmet and switched on the headlamp. He waved to her and grinned before mounting the bike and pedaling off into the night. She didn't wave back.

"Be right there," she called to Mia, trying to sound as if nothing unusual had happened. She picked Timothy up and carried him, purring loudly, up the stairs. When she reached the kitchen, she pulled the curtain aside at the window. She could barely see the taillight on Josh's bike receding into the distance on the highway.

Chapter Seven

Josh didn't stop by the next day, nor did he make an appearance on the next. Gina found herself glancing toward the driveway at odd times, especially when she didn't have a customer. She was distracted when ringing up sales to the point that twice she had to void them. Worst of all, Mia kept prattling about Josh, how he laughed when she said something funny, how he'd complimented the salad dressing she'd made for dinner.

"I like him," Mia said. "I'm going to invite him to my skating party."

"I wouldn't do that if I were you," Gina told her, trying her best to sound firm.

"Why not? I bet he's a good skater."

That wasn't all Gina would bet he was good at, but she held her tongue.

And when she dropped by Mia's skating party the next evening to take her a birthday present, there was Josh at the center of a clutch of male relatives, regaling them with some story about scuba diving in the South Pacific. Gina pointedly ignored him, returning his smile and genial wave with a slight nod, and she made excuses to leave the rink as soon as she could.

As if that weren't enough, he turned up at her aunt Victorine's family dinner the following Sunday, escorted by

Rocco and an enthralled Frankie, who seemed to hang on Josh's every word. This appearance rated a bit of stilted conversation with him about the weather before Josh retired to the den with the guys and started talking antique cars. Though she couldn't help walking past the room and even made eye contact with Josh twice as she helped clear the table, Gina kept her distance.

Her cousin Jaimie's questions about Josh and why he was there soon became annoying.

"Ask Rocco" was Gina's terse reply, after which Jaimie merely slid puzzled glances at her out of the corners of her eyes until she, too, disappeared into the den. Gina volunteered to hold her cousin Rosalie's colicky baby, thus saving herself from having to make nice to Josh or the other guys when they finally emerged from the den and went outside to shoot baskets.

Afterward, Gina realized that she was spending far too much time obsessing about Josh Corbett, worrying about what Angelini family functions he'd honor with his presence next. When she accosted Rocco, he fluffed off her objection to his including Josh at events that he had no right to attend.

"Frankie's crazy about Josh," Rocco said. "Besides, I suspect Josh still likes you."

"The question here," Gina replied stiffly, "is whether I like him."

"Listen, Gina. You don't like the guy, you don't have to hang out with him. The point is, Frankie and I think he's great, and so does everyone else. I'd be the first to make life difficult for Josh Corbett if he disses you again, but telling him to get lost because you don't like seeing his face at family gatherings? No way."

Gina didn't understand how Josh managed to hold sway over her relatives, other than the fact that he was personable, charming and, yes, good-looking. Still, his return to her life was a bit much to deal with.

"What's the matter with you, dear?" her mother, Maren,

asked a day or so after Mia's skating party when she came
by Good Thymes to pick up fresh mint to serve with the lamb
that Aunt Dede was preparing for a banquet.

"Nothing," Gina told her. "I've got a lot on my mind
right now, that's all."

"Oh, the bachelor auction. I heard that only twelve men
have signed up."

This was true, and it didn't bode well for the event. "We
need at least fifteen. I've a good mind to sign up Rocco. I
could get even with him for sending my application to *Mr.
Moneybags.*"

"Was that so bad? You had a very nice vacation in Scotland because of the show."

Maren could always be counted upon to play the devil's
advocate, but Gina didn't always appreciate hearing an op-
posing view. She made a face and decided that she'd avoid
the obvious—mentioning Josh. "It was cold in Dunsmoor,
and I had a miserable time at Loch Ness when we all went
to see if there was really a Loch Ness monster."

Maren countered with "Only because that mean girl from
Ohio tripped you and you fell into a puddle."

"That's how I found out that there really is a Loch Ness
monster, and her name is Heidi." Heidi had been eliminated
from the game only one day after causing Gina's inglorious
sprawl in the mud.

Maren picked up her bags of mint. "Give me a call when
you're not so busy. We'll have lunch."

"Okay," Gina said, kissing her mother on the cheek.
"Maybe Barbara can come with us."

"I'd love that. She can leave the kids with Nick, and we'll
go to Volare." It was the most elegant restaurant in town,
and it was owned by Angelinis.

Her mother turned when she reached the door. "Oh, Gina,
don't forget Frankie's accordion recital. It's tomorrow
night."

"I wouldn't miss it," Gina assured her.

After Maren left, Gina spent some time going over her accounts, and then she ate lunch. It was a solitary meal consisting of cold pizza, and she kept remembering the day that Josh had brought meatball sandwiches. For the life of her, she couldn't recall what it was about him that had irritated her so much on that day. Or any day, come to think of it.

Sighing, she checked her appointment book to see what the rest of her week looked like. A committee meeting for the bachelor auction tonight, and tomorrow, Frankie's accordion recital.

Nothing really exciting. Nothing really new.

Well, there could have been something—and someone—exciting in her life, but she had sent him away. Which was no more than he had done to her back in Scotland, but still. Reminding herself that the reason she'd sent him packing was self-preservation didn't help a whole lot. The comfort that fact afforded was as cold as the pizza she'd eaten for lunch.

WHEN GINA TRIED TO START her car that night to go to the committee meeting, something whirred under the hood and died.

She got out, slammed the door and raised the hood, then regarded the engine with trepidation. She could check the oil and the radiator, and that was the extent of her car care knowledge. She'd learned from past experience that the best thing to do under such circumstances was to phone Rocco, so she stumped back inside the cottage and dialed his number.

"Rocco," she said without preliminaries. "My car just quit." In the background she could hear Frankie practicing the accordion.

"Okay, calm down and tell me what happened," Rocco said.

She described the car's death rattle, told him there was no smoke and no fire. "Sounds like the battery," he said.

"We put a new one in only a couple of months ago."

"I'll take a look at it tomorrow. I can send the tow truck to your house. They'll pick your car up first thing in the morning."

Gina sighed. "All right, Rocco, and thanks. I'll watch for the tow truck." After she hung up, she called one of her committee members, who fortunately was happy to swing by to pick her up.

The next morning, Gina's car left, ingloriously towed. She had no idea when Rocco would have it ready for her, and when it wasn't back by dinnertime, she knew she'd have to find a ride to Frankie's recital. She called Rocco first.

"No problem," he told her. "You can come with Frankie and me."

"That's good, but doesn't he have to be at the school auditorium early?"

"Only fifteen minutes or so. Leo Buscani has those kids so well prepped for this recital that they all understand exactly what to do."

"I can't wait to hear Frankie play," Gina said, and she meant it. The boy's obsession with the accordion was mind-boggling for her as well as the rest of her family.

"Yeah, well, he's not the Boy Scout type, and he isn't into sports all that much, so I'm glad he has an activity that keeps him busy. A kid like Frankie needs to have worthwhile things to do, you know?"

Gina did know. Too many kids in Rio Robles got involved with things they shouldn't, which was why building a teen center was one of her top priorities.

When Rocco stopped by to get her, Gina was pleased to see that Frankie was all spruced up, his hair carefully slicked into fashionable spikes, his new jacket hanging loosely on his compact frame and his white shirt spotless.

"Are you psyched up for this recital?" Gina asked him.

Frankie replied with a wide grin. "You bet. I know my piece inside out."

Rocco dropped Frankie off at the back door of the auditorium. As Rocco and Gina walked into the school, people called out greetings.

"Hi, Gina. Hi, Rocco. Lovely night, isn't it?"

"Yes, and we're going to hear some good music," Rocco called back.

"Can't wait to hear that boy Frankie play."

Gina smiled up at Rocco. "Are you excited?"

"Nervous," Rocco grunted. "I remember how hard it was for me."

Gina laughed. "Ditto the violin." Almost every Angelini, unless he or she could show just cause, was supposed to learn to play one or the other.

Being back inside Rio Robles Elementary School awakened memories for Gina, who had been a student there years ago. The scent of floor wax, the smell of chalk dust wafting outward from the classrooms, seemed so familiar. The auditorium was exactly the same, its blue velvet stage curtain only slightly more frayed than in the old days. Gina and Rocco found seats in the middle section, and Gina, after greeting one or two friends who sat nearby, glanced over the program. Many of the children who were playing in the recital were relatives. She scanned the faces of her fellow audience members. Her mother was there, and her sister, Barbara, with her family down in one of the first rows, and—but who was that sitting beside Mia?

It couldn't be. Why would Josh be here? Yet she didn't know anyone else whose hair was shaped exactly that way or who wore such a well-cut blue blazer. Almost as if he could feel her gaze on the back of his head, the man in question swiveled in his seat and smiled directly to her eyes.

Why? How? She could only assume that Mia, the little minx, had something to do with this.

Beside her, Rocco waved at Josh. "I didn't know Josh was coming tonight," she said.

"Oh, yeah. I invited him. I told you, Frankie thinks he's a cool guy." Rocco shrugged offhandedly.

"You *invited* him?" She couldn't keep the incredulity out of her tone.

Rocco's expression was bland. "Sure. Why not?"

Gina let out a long sigh. "Don't you realize that I've been trying to get rid of him?"

Rocco pretended to be aggrieved. "When he's just getting the hang of bocce? Why would you do that?"

"Maybe," Gina said through clenched teeth, "because I don't want anything to do with him."

"Ah, Gina, you're awfully prickly about this thing. The *Mr. Moneybags* show was just a game, right? When the guys and I are playing bocce, we don't hold a grudge. We can get together for a few beers the next day and never think about who won or lost."

"It's hardly the same," Gina said. "My heart, for instance, is not a bocce ball." This was as self-revelatory as she wanted to get.

Surprise filtered across Rocco's features. "I didn't think you were in the game for love. I thought it was for the money. And didn't you tell everyone that you didn't really care that Josh chose Tahoma?"

Gina was saved from having to reply when the young musicians, seventeen of them, filed onto the stage.

Rocco, their previous conversation forgotten, leaned forward in his seat. His eyes were focused on his son, who fidgeted before aiming a confident smile in his father's direction.

Throughout the preliminaries and the playing of the beginning students, Gina tried to avoid looking in Josh's direction. But she couldn't face the stage without his being in the center of her field of vision, and once Josh turned his head slightly to the side so that she could have sworn that he was studying her out of the corners of his eyes.

Then Frankie stood up to play, and she forgot about Josh Corbett. Frankie exuded an aura of mastery as he began his piece, and Gina was spellbound by the transformation of the familiar scrawny kid into a competent musician. His fingers dancing across the buttons of the accordion were quick and sure. He didn't make a single mistake.

"Wow, Rocco," Gina whispered as Frankie bowed and the audience applauded. "He's good."

"He's terrific," Rocco said, beaming with pride.

Frankie, when he reached his seat, looked straight at Josh, who gave him an exuberant thumbs-up.

Gina frowned; not that Josh could see her, since he was facing front. But what right did Josh Corbett have to barge into a family occasion and act as if he belonged? To be grinned at by Frankie? To sit right down in front next to Mia, her own niece and godchild?

The more Gina thought about it, through the performance of three more advanced students, the more irked she became. By the time the kids marched off the stage, she was sure that she wouldn't be able to hold her tongue when she came face-to-face with Josh, which she was sure would be inevitable despite the crush of people leaving the recital.

The whole time she was smiling and greeting family members and friends as she preceded Rocco up the aisle, Gina was doing a slow burn. She'd told Josh that she didn't want to see him around, but he'd managed to figure many ways around her. Insinuating himself into the good graces of her family bordered on the diabolical as far as she was concerned. Who did Josh Corbett think he was, anyway?

If she'd been driving her own car, she would have bolted as soon as her feet reached the vestibule. But she wasn't driving her own car, and she wanted to talk to Frankie, who had made them all proud. To discover that Josh was smack-dab in the middle of the family group surging around a jubilant Frankie didn't soothe her at all.

She swallowed her anger, which wasn't easy under the circumstances. "Congratulations, Frankie, you did a great job," Gina said. Josh smiled at her in that genteel but predatory way of his and somehow managed to blend into this group of Angelinis.

"Josh, may I speak to you privately?" Gina said through tight lips.

"I thought you'd never ask," Josh said. She started to walk away, her fury barely contained. Josh shouldered after her through a bunch of her male cousins, all of whom seemed to have an affable word for him.

By the time she reached an alcove where they could remove themselves from people streaming out the front doors, she was spitting fire. "You shouldn't have come here," she said, her words stinging the air.

Josh, as if oblivious to her anger, lifted his brows and spoke in a stage whisper. "Right. If the agency finds out, they'll have to kill me."

She stared. "What…?" Too late, she figured out that he was joking. This only made her temper rise. "There is no agency, and if anyone is going to kill you, it will probably be me," she said furiously.

"I know of a couple of ways you could do it," he said speculatively. "Like—"

"I suspect that you're about to make an indecent suggestion," Gina said. "I don't want to hear it."

"Too bad. Your life is much too dull. I was hoping you'd want to spice it up a bit."

"If I ever do, it won't be with you."

"What? Haven't you started liking me?"

Liking him? She'd fallen in love with him. She wasn't about to make the same mistake twice.

She could barely think over the pounding of her pulse at her temples. "I believe I'm getting a headache," she said, pinching the bridge of her nose between her thumb and forefinger. Her favorite herbal remedy for headaches was lavender. Too bad she didn't know a remedy for love gone awry, misplaced trust or persistent suitors who needed to be discouraged.

"I'm sorry," Josh said, sounding as if he meant it.

She blew out a long breath. Maybe Rocco would take her

home right away. On second thought, she doubted it. More than likely he'd want to bask in Frankie's moments of glory as long as they lasted.

"I'd better go," she said, whirling away from him. "I need to—" She stopped talking as soon as she realized that if Josh knew she didn't have a ride home, he would probably insist on providing it.

"I need to take care of my headache," she finished lamely. She began to walk swiftly toward the big double doors.

Mia came running up. "Aunt Gina, Frankie's dad says he's treating everyone to ice cream. He wants you to come, too, Josh."

"I'm sorry, Mia, I can't go," Gina said hastily. Although if everyone in her family was going to get ice cream, there would be no one to drive her home.

"Josh, you'll come, won't you?" Mia tugged at his hand.

"Sure, Mia, it sounds like fun."

"Not for all of us," Gina said, not quite believing that Josh had the gall to horn in on another family function. Before he could reply, she stomped off in search of someone who could drop her off at her cottage.

A few inquiries of family members produced no offers to forsake the ice cream parlor for the chance to drive Gina home, but Barbara suggested an aspirin, which she produced from her purse.

"Anyway," Barbara said soothingly, "you really should go with us. Frankie will be hurt if you don't, and you and I are sort of his acting mothers now that Cissy's gone."

That was a guilt trip that Gina couldn't resist; she had promised Cissy before she died that she would always take an interest in Frankie. And then Shelley, who also played the accordion, came out of the ladies' room and was invited by Barbara to accompany them, and Gina thought that maybe she'd better ride with Shelley and talk up Rocco, who, Gina was convinced, still liked her.

And that was how Gina found herself bumping knees with

Rocco, Shelley and Josh Corbett at a table at Baskin-Robbins while halfheartedly trying to eat a sugar cone heaped with bubble gum ice cream—Mia's choice for her.

Rocco and Shelley were hitting it off magnificently; Frankie was at another table, impressing Mia and a host of younger relatives with descriptions of his feats on his skateboard; and Josh kept smiling at her in that infuriating way of his as she did her best to force the ice cream past the lump of fury in her throat.

"Stop it," she hissed at Josh when Shelley and Rocco were deep in a discussion about Shelley's old car, which Rocco had insisted he'd repair free.

"Stop what?" Josh said, putting on an innocent expression that was pure fake.

"There are no cameras here the way there were on the show. You don't have to pretend." Thank goodness the aspirin was kicking in. The throbbing in her head had subsided to an ache.

"Pretend? Me?"

"Yes, you."

"And what am I pretending?" His eyes took on a devilish gleam as he treated himself to a long, languorous lick of pistachio. A runnel of it dripped down his wrist, and Gina imagined licking it off. She made herself look away.

"That you—that you—" Words failed her. She averted her eyes, suddenly no longer angry. She was exhausted, though. Anger could do that to a person.

"That I'm fascinated by you," he supplied.

People were starting to leave, and Barbara stopped by to give her a hug. "Mia won't be coming to Good Thymes after school on Monday," she said. "I'm taking her to shop for shoes. We'll see you at the Bootery, Shelley."

Shelley smiled. "Good. We carry a new children's line that you might want to check out."

Mia, wearing a smear of chocolate ice cream on her face,

danced up in the company of her sister, Stacey. She insisted on hugging Josh goodbye.

"See?" Josh said. "Some people like me."

Gina rolled her eyes. "I like you well enough, Josh." Now that she had calmed down, now that she understood what her lingering grudge against him could do to her, she could admit it.

"This is progress. This is good." He finished off the last of his ice cream cone and tossed his napkin in a nearby trash can. "Can I give you a ride home?"

"I'm with Rocco."

"Rocco is making time with Shelley. Do you really want to disturb that?"

"He's got Frankie with him. I seriously doubt that he and Shelley are going to get together until they can count on privacy."

Rocco turned toward them. "Did I hear my name?"

"It must be time to go. I have to be out in the garden early tomorrow morning as usual," Gina said, trying to sound bright and cheery while simultaneously telegraphing her urgency.

Rocco scanned the room to find Frankie. "Yo, Frankie. Let's split."

"Aw, Pop, do we have to?"

"It's getting late, son."

"Okay, after I get a drink of water." Frankie headed toward the water cooler at the back of the store.

Gina stood to leave. Josh stood, too, and Rocco was distracted by Uncle Fredo, who was waxing enthusiastic about the benefits of playing the accordion.

Josh spoke close to her ear. "I haven't been to see you at Good Thymes, but only because I'm honoring your request." His steady gaze unnerved her, and she felt herself trembling on the edge of something that she'd rather not confront.

"I'd like to buy a copy of the cookbook that benefits the teen center, though," Josh continued. "My sister in Brazil would love to have it. She's attempting to train her cook in American cuisine, and it's been slow going from what I understand.''

Gina felt absurdly grateful for this mundane conversation, one that held no threat. "I'm waiting for a new shipment of copies, but I'll be glad to send one to her," she said.

"I don't have Valerie's address with me here—I'll have to call my office. Do you suppose you could drop a copy off at my place? You could give it to Judy Rae."

"I'd be glad to. Maybe the first of next week?"

"Val's birthday is coming up soon. I wouldn't want to wait any longer than that."

"You won't have to. I'll see that you get it." Her voice had returned to normal now, and she had almost banished her disturbing thoughts about kissing him at the bottom of her cottage stairs.

Josh reached for his wallet. "I'll pay you now."

She waved him away, and as Rocco approached, she said to Josh, "Mail me a check."

Josh looked as if he might have more to say, but Rocco didn't give him a chance. "Okay, Gina, let's get the show on the road. Josh, thanks for coming. It meant a lot to my boy."

"I had a great time." Josh smiled and shook Rocco's hand, and in that moment Gina felt a stab of regret that she and Josh had not reached the same stage of amiability. Quickly, she turned away and slid her arm around Frankie's shoulders, unwilling to let regret morph into other, more disturbing emotions. "Ready, Frankie? Let's roll."

"Not before I say goodbye to Josh." Gina watched as he went and shook Josh's hand, wondering if she would be expected to do the same. But no, Josh merely gave her a nod and a smile before greeting her uncle Albert. She would have liked to come up with a flippant comment that would show Josh that she was taking all this in stride, but she could think of nothing to say, so instead, she wheeled and followed Frankie out of the ice cream shop.

Frankie chattered all the way to the car. "Mr. Buscani said I played better than he even expected, and he told me before the recital that he thought I'd do great. He says he wants me to join the real accordion band, and we'll play just for fun a couple of times a week or so. I'll be the youngest member ever. Can I, Pop? Can I?"

"Tell me more about it," Rocco said. And father and son kept talking while Gina, alone in the back seat, stared bleakly out the window at the passing houses all the way home.

Paramount in her mind was the knowledge that she wouldn't have had to be riding in the back seat of Rocco's car, dependent on him for a ride. She could have been sitting beside Josh in the BMW, laughing at something that they both thought funny, commenting on the recital and maybe sharing a leisurely glass of wine at her place.

Except that there was no way they'd stop at a glass of wine, and therein lay the reason that she was riding home with her cousin.

"YOU MEAN MY CAR'S NOT going to be ready today, either?" Gina asked wearily.

On the other end of the phone, Rocco cleared his throat. "No, it's a complicated electrical system problem, and I'm doing the work myself. I might have it ready tomorrow."

"You said that yesterday. I'm so disappointed."

"I know, I know. What can I say?"

Rocco, generous to a fault, was not planning to charge her for the repairs to her Galaxie. She didn't feel comfortable taking him to task for not having it ready, especially since she knew he was shorthanded at the shop.

"It's okay. I'll find some other way to get Mia to her dance class," Gina said distractedly. The school bus had stopped in front of Good Thymes, and Mia was disembarking.

"I'll do my best for you. I hope you understand that." Rocco sounded extremely apologetic.

"I do. Mia's here, so I'll talk to you later."

Mia bounced through the door as she hung up. "Hi, Aunt Gina. I can't wait to go to my dancing lesson today. Madison Cleary got new tights, and she thinks they're way cool."

With a sinking heart, Gina remembered that her mother was supposed to stop by to sort herbs for the catering business and had volunteered to mind the shop while Gina ferried Mia to dance class. Barbara couldn't provide transportation for her daughter because she was still working long hours at the winery for Uncle Fredo and using her car for errands, while Maren was being dropped off by a friend who had borrowed her car while her own car was, guess where, at Rocco's being repaired.

Her glance fell upon the cookbook that she had placed on the counter earlier. She'd been planning to take it by Judy Rae's house that afternoon so that Josh could send it to his sister.

Well, maybe Maren's friend, who was also her aunt Sophia's bridge partner, would drop Mia off at dance class. It would be out of the way, however, for her to deliver the cookbook to Judy Rae. Things certainly got complicated in this big family, but perhaps if she called her mother...

Maren, though, was strolling jauntily through the parking lot at that very moment and continued on into the store before Gina could even pick up the phone.

"Oh, Mother, I'm really in a bind. I promised Barb I'd take Mia to dance class and I intended to take this cookbook to Judy Rae's, and Rocco still has my car. Have you ever had one of those days that you had so much to do you met yourself coming and going?"

"Yes," Maren said serenely. "Yesterday, when my bridge club met at my house and Gayle asked to use my car because hers is being repaired, and the electricity went off for two hours for no reason at all, and Fredo wanted me to stop by the plant and pick up the winery's new financial report—well, you get the picture. Oh, and by the way, here's your copy of the report. Fredo says to read it because he wants all of us to be informed about the situation at the winery."

"Like I'd really have time today," Gina said with irony as she put the folder in the basket to carry upstairs to her apartment later.

"It doesn't matter as long as you attend to it in the next few days. How about if I call around on my cell phone to see if one of the mothers of the girls in Mia's class can stop by to pick her up, and you phone Judy Rae and ask her if you can take the cookbook to her after you get your car back?" Maren had a reputation for being unflappable.

Gina thought through Maren's plan. "The first part is fine, the second part won't work. The cookbook isn't really for Judy Rae. It's for Josh Corbett."

Her mother's eyes grew round, but she was already entering numbers on her cell phone and didn't comment.

Josh's payment check for the cookbook had appeared in Gina's mailbox yesterday, but he'd written it for too much money. She intended to refund the extra two dollars to him, so she grabbed two one-dollar bills from the cash register and folded them into the book.

Maren clicked off her cell phone. "Bette Anne Lovvorn has already left to drive the dance class car pool, according to her son. Corby Wallace says that her little Katy isn't going today—she has the sniffles. That leaves Nola Miles, and she's not answering her phone."

Mia, dressed in a leotard, her ballet shoes slung over her shoulders, came down the stairs from Gina's apartment. "Hi, Gramma. I didn't know you were here. Are you taking me to dance class?"

Gina's mother held out her arms. "No, sweetie, I can't. I don't have my car."

"And I don't have mine." Gina hung up, having reached Judy Rae's home phone, only to be asked by the answering machine to leave a brief message. She'd thought that if Judy Rae were out and about running errands, she might do her the favor of picking up the cookbook for Josh and perhaps drop Mia off at dance class.

"Well," Mia said, "how am I going to get to dancing?"

"We'll get you there, don't worry," Gina said. She picked up the phone to dial her cousin Maureen's number. Maureen lived around the corner and could be counted on in an emergency to provide instant transportation now that she was an empty-nester.

The phone had no dial tone. Instead, a male voice on the other end of the line said, "Hello?"

She recognized Josh's deep voice immediately. "It's Gina, Josh. What do you want?"

Mia climbed up on the stool next to the counter. "If it's Josh, can I talk to him?"

Gina shook her head warningly at her niece.

"I dialed your number, Gina, but the phone didn't ring, and then you answered. I was calling to find out what happened to the cookbook you were going to bring by. I never got it."

"Josh, I'm sorry. My car's still in Rocco's shop, and it's causing all kinds of havoc."

"No need to be sorry. It's just that Valerie's birthday is soon and I have her address, so I was hoping to get the book in the mail today."

"Please can I talk to Josh?" Mia was jumping up and down, her ballet shoes bouncing on the strings around her neck. Gina looked for Maren, but she was already outside in the potting shed, apportioning herbs into plastic envelopes.

Gina waved Mia away. "As soon as I figure out how to get Mia to her dancing class, I'll see what I can do about delivering the cookbook. This has been a busy day."

Josh surprised her by being quick on the uptake. "Mia needs to go somewhere? That's no problem. I can provide the wheels and get the cookbook at the same time." Josh's tone was exuberant, and she almost hated him for it. She didn't think he had the right to sound happy when she had her hands full of problems.

"Well, um," she began.

"I'll be there in a few minutes." Josh hung up.

Her mother came inside. "Gina, where's the stapler? I couldn't find it. Did Mia get a ride?"

Gina reached under the counter and handed the stapler to Maren. "Josh said he'll take Mia to her class. He can pick up the cookbook at the same time."

"I'm pretty excited about this, Gramma," Mia said. "Lately I like Josh more than anybody in the world."

"That's nice," Maren said. "Gina, did you know that it's visitors' day at the dance studio?"

"No," Gina replied. "Barb failed to mention it."

"Well, it is," Mia said. "We're going to have cookies and punch afterward, and we can ask anyone we want. Can you go, Aunt Gina?"

"Aren't you going?" Gina asked her mother.

"I went to the last one and today I'm on a mission for Dede's catering service. The herbs," Maren reminded her.

"Well, Aunt Gina, that means you *have* to go," Mia said imploringly.

"Of course she will," Maren said sternly. "Your aunt Gina wouldn't miss visitors' day for the world."

"Mother," Gina said in protest at the precise moment that Josh's car pulled into the parking lot.

"Here he is," cried Mia. The front door of the shop slammed as she ran outside to meet Josh.

"Mia *has* to take someone," Maren said. "You wouldn't want her to be the only child without a relative present, especially since there are so many relatives."

"Where are they when I really need them?" Gina said with exasperation, but her mother gave her no quarter.

"They're usually right there, being supportive."

"I was only joking," Gina informed her, and Maren's answering grin told her that she'd known that all along.

Josh walked into the shop. He was wearing faded jeans and a red polo shirt, and he looked wonderful. Gina's heart did a little flip at the sight of him.

"Hi, Mia. Let's go. Oh, hello, Maren. Helping Gina today?"

Maren smiled back. "Yes, Josh, I am. That's why she's free to go with Mia to her class."

"You're going, too, Gina?" Josh beamed.

Her words came out more stilted than she'd intended. "It's visitors' day at the dance class, and I hope you don't mind dropping me off with Mia."

"Josh could visit my class, too," Mia said, taking his hand. "Will you, Josh?"

Josh, clearly surprised at this turn of events, looked from Gina to Maren and back again. "I'd like that," he said.

Maren shooed them away. "Go on, all of you. Gina, I'll hold the fort until you get back."

Josh plucked the cookbook off the counter. "Is this one for me?"

"Yes," Gina said, flustered.

"We'd better leave now," Mia said. "I don't want to be late."

"Okay, okay," Gina said. She knew the folly of trying to stop a runaway freight train, and that was exactly how this felt.

Josh held the door open for her and she preceded him out. She was halfway to the car when he spoke. "I didn't have anything to do with how this is turning out, Gina. Honest," he said.

"I know," Gina said with a sigh. She glanced at Josh. "At least you got the cookbook. You overpaid, by the way."

"I added the extra because I asked you to deliver. I didn't think that should be included in the price." He waited while

Mia climbed into the back seat, then he got in front beside Gina.

"That was thoughtful," Gina said, looking straight into his eyes. She didn't know what to expect—a crinkling of humor, a lift of a brow, that jaunty but maddening grin.

But all she saw in his eyes was a sincerity, and in that moment, she realized with astonishing clarity that she didn't want to push him away. She had tried that, and it hadn't worked. Moreover, she was the one who stood to lose if she refused to see him. She liked the guy, had loved him once, and there was presently nothing in her life to compare with the wildly exhilarating emotions that Josh had sparked in her in those days not so long ago.

She wanted to be, if nothing more, his friend. At least for a while, until he left the valley.

Did Josh want a friend, though, or did he only want a lover? Gina was certain that she couldn't be both, and she doubted that Josh even knew the difference.

Chapter Eight

The woman was driving him crazy.

Lately, Josh had stayed away from Gina as she'd requested, all the more intrigued by how she kept her distance. He'd lusted after her from afar, wanted to engage her in conversation, started to walk over to her at Mia's skating party but pulled back. He'd endured her stares at Frankie's recital, sat by her side as they'd observed Mia's ballet class and dropped her niece and her off at the herb shop afterward. On that last occasion, Gina had at least rewarded him with a tentative smile and thanked him pleasantly. She'd said nothing about getting together in the future and hadn't invited him in. If she was softening toward him, she'd shown few signs of it.

The only good thing about his present low-key strategy was that he was getting to know her family even better: Rocco, whose robust style made him a good companion; and at the skating rink, her cousin Jaimie, who flirted with him shamelessly, even though he didn't respond. After all, Jaimie was only eighteen years old and much too young for his taste, plus she wore a round silver ball in her pierced tongue, which he didn't find appealing at all.

What he found appealing was Gina Angelini, he decided as he stared broodingly out his apartment window at the Napa River flowing past. The way she looked, the way she laughed, even the way her dark eyes lit with the gleam of righteous anger when she didn't like how things were going.

And that seemed to be most of the time where he was concerned.

Since he was making little or no headway with Gina, it was time to tend to the business that had brought him to Rio Robles in the first place. He picked up the phone and dialed Walter Emsing, who had a private line whose number was known only to a few people.

"Hi, Walt," he said. "Checking in from the beautiful Napa Valley, where I've turned up a few deals that might interest us."

"Go ahead, tell me," Walter said impatiently. "I'm busy with a dozen things this morning, including acquiring a vineyard in Chile, but I've always got time to consider this expansion of ours."

Reading back copies of *The Juice* in the public library had paid off, and Josh rattled off the names and situations of four or five wineries that he'd read were in trouble.

"Which is the best fit for our company?" Walter asked. Josh heard him scribbling and shuffling papers back in Boston, which reminded him of how far away he was. He'd been here a couple of weeks, and New England seemed like another world.

"I'd say it's the Angelinis' operation," Josh replied without hesitation. "The only trouble is that it's run by a tightknit family, and they wouldn't like someone else's team coming in to call the shots."

"If Vineyard Oaks has problems, the best thing that could happen is for our guys to buy them out," Walter shot back. "We'd get rid of deadwood, pare down expenses—you know the drill."

Eliminating deadwood meant that family members would be laid off, and lowering expenses meant that salaries might be cut. He was sure that none of the Angelinis would approve of those measures.

"Josh? Are you still there?"

"Yes," Josh said, but he didn't like to consider what Starling's acquisition of Vineyard Oaks would mean to Gina's family. He realized that maybe he shouldn't have put the Angelinis' winery on his list of possible acquisitions. But his loyalty was supposed to be to Walter and to Starling Industries; they were the ones who were paying him to write an article, and he had agreed from the outset to research potential objects for a takeover. The only thing was, at that time he hadn't expected that Gina's family's business would be a candidate.

Walter rambled on, unaware of Josh's misgivings. "After all," he continued jovially, "all those Australian wine executives have to work someplace. It might as well be Rio Robles."

"Sure, Walter," Josh said. He hoped he didn't sound as halfhearted as he felt.

They hung up, and Josh sat vacillating over the information he'd given Walter. Though he hadn't done anything really wrong, it didn't feel right, either. Finally, when he realized that there was nothing to be done about it, he decided to head over to Mom's for the blue-plate special, which tonight happened to be meat loaf, his favorite.

He was scooping the car keys off the console beside the door when the phone rang. Thinking that it must be Walter again, he grabbed the phone and clicked it on. But it wasn't Walter at all. It was Gina. The lilt of her voice halted him in his tracks.

"Josh, it's me. I was wondering if you'd be free tomorrow afternoon?"

Free? Of course he could be free, even though he'd have to postpone an expedition to San Francisco to meet his friend Brian, who had finally returned from his trip.

"I—yes," Josh said, feeling ridiculously happy that she had called.

"If you'd like, I could conduct a wine-tasting tour of some

of our best wineries.'' She seemed slightly tentative, as if she thought he might refuse.

Never. In that moment, he would have gone to the ends of the earth to see Gina. He would have canceled any prior obligation.

''That would be great,'' he said.

''Wonderful. If you'd like to stop by around one-thirty, I should be ready.''

''I'll be there.'' He paused. ''And, Gina, thanks.''

She laughed, a relieved sound. ''Don't thank me. I haven't done anything yet.''

''Does that mean you won't?'' he asked mischievously.

''For me to know and for you to find out,'' she retorted, and he was laughing as he hung up.

He could hardly contain his exhilaration as he drove through the quiet streets to the diner, where he would most likely eat alone tonight, as he did every night that Rocco and Frankie didn't show up. He was tired of being lonely and alone, not that the two things always applied to his situation. Tomorrow night would be different. Tomorrow night he intended to be with Gina, and in more ways than one.

THE NEXT DAY, JOSH THOUGHT about keeping Gina waiting, cooling her heels while he took his time getting there. But in the end, he couldn't. He had wasted so much time by staying away from her, and this was no longer a game. This was real life, and he didn't want to screw up.

When he picked her up at one-thirty as planned, she was wearing a black clingy knit top with three-quarter sleeves and a pair of slacks that showed off her pert derriere. Her hair was piled on top of her head, pale wisps framing her face, and she looked spectacular. The *Mr. Moneybags* camera had loved her face, had imparted a certain glamour to its well-proportioned curves and angles. In person, she was even more beautiful, a classy woman who would be a standout anywhere. Briefly he wondered how she'd look against any of

Boston's elegant old brick buildings, leaning on a wrought-iron fence in the park near his house, riding a swan boat in the Public Garden.

"Hi," she said. He discerned a new shyness in her greeting, and his antennae went up. Something in her attitude had changed, mellowed, and he wasn't sure why. It seemed to bode well. After all, they'd been going nowhere earlier, and now they would be together all afternoon. And who knew about tonight?

He decided not to let on that he'd perceived anything different in her manner. "Hi," he replied. Then, like two idiots, he and Gina stood staring at each other, both tongue-tied.

She regained her voice first. "We'd better be on our way," she said. "Before something happens so I can't leave. Bye, Mother. You'll lock up the shop when you go home, right?"

"Right," Maren called back, pausing in her work in the garden to wave through the window at Josh.

Gina grabbed a leather jacket off a chair, but when they reached the BMW, she tossed it into the back seat instead of putting it on.

"It's for later, when the air cools down," she explained in response to Josh's inquiring glance. California weather was warm in the daytime but could grow notoriously cool at night. The jacket, Josh decided, was an indication that she didn't intend to get home before nightfall. A promising sign.

Gina sat straight beside him, her hands clasped in her lap as he drove out of the parking lot, then stopped at the two gateposts before the highway.

"Which way?" he asked her. She seemed a little nervous.

"North on the Silverado Highway," she said.

"Relax," he told her. "The Big Bad Wolf is on his best behavior."

"And Little Red Riding Hood wouldn't be scared of him, anyway."

He spared her a look. "Is that true?"

"Basically. I don't think the wolf ever studied karate."

"And you did?"

"Yes. With Rocco some years ago. He thought I might need to give a guy a clop in the chops every once in a while."

"And you've always seemed so nice."

She grinned and settled back in the seat. "I thought we could go to San Elmo Vineyards first. Then we'll move on to a small winery, Vincenti Brothers, between there and our final destination, Century Vintners."

"You're the tour director. I'm only the driver. By the way, when will your car be ready?"

"Ask Rocco. You're on good terms with him." She flashed him a look, shifting her eyes away quickly as if she didn't want their gaze to catch and hold. *Fine,* he thought. *I can play that game, too.*

He kept his eyes focused on the highway unwinding in front of them. Dappled shade created patterns on the car's hood; they passed three bicyclists who waved.

"Are they friends off yours?" he asked.

"One of them was my aunt Gayle. She's a serious biker. Does it for exercise."

"Is it true that everyone in the valley is related to you in some way or another?"

She chuckled. "Who told you that?"

"I'm not sure. It was either your first cousin once removed or an uncle you've forgotten about."

"Believe me, we Angelinis never forget about any of our kin," she said. He could tell by the twitch at the corners of her mouth that she was suppressing a smile.

"Are you related to my landlady?" he asked her. "To Judy Rae?"

"No, she and her late husband moved to the Napa Valley from San Diego after he retired. How is she?"

"Hard to tell," Josh said. He hadn't seen either her or Sadie for a couple of days, but Judy Rae had told him that she often went out of town to visit her daughter.

"Judy Rae's husband died a few years ago when they had

just moved into that big house on the river. I get concerned about her because I went through a lot with Mother after she was widowed, and I don't think Judy Rae's quite as resilient.''

''She said she's had a difficult time paying her expenses, and that's why she had the house converted to include a couple of apartments.''

Gina sighed. ''I know. I hated it when she changed the house. It was so perfect—the most wonderful house in Rio Robles, I always thought. I grew up admiring it as I walked past on my way to school as a kid. I was sure I'd live there someday.'' She pictured the house's carved front door and sharply peaked roof; she'd always imagined herself waving to her friends through the front mullioned window.

''Maybe you will live there,'' Josh said. ''You never can tell.''

''If she ever sells, it would be too expensive for me, and I'm not sure I'd like the way she's chopped it up in remodeling it.''

''Judy Rae said it would be easy to remove the partitions that created the apartments so that the house will be the way it was in the past.''

''I didn't realize that. Do you like living there, Josh?''

''So far. Judy Rae is a nice person—though a bit talkative—and her dog's a lot of fun. Sometimes I take Sadie out and throw balls for her. Judy Rae says she doesn't play with Sadie as often as she'd like because her arthritis bothers her too much.''

''I'll take her some angelica root tomorrow, and maybe some willow bark with instructions on how to use them. Both are useful for treating arthritis pain.''

Josh pulled out to pass a large motor home and didn't speak until he was back in the right-hand lane. ''How did you learn so much about herbs?''

''My grandmother was an herbalist. She treated a lot of people around here.''

He glanced over at her. "Do you know what an interesting person you are, Gina?"

"Just because I know what to do with a few herbs? It's no big deal, Josh."

"Why'd you decide on these particular wineries today?" he asked. As he spoke, he opened the sunroof, so that a ribbon of air stirred the tendrils on Gina's forehead. She brushed the hair back, seemed to think better of it and let it go.

"The first one is because we'll get an interesting spiel that might interest you. The second, Vincenti Brothers, is so that you can taste their chardonnay, which is exceptional. And the third, Century—well, you'll see."

"Okay, so Century is something special," he said, guessing.

She nodded. "The site is a favorite of tourists. I won't tell you any more than that."

The rolling landscape was bathed in mellow golden sunlight, the coastal range to the east bright against the shimmering blue sky. On either side of the road stretched a patchwork of vineyards, one beginning where the last one ended. Now, in autumn, the vines were changing from green to scarlet, russet, gold and yellow. He wished he'd brought his camera. The play of light and shadows on the mountains and the valley was fascinating.

"I've been to California before, but never here. It's beautiful," he said.

"I may have mentioned it when we were at Dunsmoor."

If she had, he wouldn't have paid attention, blinded as he was at the time by her beauty. "I don't recall. I only know how much you missed home."

"Was I that obvious? I thought I concealed my homesickness rather well."

She shifted slightly toward him, a frown furrowing her forehead.

"Everyone concealed something or another. Especially you women."

"Oh? And what was your secret?" She slid a sly look at him from behind her lashes.

"Nothing—at least, at first. As the game went on, I hid things, too."

"For instance?"

"For instance, my true feelings."

"Ah," she said, growing pensive. "Anything else?"

"Nothing I want to talk about now."

They rode for a few moments in silence, passing a winery that looked exactly like an old Spanish mission, complete with a bell tower. They whipped past a hedge, and another winery's sign appeared, and farther on, another.

"So many wineries," he said. "Each one different."

"As different as the wines they produce. That's what makes a tasting tour so much fun." She paused, and he was unprepared for her next remark because it didn't follow his train of thought.

"Why did you do it, Josh? Why did you play the *Mr. Moneybags* game?"

"Now, that's a non sequitur if I've ever heard one," he said teasingly.

"Maybe, but I'm curious. You don't have to answer," she said, but he figured he might as well be honest.

"I was looking for love," he said.

She gave a ladylike snort to signal her disbelief. "No, I mean really. You already had money. You could have found love in any of hundreds of places. Why there? Why subject yourself to the media scrutiny and speculation, the inconvenience of being recognized everywhere you go from now on?"

For a moment, he considered glossing over his answer, but in light of his determination to be honest, he decided he'd better not.

"I did need the money," he said quietly.

Gina's eyebrows lifted, a sign that she was unconvinced.

"What was all that ballyhoo about your being from a prominent New England family with money up the wazoo?"

"The truth," he said. "What the publicity didn't say was that my parents expect me to make it on my own. Unlike many wealthy families, they don't believe in trust funds or handouts. They put a lot of stock in the value of working to earn your own living. I wasn't making much money as editor of a newspaper in Woods Mill, Massachusetts, and I had a couple of books I wanted to write but no assurance of income if I took time off from my job to write them. That's why I signed on to be Mr. Moneybags."

"No kidding," Gina said as if he'd knocked the wind out of her sails. "How did you get to be an editor in the first place?"

"A family friend recommended me to the publisher of a string of small-town papers after I graduated from college. The job seemed like a way to make a difference in the world, so I took it. Every time I decided to leave, I got promoted." He laughed. "Anyway, when I learned that the *Mr. Moneybags* show's producers were going to be interviewing in Boston, I camped out in line to audition. I had no doubt that the successful candidate would receive offers of endorsements, interviews, ways to change his *Mr. Moneybags* fame into real money. No one was more surprised than I was to be chosen, but as soon as it happened, I left my job in Woods Mill and hired an agent. The rest is history."

"I saw you in television commercials for a big bank after the show," she said.

"Yes, and before the show aired, I appeared on college campuses, at state fairs, and all sorts of other events to promote it. I was happy to recede into oblivion after it was over, and financially, I was flush. My parents were thrilled, since my brother had already made his bundle and my sister was on the way to becoming a well-known model when she married a businessman from Brazil who manufactures shoes.

She'll never have to worry about money again—or footwear.'' He smiled.

"And you?"

"I'm doing okay," he said. "I've invested most of the money I made with a friend who managed to parlay it into a windfall. I do some consulting work for the family business. When my life settles down, I'll get started on those books. For now, I'm content writing the occasional article."

"Like the one you're writing about the wine industry," she supplied.

He felt a stab of guilt over that. His recent conversation with Walter Emsing still weighed heavily on his mind.

Fortunately, they soon reached San Elmo Vineyards, where they entered the parking lot through a high stucco arch. Following others who were there for the tasting experience, they proceeded to the building, where a long polished counter held glasses of wine poured by a friend of Gina's from school.

His name was Shawn, and he escorted a small group outside to an arbor-shaded nook and told them the story of San Elmo.

The winery had been started by Italian immigrants, like Vineyard Oaks. But unlike Vineyard Oaks, San Elmo had gone through many owners. The Italians had sold out to a German family in the early 1900s, and the winery had almost failed under their ownership during Prohibition in the twenties. Somehow it had managed to stay afloat in the thirties, when a San Francisco firm had taken it over. The winery had enjoyed relative prosperity in the 1940s and then had been snatched back from the brink of bankruptcy twenty years later. The San Francisco firm had sold out to another company, but San Elmo had kept its name, and now it was owned by a group of European businessmen.

Josh wondered if Starling would allow Vineyard Oaks to keep its name if they bought it from the Angelinis. He slid a glance in Gina's direction, but she was paying rapt attention to Shawn's talk.

When he'd finished his spiel, Shawn poured a glass of sauvignon for everyone in the group. Josh put all thoughts of Walt's interest in Vineyard Oaks out of his head and followed Gina's lead in the wine-tasting ceremony. She taught him to study the color of the wine and then move the glass in a circular motion.

"This releases the wine's vapors," she said, demonstrating. Then she held the glass close to her nose and inhaled deeply.

"That's how to detect the wine's bouquet," she told him, and he followed suit. Gina took a sip of the wine and slowly swished it from one side of her mouth to the other. Then she spit it into a container provided for this purpose. This, she explained, was perfectly proper wine etiquette for tasting purposes. Josh did the same.

"What flavors do you detect?" she asked him.

"A certain fruitiness," he said carefully.

"That's very good," she told him with a nod of approval. "This is a crisp wine, slightly herbal with a hint of oak."

They tasted two more wines, and Josh learned to distinguish certain flavors—citrus as opposed to currant, for example. To think that he had been drinking good wines for years but had never known how to discriminate among the distinct and separate flavors that comprised each one was mind-opening.

When they were headed toward Vincenti Brothers, Josh asked Gina about the varied history of San Elmo.

"It's not unusual for a winery to be passed from one owner to another many times," she said. "Vineyard Oaks is lucky. We've managed to hang on to it all these years."

But maybe not much longer, he wanted to say.

She went on talking, which kept him from giving himself away. He listened, his guilt mounting. "Vineyard Oaks has been a success because we all believe in the winery's importance. When my grandfather came here from Italy to grow grapes, he pinched pennies until he and his brothers and sister could buy land. Then they worked it themselves, planted the vines, cultivated them, saved them from insects and fungus and all the things that can destroy a vineyard, and finally, they learned to make some of the best wine in the valley.

"And they taught everyone in the family to depend on one another, and we all help out when we're needed. My sister, Barbara, for instance, works many long hours at the winery office for no pay because times are hard right now. That's okay, though. She doesn't mind."

He couldn't imagine his sister, Valerie, working in their family business for no pay, and he doubted that he would, either. He had been raised with values that didn't emphasize the importance of family in the same way Gina's did.

"As I mentioned," Gina said, a frown pleating her forehead, "the winery is going through some tough times. That's okay. It happens. Uncle Fredo always figures out how to solve these problems."

"He seems capable," Josh ventured. "And very sharp."

Gina nodded in agreement. "No one's smarter than Uncle Fredo. No one makes better wines than we do."

When she saw his questioning look, she hastened to fill him in. "It's a fact, Josh. Our wines win lots of awards. Quality has never been a problem, but production is. Unfortunately, our plant machinery is old and some needs to be replaced. Operating expenses continue to rise, even though the price of wine is depressed. The low prices we get for our wine keep us from producing more. It's a vicious circle."

"Business is usually cyclical. Isn't that the case here?" Josh didn't want to seem too interested, and he didn't want to press Gina for information. She didn't seem to suspect that he might have serious reasons for wanting to know more about the problems at Vineyard Oaks.

"The atmosphere surrounding the industry is scary right now. The trend is for the smaller wineries to be bought out and torn down. Then the land is planted with more vines. We would all hate to see that happen to us. Fortunately, we have faith in Uncle Fredo, and Uncle Albert, and in everyone who's pulling together to bring Vineyard Oaks out of its slump. We all want the winery to survive and be passed along to the next generation. And it will survive. It has to.'' Gina spoke eloquently and with the passion that he had always sensed in her.

''I hope so,'' Josh said quietly. He hated to see that white line of worry etched between Gina's lovely winglike brows. He resisted the urge to reach over and pat her hand or slide his arm around her shoulders in comfort. Gina had told him nothing about the Vineyard Oaks situation that he didn't already know from scuttlebutt that he had picked up here and there around town, but today she had raised his awareness of the personal aspects of the situation. In light of that, he made up his mind to ask Walter to cross Vineyard Oaks off his list. There were other equally interesting wineries available, and Josh decided to find out more about them as soon as he could.

''Take a right turn at this sign,'' Gina said. ''That's it— the one with the arrow.''

He was glad that Gina wasn't aware of his involvement with Starling Industries as she swung along beside him on the path to the big Victorian house that housed Vincenti Brothers' tasting room. The house had been meticulously restored to its former glory, and the tasting room occupied the former parlor. They sat at a large oak pedestal table while an employee poured the wine. Josh couldn't help contrasting this tasting room and the one at San Elmo with the small one at Vineyard Oaks. Here there was even a gift shop where people were buying things like corkscrews, wineglasses and T-shirts printed with the winery's name. If Vineyard Oaks had a gift shop, it would produce revenue for the company, and he wondered why the Angelinis had never pursued this avenue.

Despite her worries about her family's vineyard, Gina appeared to have put them behind her as they tasted a zinfandel, a cabernet and a chardonnay so impressive that Josh later bought a couple of bottles for his parents at the gift shop.

After they left the shop, he and Gina sat on the porch swing overlooking the rolling vineyards. Behind them, people chatted at picnic tables on the patio and strolled in the extensive gardens.

"I'm sorry if I vented about the winery a while ago," Gina said. "I shouldn't be discussing family business."

He could have mentioned his phone conversation with Walter Emsing, but he didn't want to spoil their outing. He was sure that he'd be able to deflect Walter's interest in Vineyard Oaks, and since that was the case, he saw no point in alerting Gina. She'd only spread the word that someone was interested in buying the winery, and then he, Josh, would most likely be banned from all future family gatherings, which would effectively cut him off from Gina. No, he couldn't say anything. It would be a huge mistake.

And so Josh kept silent. What Gina didn't know wouldn't hurt her. Or him.

Once he'd made this decision, he felt more comfortable with himself and freer to concentrate on her. On the way to the car, he took Gina's arm to help her over a rough spot on the path. She didn't resist, even leaned into him a bit. "Josh, I haven't done a wine-tasting tour in a while. It's good to be doing something fun," she said, smiling up at him as he opened the car door for her.

"I have to admit that I wasn't expecting your invitation," he told her.

For a moment, she seemed disconcerted, and while he waited for her reply, he walked in front of the car and slid behind the steering wheel.

She shifted in her seat so that she was angled toward him. "I don't see how you can write about our industry without going on a wine-tasting tour, and I know the best places to go."

"Thanks," he said, "for making the time."

"Maybe I should be the one to thank you. For giving me the excuse to leave work for a change."

"You're indebted to me, right? You're so grateful that you're willing to do almost anything I'd like, right?" He grinned at her.

"Not exactly," Gina said, but she smiled back at him.

He eased the car out onto the highway and accelerated, keeping his eyes on the road but sparing a glance at the woman beside him. Gina's hair, fluttered by the breeze from the sunroof, was gilded with the slanting rays of the afternoon sun, and her eyes, darkest brown with shimmers of amber, were clear and bright. Neither one of them spoke until they rounded a curve in the road lined by fences encircling a variety of houses and gardens. "All right," he said, "tell me about our next stop on the tour."

"It's straight ahead up that mountain," she said, and when he followed her gaze, he saw an enormous white villa perched on the mountain. In the distance, a small herd of black-and-white cows drifted down a hillside; overhead, a hawk rode a strong wind current.

She directed him down a narrow road, and as they got out of the car, he saw a ski gondola conveying people up to the villa.

Josh took it all in. "You saved the best for last, right?"

"Surprised?"

"I was expecting another place similar to the last ones."

"Oh, Century Vintners is special," she said.

They got in one of the gondola cars and were ferried smoothly and effortlessly upward to a platform where passengers disembarked. Leading away from it was a pathway that ended in front of two heavy oak doors, and inside the villa, artful black-and-white photographs lined the walls. When Josh moved closer, he saw that all of them had to do with growing grapes or making wine.

"Century has been here longer than almost any winery," Gina told him as they made their way to a huge outside deck overlooking the valley. They were shown to a table under a yellow-and-white-striped umbrella, where they could watch he sun sinking slowly behind the mountains in the west. 'This place is a big tourist attraction.''

"I can see why," Josh said. The scenery reminded him of some of the more picturesque and charming places he'd visited in Italy.

Some of their fellow wine tasters were getting up from their tables and taking turns at a large telescope set up at the edge of the terrace.

"Ready for even more spectacular scenery?" Gina asked. She led him to the telescope, then demonstrated how to train it on the vineyards down valley. He studied their patchwork pattern for a long time. "I feel as if I can see for miles," he said, moving aside so she could look, too.

"If you try really hard, you can spot the top of the Vineyard Oaks office building," she said. "It's below the mountain shaped like an anvil."

He looked again and found the Vineyard Oaks property on its hilltop right away, including the doors to the wine cave. Again, he wondered why Vineyard Oaks didn't maximize its advantageous location, add a terrace where wine tasters could sit and look over the valley, give tours of the wine cave.

"I didn't get a chance to go inside the cave at crush," he said.

"It tunnels way inside the hill," Gina said. "We have parties there sometimes, surrounded by the big wine casks, food spread out on wide tables."

"Sounds like fun," he told her.

When they went back to their table, a server came to take their order, and after their wine came, Gina smiled at him over the rim of her glass. "Look, Toto, we're not in Boston anymore," she said jokingly.

He smiled back. "There are vineyards in New England. I've never visited any of the wineries, though."

"What's it like, New England?"

"Extremely cold in the winter. Beautiful autumns. All kinds of people. You might like it."

"Maybe." She toyed with the stem of her glass. "Do you miss it now?"

"At this precise moment, no," he said, gazing deep into her eyes.

He thought he detected the first signs of a blush creeping up from her neck. "Stop staring at me," she said.

"Why? You're a treat."

"When there's so much scenery out there?" She waved her hand in the direction of the valley. "Don't be silly." She sipped her wine.

"You shouldn't undervalue yourself, Gina."

"I don't."

He thought she did, though, and wanted to reassure her. "The producers of the show considered you gorgeous enough to compete against some of the most beautiful girls in the country," he said, remembering the first time he'd seen her walking down the stone staircase at Dunsmoor Castle, wearing a white flowing gown, her face illuminated by candlelight. He'd been tempted to choose her right then and there.

"I suppose that's true," she allowed. "It's—um, maybe I don't want to say that."

"Say what?"

"What I was going to say. Tell me about your family, Josh. I'd like to know more about them."

"Wait a minute. We're not finished with the topic at hand. You should feel comfortable saying anything to me, anything at all. I don't want you to censor your thoughts. That might have been necessary on the show, but it isn't now."

"Oh, Josh, there's no point in raking through the rubble of our past relationship." She cast her gaze downward.

"I wouldn't call it rubble. We're rebuilding." He smiled at her in what he hoped was his most encouraging manner. "Out with it, Gina. I want to hear what's on your mind."

She sighed deeply, then regarded him doubtfully. "Against my better judgment, I'll tell you what I wanted to say a few moments ago. Josh, I did feel great when I was chosen to compete on the show, but I'd never considered the emotional fallout.''

''Are you sorry you did the show?''

''Not exactly. I had a lovely vacation in a Scottish castle, and I met some fine people. I just needed a while to recover, that's all.''

''Recover from the experience, or from something else?''

She seemed to think this over, appeared to come to a decision. She looked him straight in the eye. ''Josh, I might have smiled when I walked away from you that night in the parlor, but inside I was very sad. Your rejection hurt. I didn't let on to anyone, but the whole situation affected me deeply.'' She shrugged—a valiant little motion of her shoulders that went to his heart.

''Gina,'' he said, saying her name slowly. ''I'm sorry.'' He reached over and took her hand. It was small, the fingernails short and lacquered with clear polish. He turned it over and traced the lines with his fingertip. ''I shouldn't have listened to the producers. They kept telling me the show was just a game, and I even convinced myself of that when I was playing it. I never worried about whose hearts would be broken or who would hate me afterward.''

She pulled her hand away. ''Hate you? Did someone?''

''Not any contestants, as far as I know, but I got all kinds of nasty viewer mail afterward. Mostly, people sounding off about my lack of good judgment.'' He laughed ruefully. ''They were right, of course.''

''Now you tell me.''

''You've never given me a chance before now,'' he said gently.

''Maybe because I didn't want to hear what you had to say.'' Her voice faltered, and she bit her lip. He was stunned when her eyes flooded with tears. She fumbled in her purse for a handkerchief.

Shaken at this unexpected display of emotion, Josh leaned back in his chair, gazed out over the vineyards dotting the valley floor, waved away a bee that was headed for the pots of geraniums near the terrace wall. To think that he had caused Gina any pain at all tore him apart. He had never considered the consequences of the *Mr. Moneybags* game from any perspective but his own, and he was rocked to his core as the true reality of the show struck home.

"I'm sorry, Gina," he said helplessly. "More sorry than you can imagine."

"Well," she said, putting her handkerchief away. "Let's not go there, Josh. It serves no purpose."

With great effort, he pulled himself together. This was the first time that he had been confronted by a woman he'd pursued after he broke a relationship off. He had never seen the results of his moving on or understood the impact of his decision on the other party. "You're right," he told her. "We've said enough." He forced a heartiness into his voice that he wasn't feeling. "What do you say we order more wine?"

"That's a very good idea," she said, and he was rewarded when she smiled.

She had rallied, he had recovered, and maybe that was all they needed to put the past behind them. Still, at the moment he couldn't have felt worse.

The unexpected idea blossomed that if only they could spend enough time together, he could right past wrongs. "I don't want this afternoon to end," he said.

She studied his face, looked away, seemed confused. "You want to make it up to me," she said, obviously guessing but right on target.

"Will it work? Is it worth a try?"

"It's hard to get over the past, Josh. I'm sorry, but it is. Now that I've told you that, I also want to tell you that I regret the way I've treated you since you came to Rio Robles. I wasn't very nice, and I'm sorry."

He studied her expression for a long moment. "You're not saying it's a wash between us, are you?"

She hesitated before speaking. "I suppose it could be," she said with utter seriousness, "if you'd take me to dinner tonight."

It was a few moments before he understood the import of her suggestion. When he did, he would have liked to fling his arms around her. He would have liked to kiss her.

But he didn't do either of those things. "Yesss!" he shouted, and several people twisted their heads in their direction. He didn't care. He hardly noticed anything else because Gina was tremulously smiling her beautiful incandescent smile at him, and in that special moment, all was suddenly right with his world.

Chapter Nine

"That's Volare straight ahead," Gina said as Josh tried to figure out the tight parking situation on this narrow downtown street in Rio Robles. It might be a small village, but the population was swollen with tourists.

Josh braked to a stop. "Hmm, no parking places. Do you want to get out and ask the restaurant to hold a table while I park the car?"

"That's actually an alley where the blue car is turning onto the street. Take a right."

Josh did as she suggested, and Gina directed him behind the building into a vacant space that was a loading zone during daylight hours.

"See?" she said. "No problem."

He got out of the car and held the door for her. "This way," she said, leading him through a narrow arcade to the street.

"We should have called ahead for reservations," he told her when he saw the line at the door. This was a popular place with tourists, if the women in Reeboks and men with cameras suspended around their necks were any indication.

"I always have a reservation here," Gina said mysteriously.

They crowded past everyone in line and presented themselves at the hostess's desk inside.

"Gina! How nice to see you!" exclaimed the dark-haired woman in charge of the seating chart. She flew around to the front of the desk and took Gina's face in her hands, kissing both cheeks.

"Aunt Laura, you remember Josh Corbett," Gina said.

"Ah, indeed. Margo will seat you. Margo, our Gina's here!"

Margo emerged from behind a curtain, and again, the cheek-kissing was repeated. "Come with me," she said after an openly curious flick of the eyes in Josh's direction.

They followed Margo to a table that Josh quickly judged the best one in the house—away from the kitchen and at a window in the corner overlooking a garden with a gently splashing fountain. A man appeared magically in time to hold Gina's chair for her, and another shook out her napkin with a flourish and spread it across her lap. This was followed by a wink for Gina and a long stare at Josh, after which the man disappeared behind a screen.

Josh recognized the man as Uncle Aldo, one of the people tending the barbecue at crush.

"Your family's restaurant?"

"Exactly," Gina said. "The man peering through the screen and frowning is Paul. The one with the napkin is my uncle Art, who is married to Aunt Laura, the woman we met when we arrived."

Josh cocked his head toward a girl who was bussing tables. "All right, let me guess. That one's Laura and Art's eldest daughter. She works here most nights when she isn't practicing for the school play."

Gina giggled. "You're almost right. Vicki's their daughter, but twirling is her thing, and she's head majorette at Saint Vito High School. The boy filling water glasses over there is her brother, Marco. And the waiter carrying that tray toward the front of the restaurant is Lee, a cousin who fills in sometimes for the regular staff. And—"

"Enough," Josh said. "If you keep on, we'll be discussing

the Angelini family for the rest of the evening. We could talk about other things, you know.''

"Oh? Like what?'' Gina's eyes were dancing.

"Like what a good time I had today.'' He kept his gaze steady.

"I did, too, Josh,'' she said, but before he could reply, yet another relative of Gina's appeared with the menu and the wine list. This time it was Gina's cousin Little Tony, whom Josh remembered from playing bocce.

After the necessary polite remarks, Josh scanned both the wine list and the menu, then turned to Gina. "I'd like you to choose the wine,'' he told her.

"Hmm, what do you think your entrée will be?'' she asked.

He'd already decided. "It'll be the roasted duck breast with cranberry-and-orange relish,'' he said, and after a few moments' consideration, she ordered a Vineyard Oaks zinfandel. He could tell she put a lot of thought into the selection, and when the wine arrived, he was impressed that she'd discerned exactly what he would like.

Tony returned and suggested before he took their order that Josh stop by Rocco's some night when they were all there playing bocce. Josh told him that he meant to do that soon, which was true.

"Has Frankie's dog had her pups yet?'' Josh asked.

"It'll be any day now,'' Tony said before rushing off toward the kitchen.

"Have you changed your mind about wanting a puppy?'' Gina asked.

Josh shook his head. "I'd love to have one, but it wouldn't be fair to keep a dog in my small town house.'' He spoke regretfully because he'd always had dogs when he was a kid and would like to have one now.

"Oh, there's Aunt Donna,'' Gina said. She smiled and waved, and an attractive fortyish woman came tripping over to the table.

Josh hadn't met Donna before, though he knew this was the aunt Gina had suggested he might like better than her. No way, though Donna was certainly attractive, with her short dark hair and clothes straight out of a fashion magazine.

And then Gina unexpectedly invited Donna to sit down and have a glass of wine with them.

"I can't," Donna said with unmistakable regret. "I only stopped in to check out the new fountain." She nodded toward the garden outside the window. "Nice, isn't it?"

"Wonderful," Gina said.

Donna scrutinized Josh. "I didn't think we'd see you again," she said with the manner of someone who prizes frankness. "I thought that by this time you'd be back in—where was it, New York?"

"Boston," he said with reluctance.

"That's right, Boston," she said. "I'd better be on my way. Gina, want to go to the ladies' room?"

Gina smiled sweetly at him. "Sure. I'll be right back." She got up and followed Donna into the nether regions of the restaurant.

For perhaps the two-hundredth time in his life, Josh wondered why women couldn't go to the ladies' room alone. Worst of all, he decided that maybe the two of them were discussing him. Not only discussing him, but critiquing him. He shifted uncomfortably in his chair, even though it was plushly padded.

With Gina gone, he could better study the restaurant, which was decorated with restrained elegance. The walls were finished with some kind of subdued paint shading that he thought might be a color wash. Stained-glass panels divided the restaurant from the bar, and on the long opposite wall was a mural with nudes carrying water jugs. One of the nudes bore an uncanny resemblance to Gina. The woman in the mural had the same hairstyle, the same blond hair. The same large breasts, voluptuous body.

He stopped gawking guiltily when Gina returned to the

table. She had refreshed her lipstick and pushed her hair back behind her ears, making her look even more like the nude in the mural. "Aunt Donna said to tell you goodbye. She likes you."

"She's the one you wanted me to go out with, right?"

When Gina nodded, he said, "Gina, she's not my type."

"I'm not so sure," she said.

"I am." He paused to take in her flushed cheeks, unsure if their rosiness came from the wine or from gossiping with Donna about him, or both. "In fact," he said, measuring his words as he watched for her reaction, "my type is that woman in the mural. The one leaning over the fountain."

Bingo. Gina's cheeks, already suffused with becoming color, turned bright red. He had been right.

He thought he'd string this out for a while. "That's a wonderful mural, by the way. The nudes are tastefully done."

"It's—well, it's okay. I don't think this restaurant needed a mural, that's all."

"And what would you rather see on that wall?" he asked.

"A wall hanging? Pictures of the beach?"

"Anything," she said tersely.

"A picture of you, perhaps?"

She stopped fidgeting with the napkin in her lap. "Listen, Josh. I'm not responsible for the wall art in this place."

He grinned. "Who is?"

"Guess," she said.

"Probably Rocco. I didn't know he had an interest in art."

"Rocco's interest is in playing jokes. I thought you knew that. Couldn't we talk about something else?"

"Not until you let me know if that's the extent of your modeling career," he told her.

"I hope so. For your information, Rocco brought one of my old yearbook photos in here when the artist was painting the mural and asked him to put my head on one of the nudes. I was furious when I found out."

Josh threw his head back and laughed. "I love that guy."

''Most people don't recognize me,'' she said stiffly.

''Most people aren't as interested in you as I am,'' he told her in all seriousness.

She only rolled her eyes and drained her wineglass, and someone else, a young man who was introduced as the nephew of a cousin by marriage, rushed over to pour her another glassful.

Josh waited impatiently until the guy retreated. Every time he started to get somewhere with Gina, one of her relatives appeared. Here they came again, a group of Angelinis bearing trays. This meant that he could not return to the topic of Gina's nude right away. Instead, he was caught up in the show of a Caesar salad being made at their table. Many flourishes accompanied this feat, which it appeared must be appreciated by onlookers, so he found himself smiling and nodding while sneaking surreptitious glances at Gina's breasts, trying to figure out if they were really as spectacular as those in the mural.

''Voilà!'' said the waiter when he had finished with the salad, and then there were salad bowls in front of them and they were eating, and he couldn't even see Gina's breasts because her salad bowl was in the way.

And then the main course was served, and Gina seemed determined to confine the conversation to uninteresting topics. For instance, the lack of rain last summer. The restoration of the old houses along the Napa River. He was almost grateful for the flurry of relatives who soon arrived at the table. One refilled Josh's water glass, which didn't need it. Another topped off Gina's wineglass, which did. A girl carrying a cello pulled a chair close, oblivious to the other diners, and a boy with a violin appeared beside her, looking serious and businesslike.

Josh glanced at Gina, who appeared nonplussed but eyed him mischievously. ''We're in for a treat,'' she said.

Josh adopted an air of nonchalance, but inside he was seething. Earlier today, he and Gina had finally gotten around to meaningful conversation. He'd hoped for a continuation of that honesty and openness, yet her relatives seemed to be conspiring against any possibility of that.

The girl with the cello, whom he judged to be about sixteen, poised her bow over the instrument. The boy adjusted his violin more comfortably under his chin. And then they were playing a wobbly melody.

Josh schooled his expression to be blank. Not that the kids were bad once they got going. Adding to the scenario were the pleased relatives lined up right outside the kitchen door to observe. A screen hid some of them, but he was well aware of their proud comments, which were whispered to one another.

The song was finished with a flourish, and Gina began to clap. Following her lead, Josh did, too.

"We can play another, Aunt Gina, if you'd like," said the boy.

Josh groaned inwardly, all the while gritting his teeth and smiling. Thus, he was treated to a dragging rendition of a vaguely familiar Italian melody that he couldn't readily identify.

Gina seemed enthralled along with the rest of her relatives, but twice he caught her casting her eyes sideways at him to assess his reaction. He kept staring straight ahead at the pattern on the boy's tie, which was fairly mesmerizing. At least it gave him something to focus on besides the captivated mothers, fathers, aunts, uncles and cousins behind the screen.

"That was lovely, Sara. You, too, Victor," Gina said. He could tell she meant it.

"Right. Here you are," Josh said, pulling a couple of bills out of his money clip and pressing them into the kids' hands. The boy's eyes widened, and the girl said, "Wow! This is great. Thanks, Mr. Corbett."

"Call me Josh," he said, pleased in spite of himself. That is, he was okay with it until he saw that he had given them each a twenty-dollar bill, not a five as he'd intended.

The kids left, thank goodness, and he saw them behind the screen sharing news of their good fortune with other Angelinis.

"That was a sweet thing to do," Gina told him, picking up her fork again.

"I'm glad you approve," he said dryly, hoping that his unintentionally grand gesture would provide Gina and him with a few minutes' respite from the continual onslaught of attention.

"Back to our conversation," he said pointedly, and that was when Tony arrived with more bread, which had to be deposited on the plate just so while Aldo solicitously inquired about their enjoyment of the meal, and fast upon his heels appeared Marco, whose job it was to replace the butter patties stamped so carefully with the Volare name.

Gina, who had watched his annoyance growing during the procedure, giggled when Aldo and Tony and Marco had gone.

"I hope you don't mind that they're treating us as honored guests," she said.

"It's impressive, but I was hoping for a little more privacy," he said.

"Angelinis don't get much of that," she said.

"I've noticed. Do you think we could resume—"

However, Victor was on the way over, carrying his violin. "Sara and I appreciate so much what you did for us that I'd like to play you a couple more songs," he announced.

Josh all but groaned aloud. "Go ahead," he said without much enthusiasm, whereupon Victor tucked his violin under his chin and proceeded to play. By the time Victor had finished this impromptu serenade, Josh could tell from the wild look in Gina's eyes that she was barely suppressing a fit of laughter.

"Thanks," he told Victor, who then shook Josh's hand and disappeared into the far regions of the restaurant.

"As I was saying," Josh told Gina, with all the patience

he could muster, and then she did lose it. She started to chuckle, which turned into a laugh, which took on knee-slapping proportions. She hid her face in her napkin to muffle the sounds.

It was a while before she lowered the napkin. "I'm sorry," she gasped. "You seem so—so ticked."

He couldn't watch her laughing so hard without laughing, too. Not as hard as she was, perhaps, but it was a release of sorts.

"I'm not ticked, as you so quaintly put it. Disappointed, maybe. Up to here with Angelinis, maybe. But they're nice people. I would never want to hurt anyone's feelings." He swept his gaze around the room to see if any Angelinis had observed their laughing fit and decided that everyone, for a change, was occupied elsewhere.

"You know, I believe I've had enough to eat," Gina said.

Josh considered this a good portent for the evening. Maybe she wanted to be alone with him at last.

Their plates were whisked away, and Tony arrived with the dessert tray. Despite the tiramisu, the profiteroles, the petites madeleines, they managed to resist, and after Josh paid the check, they were outside on the street, blessedly alone.

He took her hand and swung it between them. "Where to, Gina? How about a nightcap?"

"After all that wine, I couldn't possibly," she said demurely. "I'd better go home. I'm supposed to talk to a gift shop owner from Santa Rosa tomorrow who wants to buy herb wreaths for the holiday season. She'll be there early."

To Josh, Thanksgiving and Christmas seemed a long time away. He was much more interested in the here and now.

They got into the car, and Gina rolled down her window to inhale deeply of the cool night air. He glanced over at her and saw that her face was illuminated by the single streetlight. He loved her dark eyes, warmed to the sensuality in their depths—a sensuality that he judged to be unexplored. Gina possessed a kind of innate sexuality, an earthy voluptuous-ness that simmered slightly below the surface, though she seemed totally unaware of it. He would love to see her sexual qualities unfettered and unleashed, longed desperately to be the man who introduced her to her own passion. He doubted that she had ever given in to it, had ever discovered it.

She sat up straighter when he drove through the two pillars and pulled the car under the moon-dappled shade of the olive tree. They sat silent for a moment, listening to the rustle of the leaves overhead, the moment ripe with possibilities. He didn't want to make any suggestions; he knew he had to leave the next step up to her.

"I'd better go in," Gina said. He thought he detected a slight intonation of regret.

Hiding his disappointment was hard. "I'll walk you to the door," he said.

They made their way around the side of the cottage on the flagstone steps. Josh was prepared for Timothy to leap out of the garden, but there was no sign of the big cat tonight. Gina fumbled with her key at the door, and he helped her slide it into the keyhole. His large hand closed over her smaller one, and he was surprised at the warmth of her skin. Or maybe he wasn't; Gina wasn't one of those cool and calculating women, the kind you didn't want to touch.

"Thanks for a lovely afternoon and evening," she said. She had turned to face him, and this was the moment that he had been anticipating all night. The way her eyes were shining, the way her lips were slightly moist and parted—these weren't the signs of wanting to say good night at the door.

"I had a good time, too," he said, shifting closer. He wove his fingers though hers when he handed the key back.

"I'm sorry if my family was annoying," she said softly.

He took her other hand, and she curled her fingers into his. "Your family is part of you, Gina. Of course I didn't mind them," he said, learning to his surprise that he really meant it.

She smiled gently, which brought an amused gleam to her

eyes. This made her even more irresistible, and he drew her into his arms. The darkness shifted around them, realigned itself, and he touched his lips to hers lightly, experimentally.

"What if your family could see us doing this?" he murmured, trailing a string of kisses up to her temple. "What would they think?"

"Some of them would tell me I'd better be careful," she whispered, but she offered her lips again, and from the way she kissed him, Josh didn't believe that she cared what anyone thought.

Her lips parted beneath his, hungry and hot, and he obliged with a deep, demanding kiss. His heart commenced pounding against his ribs. That her passion was so knowing, so keyed to his, stunned him, and his hands gripped hers as he drove her back against the stone wall of the cottage.

He felt the firm outlines of her breasts pressed hard against his chest, and he wanted to caress them, to stroke them, to take them into his mouth and taste of them, learning to savor them as he had learned to savor fine wine. But there was no time to think about that now, not with her arms going around him and pulling him even closer, not with her breath hot against his skin.

"Gina," he said, shaken by his desire for her. "Let's—"

Her hand came up; her fingers touched his lips. "Don't say it," she said. "Please don't."

"Don't you want to?"

"Nice Italian girls don't sleep around," she said primly, and then hiccuped. This was followed by a low laugh, and he decided that she'd seemed giddy ever since they'd laughed about all her relatives in the restaurant. Maybe she'd caught more of a wine buzz than he'd realized.

"Of course," she went on, "I may not be that nice."

"I hope not," he muttered.

"Josh!" she said, though he suspected that she wasn't offended.

"I don't want to do anything that makes you uncomfortable," he said, sounding more like the perfect gentleman than he felt at the moment.

"Kissing me might make me entirely too comfortable," she said thoughtfully.

"That wouldn't be the case with me," he replied with great feeling.

Her eyes reflected the moonlight, the pupils enormous. "Today I meant what I said about how painful it was when our relationship ended before. I don't want to be hurt again, Josh."

Ah, so that was it. Stunned by this revelation, he removed his weight from her and pondered briefly this slant on things.

She was still so close that he felt the breath of her sigh on his cheek. "I'm sorry, Josh. I shouldn't have—"

Now it was his turn to shush her, which he did with a brief kiss on the lips. "No apology necessary," he said firmly.

"I need to reach a point where I can trust," she said. "I'm sorry if that seems unnecessary to you. To me, it's important. I don't want to rush things."

"I understand," Josh said, regretting more than ever his choice of Tahoma. He'd been high on himself in those days, hadn't thought he was capable of making a mistake because he'd started believing all the publicity hype about him. He hadn't thought Gina had been in love with him back there at Dunsmoor Castle. He'd thought it was a serious case of like, of knowing that the possibility of something more existed. Now it was clear that their flirtation, their budding relationship, had been much more than that to her. He had been a fool for not reading the signs correctly.

"Well. I guess that's a wrap." She didn't sound happy about it.

He stepped away, and she did the same. "Do you want me to call you?"

She hesitated, but only for a moment. "Of course," she said. And then as if to reaffirm it, "Of course."

He backed off, watched her go inside. As he walked around

to the front of the cottage, he caught a glimpse of Timothy crouched atop the wall, his yellow eyes gleaming. The cat let out a long, woeful yowl.

"Yeah, me, too, buddy," he said to the cat. Timothy only blinked at Josh, switched his tail and jumped down into the tall grass.

As for Josh, after he got home he lay awake in his lonely bed, imagining lying with Gina in her lavender-scented boudoir, and thinking that he'd better order a new supply of allergy pills just in case.

Chapter Ten

"All right, Gina. What's up?" Shelley cocked her head and studied Gina while Gina schooled her expression to remain businesslike. This was, after all, a scheduled bachelor-auction committee meeting in Shelley's office at the Bootery, and Gina was going over a list of food items that her aunt Dede's catering service was planning to donate to feed the volunteers.

"What do you mean, what's up? Unless you're talking about pastrami sandwiches. Aunt Dede wants to bring them over around nine o'clock on the night of the auction." Gina was all innocence, but the third member of the committee, Shelley's friend Claudia, was sitting directly across from her and didn't seem convinced.

During this exchange, Gina's cousin Emily walked in and went to grab a bottle of water out of the small refrigerator in the next room. She tossed one to Claudia, too. "Yeah, Gina, you're looking particularly happy," she said critically as she sat down beside Shelley.

"Vibrant," agreed Claudia.

"I'm pleased that I have a hardworking committee dedicated to sponsoring the best bachelor auction in the history of this town," Gina said.

"Rubbish," sniffed Shelley. "I'd say your present radiance has more to do with seeing Josh Corbett. I hear a lot of gossip in the Bootery, you know.''

Gina slammed down her clipboard. ''Oh, mercy. There's gossip?''

''Fed by all your relatives who work at Volare. They said you two were gazing into each other's eyes when you ate there. They said that Josh Corbett is a great tipper, and that he acts like he's crazy about you. They said—''

Gina buried her face in her hands. ''Oooh, spare me,'' she groaned. ''Can't I do anything in this town without everyone's knowing about it?''

''If you're planning to sneak around, it would be best not to hang out at your family's restaurant,'' Shelley informed her.

''Great point,'' agreed Emily.

''Why would I take Josh, who is accustomed to the finer things in life, to any place that wasn't as good as Volare? I mean, the Beacon Drive-In doesn't exactly measure up.''

''I'm not telling you how to run your life. I'm merely stating that if you wish to remain anonymous, you could drive into San Francisco for the evening. Or to St. Helena, for that matter.'' Shelley got up and brought another chair for the last committee member, Kasey Simms, who was breezing in through the front door as she spoke.

''Well,'' said Kasey, ''you won't believe who just signed up for the bachelor auction.'' She waved a list in front of their faces.

''Josh Corbett?'' ventured Claudia. Gina snapped to attention.

''The same. I'd left the list at Mom's Diner, like someone suggested last time, since that's where most of the eligible unattached bachelors in town eat at least one meal a day. And Josh Corbett's signature is right here on the bottom line.''

''Let's see,'' said Shelley, who tended to be skeptical. ''Hmm, looks like you're right.''

Gina tried to hide her dismay. If Josh Corbett were one of

the bachelors, women would fall all over themselves trying to bid. She would be onstage as emcee and not allowed to participate.

Shelley shot her a knowing look. She didn't say anything. She didn't have to.

Even though Gina's friend recognized her discomfort, she had no intention of owning up to it. "Now that we're all here, let's talk about who's going to work the phones," she said, trying to nudge the meeting back into focus.

Shelley produced a list of volunteers, and Emily brought up the subject of getting T-shirts screen-printed for them to wear that night, and soon the meeting was moving along as it should be.

But Gina kept thinking of how upsetting it had been to watch Josh walk away with Tahoma on the *Mr. Moneybags* show, and now that he'd signed up for the bachelor auction, that was exactly what would be happening again. Not with Tahoma this time, but with some other woman.

JOSH DROPPED INTO THE LOCAL barber shop early one morning for a haircut and ran into Gina's uncle Albert, who glanced up from the newspaper he was reading and smiled his greeting. Albert Aurelio was the chief financial officer at Vineyard Oaks.

"Josh, how's it going?" Albert asked as he folded the paper and set it aside. He appeared tired, even haggard, with deep circles under his eyes.

"Good," Josh said. "I'm getting better at bocce, Frankie wants to give me one of his puppies and I'm enjoying my stay in Rio Robles."

Albert nodded vigorously. "It's the best place on earth," he said with conviction.

"That's what Gina says," Josh said.

"It's no more than what we all think. Rio Robles was a good choice for our forebears to start a winery. Now it's up to my generation to ensure that there will still be a Vineyard

Oaks for our children and our children's children. It's not so easy," he added with a rueful chuckle.

Josh wasn't sure how to reply to this, but Albert went on talking.

"Of course, without Fredo the winery would not have survived. Never have I seen someone who is more attuned to people. My main concern is finance—that's what I was trained to do. But Fredo, he knows the grapes. And he's great with workers, understands how to manage them, how to encourage them to give their best. Our strength is our family, but our heart—that comes from our people."

"I like that philosophy, Albert."

"It has served us well." He paused. "You and Gina— you're getting along okay?"

Josh was glad for the change in subject, since he was uncomfortable discussing anything about the Angelini winery with Albert. "Gina's a wonderful person," he said. "It's good to see her again."

Albert nodded sagely as the barber beckoned him for his turn. "Fredo likes you. So does Rocco. It was nice running into you, my boy."

Josh picked up the newspaper, but he didn't read it. As he scanned the lines of print, he kept thinking of how the Angelinis would fare if their winery was bought out by Starling. The operating philosophy of Starling was different, and the corporate culture wasn't family oriented. The Angelinis would have a difficult adjustment to their new owner. More and more, he was having a hard time separating his friendship with the Angelinis from his obligation to Walter Emsing and Starling. He hadn't spoken with Walter lately, but he'd be hearing from him soon, and he didn't look forward to the conversation.

Josh was in low spirits by the time he got to the local bookstore, where he gloomily shopped for books about the background and history of the valley. On the one hand, he wanted to read them so he'd be more familiar with Gina's family's role in the Napa Valley, but he was also aware that any knowledge he gained would be interesting to Walter. Unless he bowed out of his obligation to Walt, which would certainly not endear him to his father, who sat on Starling's board of directors.

HE WAS STANDING IN THE checkout line considering all the woulds and shoulds when Maren breezed into the store.

"Josh," she said, smiling affably. "I haven't seen you around lately."

Three days had passed since he'd taken Gina to dinner, and although he'd called her, he hadn't dropped by or made a date with her. Why? Because he was concerned that he'd been coming on too strong. Because, now that he was sure that she'd truly loved him when they were on the *Mr. Moneybags* show, he needed to evaluate his feelings for her all over again.

"I've been working," he said, holding up the book he planned to buy. "Reading up on Rio Robles," he added.

"Gina said she enjoyed taking you on a wine-tasting tour," Maren told him.

He couldn't believe how this comment made his heart leap in his chest. He remained calm, however. It wouldn't do to let Maren know how crazy he was about Gina, especially since if he did, every Angelini from here to Calistoga would be in on it, too.

"It was fun," he said, trying to maintain a noncommittal tone.

"Josh," Maren said, moving slightly closer and lowering her voice so that she spoke confidentially. "I've had a brilliant idea. You may recall that I work for a caterer." She waited for his nod before she plunged ahead.

"Well, one of the things we do is prepare picnic lunches for honeymooners. They like to get away from it all in a romantic setting, and there's no more romantic setting than the Napa Valley, don't you agree?"

"I certainly can't argue with that," Josh said.

"The thing is, these two honeymooners ordered a big picnic basket for today and then canceled. We have no one else who can use it, so the food will simply go to waste. How about if you stop by our kitchen on Springwell Street and pick it up? I'll run over to Good Thymes and suggest that I relieve Gina for a while, and then you can walk in with the basket and invite her on a picnic at Lake Berryessa. It'll be fun."

"Maren, I like the way you think," Josh said. His spirits climbed at the very idea of spending the whole afternoon with Gina.

Maren smiled conspiratorially. "The catch is that you can't tell her I set this up. Promise?"

"Promise," Josh assured her.

"You've got yourself a date." Maren winked and fluttered a little wave at him as she headed out of the store, moving at a fast clip.

GINA SPOTTED JOSH THROUGH the window when he arrived at Good Thymes. For a moment she appeared flustered, smoothing her hair back, frowning, then grinning engagingly before disappearing from view. He took this to mean that she'd gone to put on lipstick or comb her hair, and he wanted to tell her that it didn't matter to him if her hair was stringy or her lipstick chewed off; she looked gorgeous to him all the time.

When he walked into the shop, Maren was pouring herself a cup of herbal tea; she winked at him.

"Gina, you have a visitor," Maren caroled, and presently Gina appeared from the back room. Two bright spots of color accentuated her cheekbones, and Josh was sure that this was a natural blush, not artificial.

"Hi, Josh. Nice to see you," Gina said in an offhand tone that didn't fool him a bit.

"I came to drag you away from your work," he said, smiling down at her. Her hair was drawn back into a knot at the back of her head, and he suddenly had a vision of his hands releasing it to fall around her shoulders.

"What are you offering?" she said. She angled a coy look up at him, and though he didn't find coyness attractive in a woman, it pleased him that she wanted to play the age-old game of luring a man. Not that he needed luring. He was already entranced by her. Still, the byplay made pursuing her more fun.

"I have a picnic lunch in the back seat, a full tank of gas, and I am prepared to sweep you off your feet."

She pretended to consider the offer. "Since it's a slow day, you're on," she said. She spoke to Maren. "Mother, you don't mind if I leave you in charge, do you?"

"Not at all. In fact, I might be able to get some real work done around here if you leave me to myself. Go on, children." Maren smiled and shooed them away.

When Gina wasn't watching, he returned Maren's wink. For some reason, the thought popped into his mind that she'd be a great mother-in-law.

"Josh, you should see more of the valley than just Lake Berryessa. How about if we eat lunch there, then ride up to Calistoga and take in Old Faithful?"

"The geyser? I thought that was at Yosemite."

"Well, it is. This is a different Old Faithful."

"Okay. It's like the other day when we went wine tasting—you're the tour guide."

"I'm sure you've traveled a lot," she added. "Old Faithful's not going to impress you that much, maybe."

"Don't expect me to be impressed by the scenery. You're all the scenery I want."

She hated it when he looked at her that way. No, she loved it when he looked at her that way. Oh, she didn't know how she felt at all, which was confusing. The other day on their wine-tasting tour, she hadn't expected to reveal so much of herself to Josh. She wasn't sorry that she had, however, because she sensed that their communication had reached a new, more honest level. She had begun to doubt whether she should have let on how much she'd cared for him in the past. She didn't want him to take off running; she didn't want to scare him away. At least, not until she'd figured out if there was still a chance for them to have a real relationship.

His gaze devoured her, admired her. "Shouldn't you keep your eyes on the road?" she asked, her voice quavering so that she hardly sounded like herself.

He faced front again, and she decided it was time to discuss something. Anything, as long as it would make her stop thinking about his rock-solid good looks and the gleam in his eye that made her want to—

Lean over and kiss him?

Well, it was true. She loved kissing Josh Corbett, and that was the unalterable truth. Suddenly, her mouth went dry, and she gripped the armrest as she cautioned herself not to actually do it.

"This reminds me of that day at Dunsmoor Castle when I came to pick you up for our planned date in a BMW much like this one," Josh said. "The main difference was that the steering wheel was on the right side of the car."

She remembered only too well. "And when I went to get in it, I automatically walked around that side, which I thought was the passenger's side, and we bumped smack into each other. I was so embarrassed."

"Why? It was a perfectly natural mistake. Our steering wheels are on the left in this country."

"The cameras were rolling, and millions of people around the world would see me bumbling around like an idiot," she said.

"They saw you acting like a perfectly normal intelligent woman. You were charming."

"I remember you said something funny, like you always hated to be right. It took me a few seconds to figure out that you meant 'right' as in direction, not 'right' as in being correct."

That had been a lovely day, driving across the moors to a charming abbey-turned-restaurant, where they'd been treated to a delicious dinner of Scottish food, most notably haggis. When Gina had found out that haggis consisted of ground sheep's innards, minced suet, oatmeal and seasonings boiled in a sheep's stomach, she'd almost tossed her cookies on the spot. But she'd summoned the courage to try it and decided she liked it.

"Those were the days," Josh said in a mock nostalgic tone before reaching over and taking her hand.

"Shouldn't you keep both hands on the steering wheel?" she asked him.

"What is it with you? 'Keep your eyes on the road. Keep your hands on the steering wheel.' Oh, there's a hot-air balloon," he said.

The balloon was big and bright red. It was sailing toward the mountains in the distance, its occupants mere dots in the large wicker basket that swung below.

"There are always balloons to be seen on fine days," Gina said.

"I bet that's fun," Josh said. "Have you ever been up in one?"

"Yes, several times. Rocco and I took Frankie up a couple of years ago for his birthday."

"I'll bet you had a great time."

"Until Frankie got sick. He upchucked down the front of my dress. As it turned out, he doesn't do well with heights."

"Would you like to go again? I promise not to do what Frankie did."

Gina laughed. "Maybe. I might even get free tickets after the bachelor auction." She could have bitten her tongue; why had she brought up the auction?

Josh slid a look over at her. "Why's that?"

"The balloon company donates them, and some people are afraid to go up."

"Not me. I signed up for the bachelor auction. Did you notice my name on the list?"

"I heard about it at our last committee meeting," Gina said with what passed for remarkable forbearance.

"You don't sound thrilled," he said.

"Of course I am."

"Does that mean that maybe you'll bid for me?" he asked mischievously.

"I can't, Josh. I'm the mistress of ceremonies."

His face fell. "I didn't realize that," he said. His surprise was evident, but he didn't seem disappointed enough.

"It never occurred to me to mention it," she said, forcing a smile. "Anyway, we're hoping that this year's auction will put us over the top so we can start construction on the teen center next year."

He seemed distracted, his thoughts elsewhere. "A teen center," he said musingly.

"It's important to me. Really important."

"Tell me about it," he said, catching her off guard.

"Like almost everything in my life, it has to do with family," she said quietly. "My sister Barbara's son, to be exact."

"Don't she and Nick have only the two daughters, Mia and Stacey?" Josh asked.

"Their eldest child, Nicky, died in a motorcycle accident four years ago. They—and everyone else in our family—were devastated. He was fifteen years old."

Now she had Josh's full attention. "I'm really sorry, Gina. What happened?"

Remembering that time in her life was always difficult. Nicky had been an exuberant teenager, adored by and popular with his peers. His death had saddened them all and been so unnecessary.

Gina needed a minute or so to collect herself and didn't answer immediately. "Nicky was riding on the back of a motorcycle that belonged to a seventeen-year-old who had been driving for less than a year. They'd gone to an afternoon movie and were casting about for something to do. Rod— that was Nicky's friend's name—suggested riding over to Sonoma, and Nicky agreed to go. Rod was speeding when they came around a curve, and they hit a truck head-on. Rod was thrown clear, and he's still struggling to learn to walk again. Nicky made it to the hospital, but his injuries were so serious that he died the next day.''

"That's terrible. It must have been hard on Barbara and Nick.''

Gina nodded. "Barb was severely depressed for a long time. Nick held their marriage together, convinced her to pull out of her depression for the sake of their girls.'' She paused and drew a deep breath. "When I grew up in Rio Robles, I found it dull and uninteresting. If there had been a place where kids could get together and do the things kids like to do—dance, and play music and games—I would have been a lot happier. And maybe if there had been someplace for kids to gather, Rod and Nicky wouldn't have gone to Sonoma. We're going to name the teen center after Nicky. We can't bring him back, but we hope we can convince kids that they don't have to head out of town for something worthwhile to do.''

"That's great, Gina. I mean it.'' Josh squeezed her hand.

Gina leaned back against the headrest, thinking that never in her wildest dreams had she suspected that she and Josh Corbett would be tooling along the open road in the Napa Valley discussing a topic so dear to her.

They drove in silence for a time until he spoke. "I was just remembering how beautiful you were on that day when we went to the abbey.''

She'd found Josh particularly dashing in a tweed jacket, his dark hair windblown and his cheeks ruddy from the wind. He'd caught her hand in his as they left the castle, and they'd raced, laughing, all the way to the car.

He went on talking. "You wore a bright red sweater."

"Actually, it was magenta. Bought at a woolen mill not far from Dunsmoor. The wool made you sneeze."

"It fit you perfectly. And you also wore jeans."

"Borrowed from one of my cousins."

"And the most beautiful smile I've ever seen."

"That," she said, "was all my own."

"And you made a face when the waiter told you what haggis was."

"I did not! I ate it first thing!" She was indignant.

"I thought you were going to do what Frankie did up there in the balloon. You should have seen your face."

"You should have seen yours. I don't recall your eating the haggis."

"I had a different sort of appetite by that time. Even though I knew there would be a cameraman in the back seat on the way home, I was sure we'd kiss."

"I wasn't," she said dreamily, recalling how Josh had seemed so sure of himself that for half the ride home it had seemed like arrogance instead of self-confidence. When they had pulled off the highway onto the lane that led to the castle, rain began to pour from the sky, and Josh had eased the car over to the side of the road. His arm tightened around her shoulders, and they felt curtained off from the world by the rain and by their own involvement. Gina forgot about her fellow contestants back at the castle, who would be lined up to greet her when she returned, and the cameraman, who was relentlessly recording their every breath and sigh. All she knew in that breathless interlude was that Josh's strong arms were around her, and his beard was rough against her cheek, and his voice was whispering in her ear so quietly that the camera would not pick up the sound.

She was brought back to the present time by a sign looming up on the right side of the road. "Here's where we turn toward the lake," she said.

Josh apparently hadn't been expecting the turn. He

wrenched the wheel, making her slide across the slick leather seat toward him. She couldn't help admiring his smooth mastery of the car, his confidence and control.

"Sorry about that," he said in a tone of apology.

"That's okay. I should have warned you the turn was coming up." She straightened, but before she righted herself, her hand grazed his thigh, earning her a quick but searching glance. Had her touch been intentional? No more intentional than his sharp turn, but it occurred to her that perhaps the turn had not had to be so sharp after all. She supposed she wouldn't put it past Josh to jolt her closer to him on purpose, and she was amazed to discover that she didn't mind.

"How far until we get to the picnic place?" he asked.

"Not long."

"The lunch smells wonderful. Your aunt Dede said you love her stuffed grape leaves."

"They're the best. We have a lot of good cooks in our family." Their talk seemed to concentrate on her family too much. Though Josh always appeared interested, maybe it was time for a different topic. "How are you doing on your article?" she asked.

"It's coming along," he said, but she sensed caution in his tone.

"That's good." They rounded a curve and saw the lake, bright blue and sparkling in the sunshine, straight ahead. "Here we are," she said.

Josh pulled the BMW into the shade of a tall pine tree and got out to take the food basket out of the back seat. A couple of picnic tables were situated on the bluff overlooking the water, and Josh had brought a blanket.

"How about this spot?" he asked when they reached a grassy mound with a panoramic view of the lake and the mountains stretching beyond.

"Perfect," Gina said. She spread the blue-and-white checked tablecloth on the table and explored the basket.

"Mmm, parsleyed roast chicken," she said. "And saffron risotto, too. Oh, and chocolate hazelnut cake."

Aunt Dede had sent along a fresh baguette, which Gina knew had been baked by her mother, and chèvre mixed with herbs from Gina's own garden. She had also included a bottle of viognier, Gina's personal favorite wine, and a small bottle of port to drink with the cake.

After they ate, they sat on the picnic blanket. Josh lounged back against a nearby oak tree, declaring himself stuffed.

"I like Lake Berryessa better than those cold lochs we visited in Scotland," he said idly as he reached for her hand.

"Well, I'm not going to dare you to wade in the water, if that's what you're thinking." That was what Tahoma had done on the Loch Ness excursion, and the loch had been frigid.

"She wanted to warm me afterward," Josh said teasingly.

"I can't believe you obliged," Gina said. But he had. He'd wrapped Tahoma in his arms and she'd kissed him, hard. To his credit, Josh had appeared taken aback, but then he'd let her kiss him again. All of which Gina hadn't known during the filming of the program but had found out months later. The incident hadn't enhanced her opinion of Josh Corbett— or of Tahoma.

"You don't like her much, do you?" A bold question on his part, unexpected.

Gina shrugged. She couldn't explain her feelings about Tahoma. She only knew that she hated visualizing the woman in Josh's arms. She realized suddenly that his arms would most likely be around some other woman after the bachelor auction. Someone of her acquaintance, perhaps even someone related to her.

Something squeezed around her heart. She didn't want Josh to be with any other woman. Not now. Not ever. Yet there wasn't much she could do to stop him, if that was his wish.

He got up and brought the bottle of port over to the blanket, along with her glass. "Here," he said. "You might as well finish this off." He poured some into her glass and handed it to her.

"Aren't you having any?"

"No, I've had enough. I'm driving."

She sipped her wine, wanting to stay more in the present and stop thinking about their past. They were having a good time now, weren't they? She was learning to trust him, wasn't she? So why did she keep bringing up Tahoma and the *Mr. Moneybags* show and all the glitches that could scuttle their present happiness?

She spilled her wine on the blanket. "Oops, I didn't mean to do that," she said as Josh reached for a napkin.

"No harm done," he said.

Gina set her glass aside. She hated it that she was so clumsy, both physically and emotionally.

"Is something wrong?" Josh asked, furrowing his brow.

"I—I have the feeling that I'm not doing anything right," Gina blurted. "I'm not careful enough, or I'm too careful, or I say things I shouldn't."

He gazed at her blankly for a moment. "Gina, what on earth are you talking about?"

Her words came out in a rush. "Only that I may be the stupidest woman on the planet. Is that a word, *stupidest?* You're a writer. You should know."

"I don't know and I don't care. To me, you're the most beautiful woman on the planet. And I think I want to kiss you, but I'm in the same situation as you think you are. I've been the stupidest man in the whole universe, and I may have handled this all wrong, too."

"You seem to know exactly what you're about," she said, her voice low and troubled.

Josh stared off toward the edge of the lake, where the long grass swayed softly in the breeze. When his gaze finally met hers, his pupils were large and his eyes were kind and caring. His voice was a rumble in his throat. "I'm not sure that's true, but I know what I want to do right now, Gina Angelini. I want to kiss you so much I can hardly stand it."

Chapter Eleven

Before she could speak, his head dipped and his lips touched hers. Lightly at first, then more surely. His hands came up to grip her shoulders, pulling her toward him and then sliding around to hold her close. He sensed the tension in her, the excitement, the urgency. What he felt bordered on desperation, because he had never waited with more patience for any woman. With anyone else, he would have been on his merry way long before now, but this was Gina. Gina Angelini, the most important woman in the world to him. Even as his hands came up to loosen the clip that held her hair, he marveled that he felt this way about her. In those moments, she might have been the first woman he ever kissed. Everything felt new and strange and wonderful, and the woman in his arms returned his kisses passionately.

His hands slid under her sweater, explored the ripple of her ribs, encountered lace, cupped the breasts contained within. They swelled to fit his hand, he could have sworn they did, the nipples little nubs beneath his seeking fingers. His breath came harder, hotter, and she stirred within his embrace.

"Josh," she breathed close to his cheek. "Oh, Josh."

His translation: she was into this as much as he was, and he was in it with his whole heart, his whole being. His whole life.

Could this be true? The idea gave him pause, and he tried as hard as he could to strike some clarity of thought. Even though he had come to Rio Robles on business, finding Gina had been in the back of his mind, and he had wondered if going out with her was possible after all that had gone on before. But what if something more was possible? A life together? Marriage?

It seemed like a wonderful idea at this moment, with Gina in his arms. And at the same time, it seemed like a very bad idea indeed.

He didn't want to toy with her. He wouldn't be able to face Rocco or any of her other family members if he did. He was trying to figure out some way of communicating his concern, when a large and wet Labrador retriever galloped up from the lake and shook himself only a foot or two away so that water sprayed all over them.

"Durango!" called a stern male voice. "Come back here!"

The dog blinked uncertainly at Gina and Josh, his tongue lolling.

Gina bolted upright, unsuccessfully trying to smooth her clothes. "He must have smelled the food," she said, brushing at the damp drops on her forearm.

Josh inserted a wide space between them as a middle-aged man holding a stick in his hand puffed his way up the path from the lake.

"Sorry, folks," he said. "Durango and I were playing down by the water, and he decided to run up and investigate."

"No problem," Josh said. He had taken the brunt of the deluge, and he wiped his face with his napkin.

"Come on, boy. Let's go chase the stick."

The dog circled the blanket, then followed his owner down the path.

Josh grinned at Gina. "I don't suppose you planned that interruption, did you?" he asked.

"No, but I have it on good authority that Durango is related to the Angelinis in some way, though I've never seen him or his owner before in my life. Only an Angelini could come up with such a well-timed intervention."

"I heard that necessity was the mother of intervention," Josh said with a straight face. He began to gather up the food and pile it in the picnic basket.

"I think you mean *invention,*" Gina retorted.

"Gina, I couldn't have invented anything more pleasurable than kissing you."

"After two years of missing me?" There was that flirtatious quirk to her smile again, and Josh thought he might be falling in love with it. With her.

The question was, did he want to run away again, before he found himself committed to this woman?

The answer, at the moment, was no. At least, not yet.

THEY DROVE AT A LEISURELY PACE toward Calistoga at the north end of the valley. Josh held Gina's hand, which rested lightly on his knee.

"Tell me about this geyser," he said.

"We might have to wait for it to erupt," Gina said. "Which it does, in theory, every forty minutes. Slow down, we're almost there."

The geyser was beyond a low building housing displays and educational exhibits. Gina took him first into the building and led him around the room, pointing out the most interesting pictures, yet what he wanted was a guided tour of something else—her body. It didn't help that when she bent close to a display case, her sweater was drawn tight against her breasts. She'd left her hair unbound so that it spilled seductively across her shoulders, and the way she moved—so graceful and so unselfconsciously sexy—drove him out of his mind.

He wanted to ravish her as no woman had ever been ravished, and then do it all over again. He wanted—

"Oh, Josh, it's time for the geyser!" Gina grabbed his hand and pulled him along with her to the outside viewing area, crowded with other sightseers. She moved closer to make room for newcomers, and he let go of her hand so that he could drape an arm casually across her shoulders. He was supposed to be looking at the geyser, but all he wanted in his field of vision was Gina.

"Excited?" she asked, and all he could do was groan. He was excited, but not about the geyser.

"It's almost time," someone said, but still Josh wasn't thinking of the geyser. He was thinking of making love to Gina, of finally expressing his desire. A capricious wind blew her hair toward him so that strands of it wafted across his cheek. As she reached up and pushed it back behind her ear, he caught her hand, brought it to his lips. At that moment the geyser began to whisper, then the water rushed up out of the earth with a fury too long contained.

Gina's eyes locked with his, and he knew that when he finally made love to her, he would choose to be looking into her beautiful face at the moment of climax, would want to see the expression in her eyes in that magic moment. Would want her to see his eyes, which would tell her how much he cared about her, how much he wanted her.

Having reached its peak, the geyser slowed to a spurt, to a trickle, then ceased. The crowd was quiet, and Gina was still staring at him. Slowly, he lowered his hand, the fingers still laced through hers.

He didn't dare speak. He didn't want to stop the magic.

"That was spectacular," Gina said. She withdrew her hand from his slowly, as if she didn't want to break contact.

All he could do was nod. The two of them together would also be spectacular. He knew it, and perhaps she did, too. Now it was up to her.

GINA WAS SHAKEN BY WHAT had happened at the geyser. In that moment of its eruption, she had lost herself in Josh's eyes, and for an instant, she had known what it would be like to lose herself in making love with him. That passion, that longing, that closeness that she had felt for him two years ago had returned full force, and this time every cell in her body seemed to be urging her to bring things between them to their natural completion.

Was it a good idea? Maybe not. But if she never knew Josh Corbett in that way, she might regret it all her life.

They drove toward Rio Robles through the golden twilight, speaking occasionally but mostly enjoying the rare communion of two seeking souls. When they reached Rio Robles, it was dark and still early. Gina wasn't hungry, but she thought Josh might be. She was contemplating inviting him to her place for a light supper and considering the consequences of such an invitation when Josh noticed the bright lights two streets over.

"Looks like a party's going on," he said, slowing the car.

"It's the street market. They block off the downtown streets on the second and fourth Saturdays of the month and allow the local farmers to set up stalls where they can sell their produce."

"I hear a band. Mariachi music, it sounds like."

Gina stopped trying to figure out what she could serve for supper. She'd just had a better idea. "We could grab something to eat if you'd like. Some of the vendors sell really great food that they cook right there in the open."

"You're on," Josh said. A minivan ahead of them was pulling out of a parking place, and he slotted the BMW neatly into the space.

Before Gina could get out of the car, Josh came around and opened the door for her. She pulled on a light jacket as they walked, and Josh slid his arm around her shoulders and drew her to him. It was nice that he was affectionate. She liked a man who wasn't afraid to show a woman that he cared when they were in public.

They passed a couple of groups, and, as always when they

saw Josh, the women did a double take. He noticed and said sheepishly, "I guess they remember me from the show."

"Maybe they think you're handsome," she said.

This seemed to embarrass him. "It could be you that they're gawking at," he pointed out.

"Oh, sure. Like I really believe that," she scoffed, but in a way it could be true. As in, look at her, she's with him, meaning that they admired her for having such a handsome escort.

Main Street stretched for six blocks, and it was lined on both sides with booths. The trees had been strung with tiny white lights, so that a soft glow suffused everything. People thronged the streets, and food from the stalls lent a combination of tantalizing aromas to the crisp night air.

"Hi, Gina," someone said, and Gina turned to see her cousin Martin with some of his friends. Her heart sank when she realized that she and Josh might well acquire an entourage of her relatives, but Martin only said, "See you around," before disappearing toward the town square.

"Are you thinking what I'm thinking?" Josh asked.

"That we don't need company? Believe me, I know." She smiled up at him, and he grazed her cheek with his knuckle.

"Not that I don't like your family," he said.

"Not that I don't love them," she agreed.

"But we deserve some alone time," he said.

"Agreed."

For a moment, all she wanted was Josh Corbett in her field of vision—to take in the little crinkles at the corners of his eyes, watch his lips as they curved into a tender smile. His lips. Oh, God, she'd better stop this or she'd be kissing him out here in the middle of Main Street with the whole town observing.

"How about a burrito made fresh right over there?" she said in a rush, angling her head toward a nearby booth.

"Good idea," Josh replied.

They let themselves be propelled by the crowd, and found

that they had to hold hands in order not to be separated. When they'd received a plate of food from the cheerful vendor, who insisted that they douse their burritos with his special hot sauce, they settled on a table in the alcove of a building and chowed down.

"This is the best burrito I ever ate," Josh said after he'd taken a bite.

"I don't suppose they have a lot of Mexican food in Boston," she ventured.

He stared for a moment. "You've got to be kidding. Every kind of restaurant is represented there."

"Boston is a place I've never been," she said. She must seem less than worldly to Josh, but that was nothing new. He'd figured out that she was relatively unsophisticated back at Dunsmoor Castle.

After they'd finished their food, they bought Italian ices for dessert and walked along the street eating them. Josh finished his first and made a detour to a stand selling handmade jewelry. "Gina, this would look great on you," he said, holding up a large amber heart swinging from an intricate silver chain. "It's so pretty against your hair."

"Oh, not really," Gina said. She didn't have any extra money to buy things like that. She plowed most of her profits right back into her business.

"I'll buy it for you," he said, and even though she protested, he insisted. Before they left, he fastened the necklace, brushing aside her hair to adjust the clasp and then arranging it across her shoulders again. "There. It's perfect for you."

"Thanks, Josh. That was a nice thing for you to do." She hadn't wanted him to buy her a present. She didn't want to feel obligated to him.

"I'm a nice guy."

"That's true," she said thoughtfully.

"Don't sound so surprised," he said, but he was grinning. "Now what would you like to do?"

"Buy fruits and vegetables. They'll be fresh, probably picked today."

"Hi, Gina. Hello, Josh," said a voice at Gina's elbow, and suddenly, Frankie was there.

"Hey, sport," Josh said. "What's new?"

"Not much. Nothing good."

"Hmm, does that mean that you still haven't brought up your math grade?" Gina asked him.

"We had a test the other day, and one of the questions was about figuring two to the seventh power. I'm not sure if I got it right or not. Josh, you want to come over and throw a baseball with me sometime? My dad says you used to play on your high school team."

"Sure, Frankie. Maybe tomorrow afternoon if you're going to be home."

"Speaking of your dad, Frankie, where is Rocco?"

Frankie jerked a thumb toward Volare, which was a half block away. "He and Shelley are eating dinner in there. Oh, and by the way, Gina, they delivered your car to your place earlier today. Pop said that now he's finished working on it, he'll have time to paint my bike."

"That's good news for both of us, right?" Gina said with a smile. Frankie had been wanting his bike painted ever since one of Rocco's customers had backed over it in the parking lot.

"Yeah, it sure is. Well, guess I'd better go, 'cause I'm here with Mia and her mom."

"See you tomorrow," Josh called as Frankie melted into the crowd.

Gina and Josh resumed their walk. "What's with Frankie's math grade?" Josh asked her.

"Rocco told Frankie that he couldn't play with the accordion band if he didn't bring his math grade up. He thinks it would take too much time away from Frankie's studies, since they'll meet two nights a week right after dinner."

"That's too bad," Josh said.

"Maybe it's the incentive Frankie needs to study more in the afternoon. That kid absolutely hates to crack the books until the last minute." Gina stopped at a large vegetable stand and began to pick up and discard eggplants, turning them over and over in her hands as she studied them. The delectable vegetables turned Josh's thoughts to how luscious Gina herself was.

I've got to stop thinking like this, he told himself in desperation.

"I've found what I want," Gina said with satisfaction. "I'll make eggplant parmigiana next week."

I've found what I want, Josh thought. *I just can't get to it.*

"Now for some pomegranates," she said, moving down the line to a bin full of them. Again, she began to browse through the fruit, tossing some back, putting others in a bag. The pomegranates were the exact color of Gina's lips. As round as her breasts, which he ached to touch at this very moment.

Stop it, Josh told himself sternly, but he couldn't stop visualizing Gina. He knew exactly how he'd approach her; first, he'd caress her rich, ripe pomegranates—no, breasts. Then her soft cheeks, and he'd explore every part of every crevice, kiss every sweet inch of her skin until she cried out for mercy.

"Mercy," Gina said in a conversational tone, which brought him back to reality. "We'd better stop by the bakery kiosk over there. They usually have the most wonderful brioches."

Josh stuffed his hands in his pockets and followed glumly along, knowing that he shouldn't get his hopes up. This night would probably end as the others had, with Gina evading his kisses and rushing upstairs. Without him.

Gina bought several brioches and some hard poppyseed rolls, and he took the bags from her to carry. Even if this evening ended in disappointment, he wouldn't consider the day a total loss. The two of them had reached a rare communion when they'd watched Old Faithful.

Damn. He didn't want the evening to be over yet.

"How about if we go check out that mariachi band?" he suggested.

"Oh, that would be fun," she said, smiling brightly.

It didn't take long to reach the town square and locate a table at the edge of the dance floor. Before long, Josh was snapping his fingers. Couples young and old circled the floor, dancing every which way. "Want to try it?" he asked.

"If you do." .

Gina preceded Josh to the dance floor, where she turned to him and flowed into his arms. The music was fast, and Josh was a good dancer. The bandleader eyed them, and Gina saw him confer with one of his musicians. After that, the music slowed to a plaintive ballad, and Josh tightened his arms around her. Her temple pressed against his cheek, and his breath fluttered against her ear. They danced, but it was more than moving their feet in time to music. It was the two of them in concert, every little movement making them more aware of each other. Of their faces, so close that all she would have to do is tilt hers toward his to find his lips. Of their hands, clasped close to Josh's chest. Of their bodies, touching each other until Gina was primed for love.

The music continued to be slow for the next few numbers, full of muted brass, plaintive violin and soulful guitar. Desire shimmered in her blood, hummed beneath the surface of her skin, made her body feel languorous and edgy at the same time. She swayed into him, felt his taut muscles beneath the fabric of his shirt. She lifted her lips to his, oblivious to the others on the dance floor, the musicians, anything.

His lips met hers, soft, sure. Tension vibrated between them. "Let's go," he said, and she nodded.

They stopped for a moment to pick up their packages where they had left them, and then they slipped away from the lights, the music, the people.

In his car she lifted a hand, brushed it against his cheek. She heard him catch his breath and then he turned to her, his eyes deep with longing, the same longing that made her nipples pucker beneath her sweater. He pinned her back against the seat and kissed her, his lips ravenous, his tongue seeking. "Tell me what you want," he demanded, his hand finding the silky inside of her thigh.

She tore her lips away, clung to him as all doubt faded. "I want—you. You," she whispered.

"Are you sure, Gina?"

Her eyes found his, saw the glitter in the darkness. "Yes," she breathed.

She didn't remember afterward how they got to her cottage, but she did remember standing inside the door, silent in her need, before Josh took the breathtaking first step of slipping his arms around her waist. In a moment, they were kissing in a flare of passion. She helped him out of his shirt, lost it on the way up the stairs, unfastened her bra as they kissed in her dark kitchen. She felt an aching readiness that couldn't be overridden by common sense. The time for that had come and gone; now she was his.

She backed toward the bedroom as he touched her breasts, circling her nipples with his thumbs, skimming his hands downward. Without speaking, she shivered out of her clothes above the waist. She felt no self-consciousness in front of him, no reticence about anything.

The only light was the glow of a street lamp shining through the cottage window. "My gorgeous Gina. You're even more beautiful than that nude in that mural," he murmured as they reached her bed. "More lovely than I ever dreamed."

"I wish—" she began, and then thought better of it.

"That this had happened in Scotland? So do I."

She considered this as she slid off her shoes, kicked them into a corner, wrapped her arms around Josh and kissed him gently on the shoulder. He slowly unbuttoned her slacks. They pooled around her feet, and she stepped away from them, only to be swung up into his arms.

He settled her carefully on the bed, lay down beside her. She reached her arms up, pulled him down to her and reveled in the textures of him. Skin, hair, teeth, tongue. Tangled with hers, then not tasting each other and lingering, and his lips exploring her throat and down, down...

His face was in shadow, but she could still see written there the wonder and the beauty of this moment—the excitement of making love for the first time. All her anticipation could never have prepared her for this. Nothing in her life had been as beautiful as wanting to become part of Josh. She heard herself murmur his name as his lips found her breasts, as they feathered across her abdomen, and she wove her fingers through her hair. He paused for a moment. "Gina," he said tenderly, "are you protected?" She shook her head. "I'll take care of it," he said, reaching for the foil pack in his wallet. Then they were lost in the sensuous tumble of their bodies, wild with pleasure, her body arching into his, pulsing toward a smooth, slick, satiny welcome. Tears of joy that finally this was happening to her. A gasp, a cry, her name, her man. Her love. Yes.

She held him tight, spiraling down from the incredible peak as gently as a whisper on the wind. Josh stroked her face, kissed her with inexpressible sweetness and did not question her tears. Then he curled his body around hers, his hand curving around her breast, and held her that way until they both fell asleep.

Once during the night, Gina drifted up out of a dream to feel him stir and asked him if everything was all right. He tightened his embrace and said, "Very," before kissing the back of her neck.

She knew from his steady breathing that he had fallen asleep again, and she snuggled even closer. With a sense of contentment and well-being, she herself fell asleep.

Chapter Twelve

Josh woke up to a huge weight in the middle of his chest. In the first moments of waking, he was sure that it was Gina, ready for more lovemaking.

However, when he finally cracked open one eye, then the other, he saw only the curious face of the cat. Timothy was purring waves of stale tuna breath into Josh's face and industriously kneading the bedclothes.

With his hopes dashed, all Josh could do was dump Timothy off the bed and sneeze loudly.

He heard Gina taking things out of the refrigerator and closing cabinet doors. "Gina?" he called. The cat glared at him balefully and, tail held high, marched out of the room in high dudgeon.

Gina popped her head in the door. "Good morning, Josh. I had to get up to let Timothy in, and I'm fixing something to eat." She swooped down upon him and kissed him on the lips. She tasted like toothpaste.

He slid his hand up and cupped her breast, brushing aside her robe so he could kiss the rosy tip. The nipple hardened, and he said coaxingly, "Come back to bed." Gina's body was all he had ever imagined, and he could hardly wait to explore it more thoroughly.

"I'll be back with the breakfast tray," she said, eluding his grasp. She hurried toward the kitchen, but by the time he had pushed himself up against the pillows, she had returned. The tray held a couple of warm brioches, butter stamped with a four-leaf clover and a bowl of pomegranates. Also coffee, which smelled wonderful.

She perched on the edge of the bed while he dug in. He patted the blanket beside him. "Scoot over here," he said. "You don't need to be so far away."

She gulped down a few bites of the brioche. "I have to get ready. I don't want to be late."

Late? Late for what?

"Uh, maybe you'd better fill me in. Are we going someplace?" He'd promised to throw a few balls with Frankie later, but this was Sunday morning.

"I'm going to church," Gina said, wiping her hands on a napkin. It was made of cloth and had lace edges, he noted dimly, but this nicety paled against what she was telling him.

"Church?" An entirely unwelcome idea, since he was of a mind to eat a quick breakfast and then make lazy love, lingering on all the fascinating bits of Gina's body that might have gotten short shrift last night.

"Angelinis always go to the ten o'clock mass." She stood and walked to the closet, where she thumbed through a bunch of clothes before tossing a blue dress across a chair. She disappeared into the bathroom and turned on the shower.

"I don't suppose you could attend a later one," he ventured.

Gina stuck her head out. "What? I can't hear you when the water's running."

"You could go to a later mass, right?"

"Wrong. They'll wonder what happened to me, and Mother or my sister will stop by to make sure I haven't met with misfortune, and—I'm sure you get the picture." Leaving the door open, she ducked back into the bathroom, and he heard her stepping into the bathtub and pulling the shower curtain closed.

He wasn't so hungry anymore. Nonplussed, he looked

around at his surroundings, which he'd been in too much of a hurry to notice last night. Everything in Gina's bedroom was a shade of yellow, from the palest buttercup, to darkest ochre. The bed was ornate brass, and the furniture, mellow pine. Somehow it all worked, and the yellow made him feel overwhelmingly optimistic in general, despite his disappointment about this morning.

After a few minutes he got up, pulled on his shorts and padded over to the bathroom. Gina was humming to herself, her body slightly visible behind the shower curtain. He turned away from this tantalizing sight and leaned against the door frame.

The dresser was beside him, and some papers were spilling out of a folder. The headings were in bold print: OPERATING EXPENSES, PROFIT AND LOSS, LAST YEAR'S PRODUCTION REPORT. He was seeing valuable information about the Angelinis' winery. He stared for a moment, realizing that this was a true crisis of conscience. If he continued to look, he could report certain facts back to Walter and win Walt's approval, not to mention his father's. And if he didn't? That would mean that he was more committed to Gina than to Walt, his father and Starling Industries combined. He felt frozen in place, unable to move.

"Josh?"

He heard Gina's voice as from a great distance, stared at her blankly as her head emerged from behind the shower curtain.

"Y-yes?"

"Hand me that washcloth on the rack, will you, please?"

He moved woodenly toward the washcloth, passed it to Gina. She smiled at him, pure sunshine. In that moment, he flashed back to last night, when she had been so eager, so willing. So sexy and beautiful and truly the woman of his dreams.

"Thanks, Josh."

Her figure was outlined in the diffuse light coming through

the bathroom window, and she was humming to herself. At one time, he might have been able to shrug off his feelings for her. He would have reminded himself that there were many beautiful women in the world and that they were his for the taking. But now he knew that only one woman had a profound effect on him, made him want to be a better man than he was.

Slowly, he backed away from the folder on the dresser. If Walter wanted to find out the information contained therein, he certainly could. But he was not going to find it out from Josh.

He sank onto the bed, feeling a sense of relief that he had resolved this issue. "Gina," he said.

"Yes?"

"How about if I go to church with you?"

Silence greeted this suggestion. Then he heard the shower curtain pull back, and glanced up to see her studying him openmouthed. "You're not Catholic, are you?"

"On my mother's side, but I was never confirmed."

"Oh. Well, even though you're welcome to attend our church, we can't walk in together. We can't sit together." She yanked the curtain closed again and resumed her shower.

He considered this for a moment. "Why not?" he asked.

"Because if we show up in each other's company, my whole family will know what happened. I'd be embarrassed."

"What do you mean, 'what happened'?" He was unsuccessful at keeping his impatience out of his voice.

"That we slept together. By this time, one of my aunts has called Mother and told her she saw us dancing at the street dance, and Frankie has mentioned to his dad that he ran into us and we were holding hands, and so on. People piece things together. You know."

He should have considered this. Her family seemed to be everywhere, all the time. He had no idea how many Angelinis lived in or near Rio Robles, but they all had two eyes, two ears and mouths that never stopped passing along family news. And he certainly didn't want to upset Gina by appearing with her at church. He had never considered the family angle of courting Gina before, but clearly, there was more to it than he could have imagined.

Gina stepped from the tub, all slick with water, her hair hanging wet down her back. He couldn't stop himself from going to her and kissing her soundly, all thoughts of everything else forgotten for the moment. She responded with an eagerness that gave him a little hope for this morning's agenda until she slipped out of his arms and said playfully, "I've got to blow-dry my hair. Scat."

"You talk to me like I'm the cat," he said, adopting a mock-wounded air.

"After last night, I know you're a lot more fun," she said, and then the sound of the blow dryer drove him away.

He retreated to the bed, where he ate another brioche and started to peel a pomegranate. This wasn't what he'd had in mind for the morning after. A pomegranate was hardly as mouthwatering as the real thing.

GINA WAS ALMOST LATE for the service, but Maren had saved a place for her. Usually, her mother sat beside Uncle Fredo, but he wasn't there today. Neither were two other key family figures: Uncle Albert and Uncle Anthony.

"Where are the uncles?" Gina asked as she and Maren were walking out of the church.

"An emergency meeting at the winery," her mother said. "It's about finances, of course."

"Oh, dear. Is there anything I should know?"

"Only that Fredo asked for our prayers."

"I mean, anything new? I took a look at the report you brought over. I have to admit that I didn't understand a lot of it."

Maren shook her head, her eyes serious. "Fredo's worried about the heavy debt load. Albert says they need a serious infusion of cash."

"This is certainly nothing new," Gina said grimly.

"I know. Don't worry. Fredo and company will come up with a solution. They always do." Despite trying to put a positive spin on the situation, Maren didn't fool Gina. The little creases between Maren's eyes meant she was more concerned than she let on.

Frankie, with Mia close behind, hurried toward them as they stepped out of the church into the open air. A large crowd stood milling around, many of them Angelinis. Some of them huddled together, speaking in low tones. They would be talking about the problems at the winery, reassuring one another that things weren't that bad, reminding one another that Uncle Fredo always performed a miracle at the last minute.

"Hey, Gina," Frankie said, "any idea what time Josh is coming over today?"

"Josh is coming over?" asked Rocco, coming up and flinging an arm around his son's shoulders.

"Yeah, I saw him and Gina last night," Frankie said. "I asked Josh if he'd stop in to see us, and he said he would."

"You and Josh saw Frankie? At the street market?" Rocco's eyes were keen upon Gina's face.

Gina, happy for a diversion from the winery's problems, felt sure her cheeks were turning pink, but she reminded herself that Rocco couldn't know that she and Josh had spent the night together. In any case, it wasn't any of his business. Uh, right. Rocco was perfectly capable of making it his business.

She cleared her throat before answering. "We stopped to talk with Frankie, but only in passing," she said.

Maren spoke up. "If I'd known you were going to go to the market on your way back from the picnic, I'd have asked you to buy me some pomegranates. They're especially good this year," she said.

"You and Josh went on a picnic?" Frankie said with an air of dismay.

"Well—"

"A picnic without us?" Mia asked incredulously. "How could you?"

"It wasn't a kid kind of a picnic," Maren contributed hastily.

"Every picnic is a kid kind," Mia said, pouting.

"Not necessarily," Gina said. "Anyway, when are we going to work on your science project?" She had promised Mia that she'd teach her about the medicinal qualities of the plants in her garden.

"Can we do it this week?" Mia looked slightly mollified at the prospect.

"Sure. Someday after school when your gramma is helping me in the shop would be good."

"I'll be there on Tuesday," Maren told Mia.

Gina's sister came to claim her daughter. "I hear Josh Corbett signed up for the bachelor auction," Barbara said.

"He did," Gina said. "How did you find out?"

"Shelley mentioned it to Rocco, who told me," Barbara said. "Such a prominent bachelor should up the take for sure."

"I hope so," Gina said, but her heart fell as it always did when she thought about Josh with another woman.

"The teen center project will profit from the wine auction this year, too," Barbara said. "They've agreed to give a chunk of their proceeds." The annual Napa Valley wine auction was the major charity event in the valley, raking in millions of dollars and attended by everyone who was anyone in the vintner set, as well as a host of celebrities. Wine would be auctioned for humongous prices. It wasn't unusual for a case of a particularly prized vintage to go for more than $100,000.

"Too bad we can't make Vineyard Oaks a beneficiary of the wine auction," Gina said. It was a lame attempt at trivializing the winery's problems. She knew, and so did Barbara, that all monies from the wine auction went to deserving charities in the valley. Vineyard Oaks wasn't a charity, at least not yet.

Barbara moved closer. "Some company has been making serious inquiries about buying Vineyard Oaks," she reported in a low tone. "I overheard things while I was working in the office."

"No!" Gina said. Why was she so shocked? She'd known that was a possibility, yet it was certainly one that she didn't want to contemplate.

"Don't tell anyone," Barbara warned as they were approached by doughty old Miss Dora, who wanted Gina to tell her what herb she'd recommend for her grandniece's morning sickness.

Once Miss Dora tottered off, Gina looked for Barbara in the hope of resuming their conversation, but she had already left. "See you Tuesday," Maren called as she went off to brunch with friends, and Gina, her heart heavy with Barbara's news, walked slowly to her car.

Who was sniffing around Vineyard Oaks? A local winery, hoping to expand? If so, surely she would have heard rumors. Or was it a large conglomerate? Or perhaps an individual? It didn't matter; she took a fierce pride in the winery, and for it to pass out of Angelini hands was unthinkable. Unthinkable, but not impossible.

When she arrived at her cottage, she was surprised to see Josh's car still parked under the olive tree. She got out of the Galaxie and hurried inside, calling up the stairs as soon as she went.

"Josh?" As she started to climb the stairs, she was halted by the sight of Josh standing at the top, wearing an apron and brandishing a vegetable peeler.

"I'm cooking dinner," he said. "Yankee pot roast."

It wasn't what she had expected—she'd thought he'd left after she'd gone to church—but she laughed, glad to see him there in her kitchen, surprised at how pleased she was. "I didn't know that cooking was among your talents,'' she told him.

"When I was living in Woods Mill, I had to learn. Come see what I've done."

He took her arm and propelled her to the stove, where beef, potatoes and carrots were all bubbling harmoniously in a pot.

"Fantastic," Gina said.

"I thought maybe you could recommend some herbs from your garden to put in it."

"Perhaps basil and a bit of garlic. Honestly, Josh, I'm impressed."

"How about if you go out and pick the basil and I clean up the kitchen." He hadn't left it particularly neat; Gina spotted potato peelings on one side of the sink, carrot scrapings on the other, and a couple of measuring cups in the sink.

"Good idea. You're a great guy, Josh, but it looks like the Russian army just marched through here."

He curved an arm around her waist and kissed her cheek. "Am I really a great guy?" he asked.

She turned and slid both hands behind his neck. "That's occurred to me in some of my not-so-sane moments," she said.

They kissed lightly. "I'd better change clothes before I head for the garden."

"You mean this is the second time in twenty-four hours that you're going to take them off in my presence? How lucky can a guy get?"

"Don't get too cocky," she warned. She twisted out of his embrace. "I let Timothy out when I left. Has he been around?"

"I haven't seen him. He's in a snit because I'm competing for your attention. Maybe you'd better let him in."

"No, he'll aggravate your allergy."

"I took a pill. He won't bother me."

"Great." She started for the bedroom, glanced over her

shoulder. "I don't suppose you've ever been allergic to women, have you?"

"No, they're the remedy, not the cause."

"You wish."

Josh only chuckled.

Gina changed into jeans and a striped shirt, and threw a sweater around her shoulders to ward off the chill in the air. When she emerged from the bedroom, Josh was sitting at the kitchen table, reading the Sunday paper.

He looked up and let out a low whistle of appreciation when he saw her. "How about a walk while this is cooking? We'll have plenty of time."

"I thought you were supposed to go over to see Frankie and Rocco today."

"I called while you were at church and left a message that I'd drop by in the late afternoon. We'll eat first."

"Okay." She hesitated at the door. "Josh, it's neat that you're taking such an interest in Frankie. It means a lot to him."

"He's a cool kid."

"It was hard on him when his mom died. Rocco's needed all the help he can get. Barbara sort of took Frankie under her wing after she lost her son, and I've contributed what I can, but he's at the age where he craves positive male role models."

"Rocco is that," Josh said.

"No doubt about it, but you know how it is with kids. Sometimes they latch on to someone outside the family circle, and it's good. Sometimes it's a teacher. Sometimes it's a friend. You didn't back off, and I thank you for that."

His eyes held a warm light. "No thanks necessary," he said.

She grabbed her basket from the top of the refrigerator. "I'll only be a few minutes," she said.

"I'll be here when you get back."

He'd be there when she got back. It was a comforting

thought. The few other men she'd invited to stay the night had always rushed off in the morning. They had been relationships, not mere one-night stands, but no one had ever cooked for her and suggested hanging out together for the rest of the day.

But then, Josh Corbett had always had a lot of class. That was one of the reasons she'd fallen for him in the first place.

THEY ENDED UP WALKING ALONG the river, scuffing through fallen leaves and holding hands. One of the houses they passed was Judy Rae's. Josh offered to show Gina his apartment.

"Some other time," she said. "I'm enjoying being outdoors on a beautiful afternoon. Besides, it might make me sad to see how it's been divided up. I'd rather look at the outside of the house."

"The place must have been wonderful in its heyday. All those old parquet floors, and the light fixture in the dining room, and that big bay window overlooking the backyard."

"I always imagined that backyard overflowing with children. And pictured silk draperies at the front windows. Also a flower garden that bloomed all year round." She laughed. "That's what it's like when you're a kid. I was always daydreaming about how wonderful life would be when I grew up."

He smiled. "So was I. Only, I was going to be a famous writer."

"You did get famous, Josh," she reminded him.

He groaned. "Sure. But not for my writing. Still, I can't complain. Eventually, I'll settle down and write those books I have in mind. My apartment in Judy Rae's house contains the former library. It would be wonderful to rehabilitate a room such as that into an office."

"You live in Boston, Josh," she reminded him gently.

"This is true," he replied, looking pensive.

On their way back toward town, they stopped at a conveniently placed park bench to take a break.

Gina leaned back and lifted her face to the sun. The Mayacamas range rose in the distance, and the river purled between its banks. "I haven't done this in a long time. It's good therapy when I'm stressed. I should do it more often."

Josh was sitting with both arms spread wide, one hand cupping her shoulder. "Tell me about the stress," he said.

She sighed. "Oh, it's the winery. Today they're having an emergency meeting. I can't help worrying."

Something in Josh seemed to go on alert. He sat up straighter and uncrossed his legs. But she dismissed it as merely changing position.

"I'm sorry to hear that," he said.

"I hope Uncle Fredo can find money somewhere for improvements instead of selling the business. I can't imagine anyone but Angelinis working at Vineyard Oaks."

"Do you think Fredo wants to sell?"

"No. He'd never want that. He might have to, that's all. And if Vineyard Oaks is sold, a lot of people will have to find other jobs."

"What are their prospects? Where could they work?"

Gina considered this. "Nick, my sister's husband, could probably find a position somewhere else. He's a good winemaker. Barbara works free, so it's not like she'd be losing income. But Uncle Fredo—the winery is his passion. And David, who has worked in the warehouse his whole life—he has a mental handicap. What will he do? And all the Mexican migrant workers who help in the fields, and Martin, who oversees their work, and Bobbi, who loves interacting with people in the tasting room. Ronnie recently became head of the sales force, and he was so proud when he took over the department. His wife is expecting their third child. He wouldn't be happy anywhere else."

Josh was quiet for a long time. "Well. At least you don't have to worry. Your work doesn't depend on the winery."

"Oh, but it does. Tourists on their way through the valley on wine-tasting tours often stop at Good Thymes after they visit Vineyard Oaks."

"If the winery had new equipment and could expand, that would help you, right? No matter who owned it?"

She didn't like the tone of his question. "I wouldn't feel right benefiting from the sale of Vineyard Oaks. Not when my family members who once worked there are hurting."

"What hurts one of you hurts all of you?"

"Exactly. That's the way it is with our family."

After she said that, she detected a quietness in Josh, a thoughtfulness. A wariness, perhaps, and she didn't know what had brought it about.

She was glad when he changed the subject. "Let's walk a bit more."

They got up and continued along the river path. Gina kept mulling over the problems at the winery, and after a while, Josh took her hand. "I want to talk to you about something," he said.

She pulled herself back from her thoughts. "Something serious?"

"I was wondering if someday soon you could come to Boston with me to meet my family. I could show you my town house, and we could do some sightseeing."

The sun working its way through the branches of a twisted oak tree beside the path played across his features as she looked up at him.

"I—I don't know," she said haltingly.

"My parents would love you, Gina," he said. "So would my friends."

The idea of meeting his parents was daunting because she pictured them as quite different from her own warm, welcoming family, but aside from that, she had responsibilities. "How can I leave here? I won't have time with this bachelor auction coming up, and there's always my garden, and I'd have to find someone to fill in for me at Good Thymes."

"All solvable problems," he pointed out. He raised her fingertips to his lips and kissed them one by one. They stopped walking beside a big rock sheltered by an enormous oak tree.

"I don't know, Josh," she said.

He reached for her other hand so that he was clasping both. "It's important to me, Gina. I'm not sure you know how much."

"I—" Her eyes searched his, saw depths there that she had only imagined before.

"I'm falling in love with you, Gina Angelini."

She stared. It was all she could do. And she took in his eyes, so expressive and so sincere; his lips, softly parted now; his dimple; his strong chin. She swallowed hard, wondering if she had imagined his words.

"Did you hear what I said?" he asked gently.

"I actually thought I heard you say that you're falling in love with me."

"I hope you feel the same way."

She closed her eyes. This was when she was supposed to reciprocate in kind. She was expected to say the magic words, *I love you,* and everything would fall into place. Yet she knew that sometimes things didn't work that way; you wore your heart on your sleeve and then someone punched you in the arm.

"It's too soon," she said with bewilderment. "How can I know if what I feel is love?" Last time, she had let her emotions run away with her heart. This time, she wouldn't allow that to happen.

"I know what I feel, Gina. There's no mistake on my part."

"You're away from home, you're having a vacation, and I'm sure the Napa Valley seems like a romantic place," she said.

"It does, but that's not why I care so much about you. I

want to take you back to Boston, let you see what it's like there. What *I'm* like there.''

"I don't know if that's a good idea, Josh. I belong here. I always have."

"I understand why this place is important to you. You have your business. You have your family."

There was more to it than that. She wondered if she could make him understand.

"Josh, the soil here loses water very quickly. Because of that, the roots of the vines burrow deep down to find moisture. I am like those roots. My family is the soil, and I've grown deep down to find what nourishes me. It is their love, and their caring, and their concern. Take me away from that and I would die."

"The vines also need lots of sun. I could be that for you."

He had never been more earnest, and she was touched. "Josh, I wasn't expecting this," she said.

"Neither was I. But I thought you should know how I feel."

"Of course," she said.

"Now that it's off my chest, suppose we go back to your place and check on dinner. I don't want to be late for Frankie."

"You're on," she said, able to return his smile.

The conversation had given her pause. If she went to Boston, not only would she feel out of place, but the differences in their two worlds would be readily apparent. Wasn't it better to enjoy what they had, while they had it?

They walked arm in arm back to the cottage, not saying much. But then, they didn't need to speak. Enough had already been said for one day, at least.

GINA HELD THE LAST MEETING of the bachelor auction committee at her shop two days before the auction. She had seen Josh a couple of times since the weekend: once when he brought lunch to Good Thymes and sat with her outside to eat it, and again on the day that she was busy helping Mia with her science project. They talked on the phone every day, sometimes twice. And she thought about him all the time—his empathy when he'd listened to her concerns about the winery's future, the simple pleasure she found in their clasped hands swinging between them. She had more erotic thoughts, too, such as the softness of her breasts as they molded to the curves of his palms, the hammering of her pulse in her ears and the slick friction of their bodies when they made love.

"Gina? Are you listening?"

She forced herself to pay attention to Shelley, who was going over their committee expenses.

"Of course I am. A five-hundred-dollar deposit for the hotel, which has been paid, and a donation of cocktail napkins from the Winegrowers Association. Doesn't that wrap it up?"

"That's it for the expenses, but I thought you might want to hear what Kasey's written for the bachelor profiles for the program."

"Didn't we go over that last week?" Claudia asked.

Shelley shot a covert glance at Gina, who kept her head down. "All but Josh Corbett's," she said.

"Read it, Kasey," said Emily. "Josh is going to be a big hit with the women, I'm sure."

Kasey made a show of shuffling papers and clearing her throat. "Okay, here goes."

"Hey, let's get on with it," murmured Claudia. Gina spared her a keen look. She had an idea that Claudia herself might want to bid on Josh.

"He says, 'I like picnics, street markets, women who don't capitulate right away and the scent of lavender. When I finally find a woman who is right for me, I'll move heaven and earth to be with her,'" read Kasey.

As Gina listened, she felt a stab of dismay. Josh had told Kasey the very things that the two of them had done together as an inducement to other women to bid on him? After he'd told her he was falling in love with her? She kept her gaze focused on the paper in front of her, but her hand came up to fondle the amber heart at her throat. She hadn't taken it off since Josh had put it there.

"Okay, keep going," said Claudia with interest.

"'The lucky woman who outbids everyone else for a date with me will be serenaded by a gondolier on the Napa River as we sip wine served with the finest cheese. Afterward, we'll eat in the private VIP dining room at Nando's Restaurant in St. Helena, followed by a drive back to Rio Robles in our limo. Then, if we're lucky, there will be time for a walk in the moonlight and plans to see each other again very soon.'"

Had Josh given this information to Kasey before he'd decided he was falling in love with her? She didn't want to ask Kasey when he'd provided it, in front of Claudia, Emily and especially Shelley, who might pick up on her concern.

"Wow," said Claudia, sounding impressed. "This guy pulls out all the stops."

"I should say so," Kasey replied as she handed a copy of the bio to Gina.

Gina had heard enough. "All right," she said. "Everyone be at the Majestic Hotel's ballroom at least an hour before the auction begins. Thanks for all your hard work."

"Oh, it was a pleasure," Kasey said. "Any time you need help recruiting handsome bachelors for this event, be sure to call me."

They all laughed as they got up to leave, but Gina wasn't amused. Fresh in her mind was the new intimacy that she and Josh shared, the warm light in his eyes when he spoke of Frankie, his invitation to visit Boston.

Gina lingered for a moment in the doorway, watching her committee members disperse to their cars. It didn't escape her notice that Claudia's hair bounced as she walked, a long curly cascade of auburn. Not until that moment did Gina realize that Claudia reminded her of Tahoma.

Chapter Thirteen

The night of the bachelor auction, Gina arrived at the hotel early. She checked to make sure that the hotel's staff were doing their job, paused for a few words of encouragement to the phone volunteers and went to assure herself that all the bachelors had arrived.

"Everybody ready?" Gina asked brightly as she entered the room set aside for them backstage. She received fifteen affirmative answers from fifteen attractive guys. None compared with Josh Corbett, who stood leaning against a wall with his arms crossed over his chest and one eyebrow raised in silent greeting.

As the mistress of ceremonies, Gina intended to maintain a professional demeanor, but it wasn't easy when every nerve in her body went on alert at the sight of him. He looked especially wonderful in his evening wear.

"All right," Gina said in a brisk tone as she adjusted the papers on her clipboard. "You'll walk down the runway in alphabetical order. I'll read your biography to the audience, and you have a few minutes to make an initial impression. If you feel inspired to break into a few dance steps, that's fine. The livelier the better."

"That's what I say about my women," Josh whispered as she hurried past him.

"Hush," she hissed.

Josh only lifted his other eyebrow and treated her to a wicked smile. She hadn't confronted him about the bio that he'd given to Kasey; she hadn't had the heart for it. All she knew was that she was going to be instrumental in getting him a date with someone else, and that was the last thing in the world she wanted.

It's for a good cause, she reminded herself. She'd been telling herself that for the past week, not that it did any good.

"Are you going to bid, Gina?" asked one of the bachelors. He was a local firefighter who had received a certain amount of fame for posing naked for a calendar.

"Not a chance. I'm the emcee, remember?" She aimed a cheerful grin at him and moved on.

"Too bad," one of them said, but it wasn't Josh. She didn't dare look at him as she left the room, but she knew he was watching her. She'd bid on him if she could. In fact, now that this event was about to happen, she'd bid every cent she had to make sure he didn't go out with anyone else. But she wasn't allowed to bid, so there was no way.

She was pondering her conflicting feelings about tonight's situation when she almost bumped into Shelley.

"Did all the bachelors show up?" Shelley asked.

Gina waved her checklist in front of Shelley's nose. "After hanging out in that room for ten minutes, I feel as if I've OD'd on testosterone. All of them are here."

"That's good. The phone lines are a go, and the volunteers are ready to roll. We've got about three hundred in the audience."

"Okay, Shelley. Let's keep our fingers crossed that this auction pays off. Are you planning to bid tonight?"

"No, Rocco and I are officially a couple," Shelley confided, her pleasure evident.

Gina beamed at her. "That's wonderful news, Shell. Is Rocco coming tonight?"

"He's picking me up afterward. I'll be too busy to pay

much attention to him until this thing's over. Say, I love your dress. Is it new?''

"I bought it the other day." It was a red chiffon halter top with a long skirt that clung to her figure and belled out at the bottom, bought because Josh liked her to wear red.

"It's a great choice for the shoes," Shelley observed. "I sold them to you, remember?"

That had been a long time ago, before Shelley moved to Oregon. "I remember. I bought them for the *Mr. Moneybags* show."

"I'm glad they've worked for you. You look fantastic. See you later." Shelley bustled off toward the bar.

It was almost time to begin. Gina checked her watch, cued the band, and when they began to play, she marched out, her long skirt swirling around her ankles.

"Good evening, ladies and gentlemen," she said.. "Welcome to the third annual Rio Robles Bachelor Auction to benefit the Nicholas Sorise Jr. Teen Center."

The audience consisted of many single women and a lot of married couples. A number of single men were there to egg on their friends, and Gina spotted several of her cousins in the crowd.

She sped through the preliminaries, knowing that people had come to see the bachelors. In fact, an air of suspense hung over the proceedings, and she almost breathed her own sigh of relief when it was time to get started.

"We'll proceed in alphabetical order," she declared as the band struck up a lively song designed to make the bachelors' introductions move along at a fast clip.

"Our first bachelor is Don Allisandro," she said as he appeared at the head of the runway. "Don is twenty-nine years old, and you may recognize him as one of our public defenders in the Napa Valley. He likes a good cabernet, sleeping late on Sundays and women who can cook a saddle of lamb—not necessarily in that order."

"Whooeee," called one of the women in the back of the room. "What a stud!"

Don had begun his walk into the part of the runway that bisected the audience. He must have liked that comment, because he gave it a hearty thumbs-up and did a little boogie step, which made everyone laugh.

"Don's dream date is a trip to Morro Bay, where you'll watch the sun set as you feast on a fine bouillabaisse. After that, he suggests a slow ride along the coast highway and a visit to a cozy little nightclub where they'll be holding a table for two."

She interviewed Don for a few minutes. He obliged his admirers by grabbing the microphone and reciting a bit of poetry he said he'd composed himself. He departed after a soulful wink at someone in the audience—Gina's cousin Donna, as it turned out.

Gina waited for the applause to taper off before she introduced the next bachelor, who was Josh Corbett.

His walk was supremely confident, with one hand in his pocket and a cheerful grin on his face. He treated Gina to a long look, which she returned. She couldn't help thinking that she'd tear up his bio and beg him to back out of this obligation if it were remotely possible. Which it was not, at this stage of the game.

She tried to keep her eyes on the sheet of paper in front of her as Josh began his saunter down the runway in time to jazzy merengue music. Compared with the other bachelors, Josh seemed so urbane, so experienced, so sophisticated. A lot of women in this audience would bid for an evening with him; she was sure of it.

"Josh Corbett is well known as Mr. Moneybags from the TV show of the same name," she began. "He—"

She stopped reading abruptly. Fortunately, at that moment someone called out, "Hey, what a hunk," and others echoed the sentiment. Gina might have been able to work the comment into his bio in a clever way, except that she was reading with horror what was written on the paper that had been handed to her. And it definitely wasn't the bio that Kasey had shared with the committee.

Gina felt her mouth drop open. She quickly clamped it shut as she skimmed the bio to the end. There was no way that she could say any of this, no way at all, because it read: "Josh Corbett is crazy about Gina Angelini, who has the most beautiful breasts that he's ever had the pleasure to behold. When he kisses her, he wants nothing more than to get her in the sack, and once he does, it's thrills and excitement like no one would believe. And when she reaches down and—"

Gina's hand shook as she folded the paper. Out there beyond the runway, faces were tipped toward her, the people waiting expectantly as Josh continued to strut his stuff.

What on earth was she going to say? How in heaven's name had this sheet of paper replaced the original bio?

Josh swiveled at the end of the runway and began walking back toward her, an expression of devilment on his face, which immediately clued her in to who was the author of this new and creative bio. At the moment, Josh's prank was secondary to the dilemma of finding the right words.

She cleared her throat. From his vantage point squarely in front of her, Josh could undoubtedly see exactly how uncomfortable she was, and certainly some of the audience had already sensed her discomfort, as well. She had to get through this, had to will herself to stop blushing like an idiot!

She made up her spiel as she went along, and it came out as a bunch of nonsense. "Josh is…um…six feet tall, likes…um…bubble gum ice cream and…uh…the scent of lavender. On his date with you, he will cook you some of his wonderful Yankee pot roast, which he will more than likely wish to eat in the company of your cat. If you have one. And which will make him sneeze, because he's allergic. But that's okay, because everything—everything else about him is, um, almost, well, perfect."

Josh had almost reached the place where she stood. How in the world was she supposed to interview him after the fiasco of his bio?

"You think I'm 'almost perfect'?" he whispered while she was trying to collect herself.

She glared at him, recovered slightly and held the microphone up to his face. "It's quite a pleasure for you to pay us a visit here in Rio Robles, Josh. Perhaps you could say a few words to the audience."

"Only that I'm happy to be here, and that it's good to renew my acquaintance with you. It's wonderful to meet so many new people, and I'm looking forward to my date with whoever—" and he treated everyone to a roguish grin that made Gina feel slightly sick to her stomach "—whoever my dream date turns out to be." After one last impudent waggle of his eyebrows at Gina, he fairly danced his way offstage.

By this time she'd figured out that he'd had an opportunity to insert a substitute biography in the folder where she filed all things pertinent to the bachelor auction. It would have been easy, because the files sat on the counter at Good Thymes where anyone could access them. Oh, she couldn't wait to get her hands on Josh Corbett, she thought grimly. The only trouble was that if she did get her hands on him, she knew she'd probably want to caress that certain part of his anatomy he'd cited in the phony bio much more than she'd want to wring his fool neck.

THE BIDDING, WHEN IT WAS time, was fast and furious, with Josh Corbett far and away the leader. At first a few women from the audience were participants in the bidding for Josh as well as someone bidding by phone. Then everyone fell away except Claudia, whom Gina suspected of harboring a crush on Josh, and the telephone bidder.

At one point while the bidding was proceeding without a break, Gina stepped backstage to get a sip of water. Shelley handed her a full glass.

"Looks like Josh is going to go for a good amount of money," Shelley observed with glee.

"It certainly does," Gina replied tersely.

Shelley cocked her head and studied Gina's expression. "Do you mind?" she asked. "I didn't think you two were— well, you know. Serious or anything."

"Of course I don't mind," Gina replied. "It's for the teen center, isn't it?"

"The telephone bidder is someone named Roxie. I don't know anyone named Roxie, do you?"

"No," Gina said before hurrying back onstage.

"And our telephone bidder is raising her bid to $10,000," the auctioneer announced with a puzzled frown.

"That can't be right! The previous bid was only one thousand," Gina hissed at him from behind her program, bewildered. She saw Claudia, grumpy and disgruntled in her first-row seat, and several of the audience members were whispering to one another in obvious surprise at this unusual development.

The auctioneer, a fellow brought in from Santa Rosa for the occasion, shrugged. "Ten thousand for the teen center. Do I hear another bid?" He eyed Claudia, who lifted her hands as if to say she was out of it. "Ten thousand for a date with Josh Corbett. Going once, going twice, going to Roxie on the phone for ten thousand dollars." A bang of the gavel and it was done.

Gina felt numb. Someone—someone rich—wanted a date with Josh, perhaps even desperately. The auction had been well publicized all over the Napa Valley. Gina was aware that there were plenty of wealthy women in the area whose idea of a good way to spend their money was on a date with a celebrity.

No matter how hard she tried, Gina couldn't focus on the rest of the auction. After all the bachelors had been auctioned, as she wound up the proceedings and thanked everyone for attending, she tried to maintain her bright line of patter, determined to hide the distress she felt about Josh's having a date with someone else. But when she left the stage, all she wanted was to get out of the ballroom and go home.

"Great job, Gina," someone called as she left the hotel. She waved at whoever it was and kept walking. That was when she spotted Josh standing beside Rocco's car, talking to Rocco and Shelley, who were sitting inside.

"Hey, Gina," Shelley called. "Come on over."

Josh pivoted and smiled at her, but she was still upset over the fake bio that he'd written to embarrass her.

"If I do, I'll say something I'll be sorry about," she said.

Josh hurried toward her, holding out his hand. "Gina, I thought you'd be happy about all the money you've raised tonight."

She stopped in her tracks, taking a great deal of satisfaction at his perturbed expression. "Josh," she said, "after you somehow managed to insert that fake bio into my notes, I'm not feeling too positive toward you."

"It was a joke. I thought you'd think it was funny."

"You've been hanging out with Rocco too much."

Rocco leaned his head out of the car window. "Hey, what do you mean by that? I didn't have anything to do with any fake bio. I don't even know what you're talking about."

Gina ignored him. "What I think, Josh Corbett, is that you could have embarrassed me in front of everyone tonight. What if I'd read that out loud?"

"But I knew you wouldn't, and I had faith that you'd recover and think of something appropriate to say. It's not as if you aren't familiar with my character," he said smoothly. His eyes were entirely too blue, his expression entirely too charming.

Rocco switched on his car's engine. "I'm out of here. I don't know where this conversation is going, but I'm sure I don't want to be along for the ride." He backed out of the parking space and drove slowly toward them, braking when the car drew even with them. "You gonna tell her, Josh?"

"Tell me what?" Gina asked quickly, her gaze darting from Josh to Rocco and back again.

Rocco waited, and Josh frowned. "I don't know, considering her present annoyance. Maybe I should wait for a better opportunity."

What opportunity? He thought he deserved an opportunity? After he'd embarrassed her in front of everyone tonight? As far as she was concerned, he didn't deserve any breaks. She wheeled and started toward her car.

"Okay, okay, I'll tell," Josh said, taking off after her.

"Why don't you tell Roxie," Gina said in a flash of anger. "Why don't you wait for your big date and tell *her?*" She forged ahead, drawing stares from other people heading for their cars.

Rocco idled along beside her. "Yup, Josh, you'd better spill the beans. Let the cat out of the bag." Rocco winked. Shelley, sitting beside him, was grinning, which Gina couldn't figure out. Nor did she want to, come to think of it.

Josh caught up with her when she was fumbling in her purse for her car keys.

He grabbed her arm.

"Gina, there isn't any bidder named Roxie. I bid for myself. I'm the one who is paying $10,000 for a date with me."

She might have thought this was another practical joke except for the sincere light in Josh's eyes. She stared at him, faltered, decided not to believe him.

"That's ridiculous," she said faintly. Her gaze darted from Josh to Rocco and back again. A faint suspicion burgeoned into an idea that took hold. "Unless—unless Rocco was really Roxie."

"I was," Rocco said smugly. His voice became a falsetto. "I can talk like this, and your phone volunteer never questioned that I was a—" and here he came up with a realistic giggle "—a woman."

Josh's grin was expansive. "I had Rocco—Roxie—bid for

me. And now that I own this date with me, I'm giving it to you as a present."

"What?" This was all Gina could manage to say.

"I'm giving the date to you as a present," Josh repeated with extreme patience. "I thought you'd be happy about it."

No one else had bought the date with Josh? He'd bought a date with himself and was giving it to *her*? As relief washed over her, she started to laugh. It started out a mere chuckle, then became a full-bodied belly laugh. It struck her as really funny that she had been so worried, and really extravagant that Josh had spent so much money to put this one over on her.

Josh was laughing, too. "Tell me you're happy, Gina," he said. "That's what I want to hear."

"I'm happy," Gina said weakly, wiping the tears from her eyes with a handkerchief that Josh thoughtfully provided.

"I'm glad to hear it," Rocco said. "Josh, I'll run along and leave you to explain." He reached through the open car window and aimed a fist at Josh's arm. "See you tomorrow, man."

"'Bye, Gina," Shelley called as Rocco drove away.

"So are you still angry?" Josh drew her arm through his and began to walk with her toward his car.

"I can't stay mad when you did something so wonderful. That's a lot of money for the teen center."

"It's a good cause. You convinced me of that. I never intended to go out with anyone else, Gina. You couldn't bid for me, so I had to figure out another way."

"You could have clued me in."

"Perhaps I could have, but I wasn't sure that was kosher. I thought it would be better if you, as the head of the committee and emcee, knew nothing about my and Rocco's little scheme. By the way, when do you want to have our date? We can go any time this week, but I'd like to know when. My friend Brian in San Francisco has invited me to spend several days with him."

"I can't tomorrow night. We're going to have our last committee meeting. Maybe Saturday? And what should I wear?"

"Saturday is good, and wear something frilly. After our gondola ride and dinner I thought we might check into a nice bed-and-breakfast—"

"Hold it," Gina said. "If you and I check into a place like that, it's most likely going to be owned by a relative of mine. Two of the bed-and-breakfasts in St. Helena are owned by aunts."

"Okay, scratch the bed-and-breakfast part of the plan. How about if, instead, we take off our clothes and dance naked in the moonlight? Or get tattoos on parts of our body that aren't usually visible?"

"I don't recall those activities being in either of your bios," she said, smiling.

They reached his car. He walked around to the passenger side and opened the door for her.

"Wait a minute—you're not taking me home. My car's over there."

"Oh, but I am. We'll come back and get your car in the morning." He came around and slid behind the steering wheel. "Your place or mine?"

"Mine. I'm not ready to face Judy Rae after a night of— well, you know."

He reached over and grazed her cheek with his thumb. "I do know. Can't you say it? What's so awful about saying 'making love'?"

"Nothing, except that I'm superstitious. What if speaking the words makes it all go away?" She was only half serious.

Josh studied her face for a long time, so long that she almost asked him what was wrong.

"I don't expect it ever to go away, Gina," he said. Then he turned the key in the ignition and started the car.

Gina rocked back in the seat, awed by the emotion she'd seen in his expression. As if he would do anything within his power to keep things right with her, as if nothing would deter him from this relationship. As if he'd pay $10,000 to win a date with her even when she wasn't in the running.

For the first time she allowed herself to believe that maybe, just maybe, this would work out.

"O SOLE MIO," SANG THE gondolier in an unbelievably good baritone as he propelled them on the calm Napa River. Josh spread a toast round with more of the delectable artichoke-parmesan spread, made fresh that day from locally grown artichokes. He fed it to Gina, who was reclining on a bank of cushions with a wineglass in her hand.

"Doesn't he know any other songs?" Gina asked. "He's been singing that one for about twenty minutes."

"I'll ask," Josh said. When he'd arranged for the gondola ride he'd chosen the gondolier who could sing in the most languages, but the reservations clerk had neglected to inform him that Luca didn't speak English. Sing in English, yes. Understand even one word, no.

Josh stuck his head outside the curtain that provided privacy for the interior of the small cabin. "Luca," he said. "Sing another song?" He pantomimed singing, but not very well.

Luca stopped singing and smiled from ear to ear. "*Sì, sì, signor.*" He resumed singing "O Sole Mio."

"Let me try," Gina said, scrambling toward the opening. Josh didn't think this would do much good, since she had already told him the extent of her knowledge of Italian, learned from Rocco when they were both children: Italian curses.

"*Scusi,*" Gina said. Luca stopped singing and smiled again. "Um...*per favore*...could you sing some other *melodias?* Songs? Different?"

Luca appeared puzzled as he poled the gondola along. Suddenly, a lightbulb seemed to go on in his head, and he nodded enthusiastically. "*Ah, sì, sì, melodias.*" He winked, and Gina settled back against the cushions. Luca immediately launched into a lusty rendition of John Denver's "Take Me Home, Country Roads," rife with mispronunciations but sung with gusto.

Gina and Josh looked at each other and burst out laughing. Josh passed the bruschetta. "Try some of this," he said. "It's good."

"I still can't get over the trick you and Rocco—I mean Roxie—played," Gina said. "I didn't have a clue what was going on until you told me."

"I have to admit that bidding for myself was my idea. When I found out you couldn't bid, I had to figure out some way for us to get together. I definitely wanted to participate in the auction because I knew you were working hard to make it a success. Plus I'd already signed up."

"I'm sure you made at least a couple of women's hearts go pitter-patter when they saw your name and picture in Kasey's brochure."

"Only a couple? I must be slipping. Anyway, I had the idea of bidding for myself, but I couldn't figure out how to do it. That's where Rocco stepped in."

"I was blindsided."

"Hey, it was fun. And so is this." He pulled the curtains around the cabin of the gondola, enclosing them in their own private world. "How about another appetizer? One that wasn't on the menu?"

"Show me what you have in mind," she whispered, raising her lips to his.

Luca, having done the worst he could to "Take Me Home, Country Roads," burst into another verse of "O Sole Mio," and Gina, giggling, broke away from their kiss.

"Stop it," growled Josh. "Kissing isn't supposed to be a laughing matter."

"Neither is 'O Sole Mio.' And if this is the appetizer, what's the main course?"

"Never mind that, but I'm eager for you to try dessert,"
Josh said.

"I can't wait," Gina murmured close to his ear.

LATER, AFTER DINNER IN St. Helena, Gina lay in Josh's arms
on his bed at his apartment. She had agreed to go there only
after he assured her that Judy Rae had gone back to her
daughter's house in San Diego that morning.

"I'm so sleepy," Gina said, yawning.

"You mean I can't convince you to—"

"No. Not again. Maybe tomorrow."

"We'll go out for brunch after church. Someplace fancy.
How about it?"

"Sounds good. By the way, do you want to come to
Mother's birthday dinner on Wednesday night? We're having
it at Barb and Nick's."

"I'd love to, but I'll have to let you know later. I want to
see Brian this week because he'll be leaving on another business trip soon. I'd like to come to Maren's party, though."

"It's not exactly a party, only a family gathering. We'll
end it early because it's a school night. Don't worry, Nick's
birthday is coming up soon. You're invited to that, too."

"It seems as if someone in this family is always having a
birthday," Josh mused.

"With so many people, that's what happens." Her eyelids
were growing heavier and heavier, and she adjusted her head
more comfortably on Josh's shoulder.

"I can't even recall the last time I had a birthday party,"
he said. Something in his tone made Gina's eyes pop open
again.

"Really?" she said.

"Really. It was when I was about ten. My parents hired a
clown to entertain us, and someone fell off the pony and
broke his arm. I remember the ambulance better than anything, all those red-and-blue flashing lights. I wanted to go
for a ride in it, but my friend with the broken arm went,

instead. It didn't seem fair. It was *my* birthday.'' He chuckled at the memory.

"When is your birthday, Josh?"

"In two weeks."

"That would be on a Sunday?"

"Yes. Why?"

She pushed aside the sheet and sat up. "Because I'm going to give you a party."

"Gina, don't get carried away. I thought you were sleepy."

"I was. Now I'm not. I can't believe you haven't had a party since you were a kid. You need a party, Josh."

"I never thought about it," he said. "I figured grown-ups didn't have people fussing over them on their birthdays."

"Maybe that's the way it is in your family, but in mine, a birthday is a big deal. We can have your party at the winery. I'll invite my whole family and some friends. It'll be fun." She settled back against the pillows, already planning.

"Now that you're out from under the bachelor auction, can't you relax? Have some free time? Maybe go to Boston with me?"

"After your party, we could discuss it," she said. She'd make a run to the coast, pick up some mussels. Then she could make her special tomato fettucine with mussels for the party.

Josh traced a finger across her bare breast. "Now that you're not sleepy anymore, we could discuss something else," he said suggestively.

"Who said I'm not sleepy?" she challenged him.

He moved his hand downward, and she rolled toward him, giving herself up to all the pleasurable sensations that Josh knew how to evoke so very well. Which was when she decided was that Josh was right after all. She wasn't sleepy. Nor would she sleep for quite some time.

"IT'S LIKE THIS, JOSH," Walter Emsing said on the phone on Sunday, a week later. "My people tell me that we can buy

Vineyard Oaks for a pittance. They make a good product. They have a good reputation. The vineyard will be a fine addition to Starling Industries.''

Josh's mind whirled. He'd figured he would have more time.

"What's the rush?" he asked bluntly.

"We don't want some other outfit to beat us on this one."

Josh thought about Fredo and his desperate efforts to save his family's winery. He thought about all the Angelinis who would be out of work if Walter went through with this plan. He thought about Gina and how much it would hurt her if Vineyard Oaks was sold to outsiders.

"The net of it is, Josh, that we're prepared to make an offer the Angelinis can't refuse."

"When?" The word almost stuck in his throat.

"Next week. Josh, I've got to run. I have a call on another line. Talk to you soon."

"Sooner than you think," Josh muttered, and then tapped out the number of Vargas Aviation, a local charter outfit that could supply him with a plane immediately.

After he'd arranged to fly to Boston that night on a Gulf-stream V jet that was ready and waiting at the local airport, he dialed Gina's number at home. She wasn't there. He also dialed her shop, but for some reason her answering machine didn't pick up. He started to pack and decided to call her later.

He never reached Gina that day. He called Barbara to see if Gina was at her house, but Barbara said that Gina was meeting with an architect to discuss the plans for the teen center. Josh vaguely recalled that she'd mentioned something about it.

He scribbled out a note explaining to Gina that he was going to be away until the end of the week, and gave it to the Vargas Aviation driver who came to pick him up, asking the guy to drop it off at Good Thymes when he drove back into town. The driver said he would do it, and Josh put the matter out of his mind.

He spent the whole flight to Boston mapping out a plan that he hoped would appeal to Walter Emsing, despite the ministrations of a buxom flight attendant who knew who he was and was determined to impress him. At one time he might have welcomed her attentions, but now they were only a distraction and, finally, an irritation. He brushed aside her offers of brunch at her hotel, cocktails ditto, and made himself concentrate. If he could just convince Walter that Fredo and the rest of the Angelinis were the best people to run Vineyard Oaks, he would be able to save the winery from being gobbled up.

He was doing this for Gina. He knew how hard she'd take it if Starling bought her family's business.

But he was also doing this for himself. If Gina found out that he was in any way instrumental in Walter's proposed buyout, there was no saving himself as he had with the bachelor auction. No practical joke would get him out of the bind, and Rocco most definitely wouldn't be on his side. Worse yet, Gina would boot him out of her life for good.

"You'll come to Josh's party, won't you?" Gina asked Shelley.

Shelley had stopped by Good Thymes to buy tincture of anise for a lingering cough. "You're giving a party for him?"

"A birthday party at Vineyard Oaks."

"I'll be there."

"We'll set up tables in the wine cellar like we do for wedding receptions," Gina said. It was family tradition to hold such celebrations there.

Mia popped up from under the counter. "I'm making a big banner that reads Happy Birthday, Josh. Frankie's supposed to help me."

"And where will you hang the banner?" Shelley asked playfully. Mia was a favorite of hers.

"I don't know yet." Mia disappeared under the counter again, where she was doing her homework with Timothy curled up beside her.

"Gina, could I talk to you for a minute?" Shelley aimed a meaningful look toward Mia's space under the counter, and Gina nodded. She followed Shelley to the other end of the shop.

Shelley continued in a low tone. "I wanted to ask you about Frankie and his math. Rocco says Frankie won't be allowed to play in our accordion band if he doesn't bring his grade up. Tell me, what's the problem? Does the kid need a tutor?"

Gina took her time answering. "Maybe," she said. "He's smart enough, but he can't seem to settle down to do his homework every night. I think his bad grades are a result of simply not doing the work."

"I've been to Rocco's house for dinner several times lately. When we're busy cleaning up, Frankie is supposed to be doing homework, but he either says he doesn't have any or that he's already finished it. Usually, he ends up outside shooting baskets in the driveway."

"Rocco has tried to check behind him, has attended more parent-teacher conferences than you can imagine, and he's at his wit's end. He sees the band as a way to make Frankie measure up. In other words, it's like a carrot on a stick. Bring the math grade up, and Frankie gets to be in the band. If the math grade is unsatisfactory, Frankie doesn't."

Shelley sighed. "Leo Buscani thinks playing in the band would be the best thing in the world for him. He says Frankie responds well to the kind of self-discipline required to play a musical instrument. He thinks that self-discipline will carry over into Frankie's schoolwork. He's seen it happen before."

"I'll speak to Rocco," Gina promised. "Maybe he needs to talk to Leo."

"I'll suggest it. Thanks, Gina."

Shelley, after a hurried goodbye, headed back to the Bootery, and Gina resumed planning the menu for the birthday party.

"When is Josh coming over?" Mia asked as Gina pored over a list of wines and made a note to ask Maren if she could borrow a steam table for the serving line from Aunt Dede.

"I don't know," Gina said absently. She hadn't heard from Josh since Sunday morning.

"I wish he'd come over," Mia said.

"Me, too."

Josh didn't call that night, either, but Gina wasn't concerned. He had told her he would be visiting his friend in San Francisco soon, and that was probably where he'd gone.

Chapter Fourteen

Josh stepped out of the taxi in downtown Boston into a driving rain. He paid the cabdriver and blinked up at the towering Prudential Building before yanking up the collar of his raincoat and marching into the lobby of the nearby building that housed the offices of Starling Industries.

Ever since he'd landed at Logan Airport an hour or so ago, he'd been overcome with the grayness of everything. Gray skies, gray buildings, and the people wore dark clothes, not the light, bright colors he'd grown accustomed to in California. He felt darker, smaller, grayer himself. And it was noisy here. A constant cacophony of horns blaring, trucks roaring and overamplified music emanated from passing cars.

He was bundled up in a wool-lined trench coat and a wool scarf, and when he caught a glimpse of his reflection in the gold-veined mirror beside the elevator, he almost didn't recognize himself.

The elevator deposited him at a reception desk on a high floor. The receptionist graciously offered to relieve him of his coat, and he was ushered into a blessedly quiet waiting room, where he cooled his heels for an uncomfortably long time. He switched off his cell phone; no point in taking the chance that a call would interrupt his meeting with Walter.

When he grew tired of sitting, he wandered over to the floor-to-ceiling window for a bird's-eye view of the city. The cars below looked like toys; the people scurried like ants. They somehow seemed insignificant, and he felt a pang of longing for the blurred outlines of the mountains visible beyond the river from the window of his apartment in Rio Robles. He missed Gina suddenly and with an urgency that he couldn't have imagined a couple of months ago.

"Josh! What a pleasant surprise. Come in, come in," boomed Walter Emsing from the door of his office.

Josh turned and tried to force thoughts of Gina from his mind. If he was going to accomplish what was necessary for the good of her family, he had to stay focused on the goal. He couldn't forget why he had come back to Boston for even a few seconds.

"Walter," he said, shaking the man's hand. "I'm here because we need to talk," he said.

Walter ushered Josh into his office. "All right," he said. "Tell me what's going on."

"Quite a lot," Josh told him. To himself he added, *Like falling in love.*

"Something that will change my mind about our plans for Vineyard Oaks?"

"I hope so," Josh said. He removed his proposal from his briefcase; he'd worked on it feverishly and had it formally prepared by an assistant this morning. He'd only slept a few hours since he'd left the Napa Valley, and his eyes were gritty. But he was clean-shaven and dressed in a suit in order to impress Walter Emsing.

"Let's see what you have," Walter said, and Josh handed the folder over.

Walter thumbed through it rapidly, then tossed the papers onto the desk between them. "You know my feeling about acquisitions," he said brusquely. "Buy 'em out and get 'em out."

"If you do that with Vineyard Oaks, you'll be ignoring one of their greatest assets—the strength that comes from a close-knit family."

"I fail to see that as strength, Josh. I believe that family cohesiveness can be a weakness when running a company."

"Not in this case," Josh shot back. "Vineyard Oaks produces excellent wines—there's no doubt about that. My report lists the prizes they've won. You can even taste the wine that recently copped a prestigious award in an international contest." He produced a bottle of Vineyard Oaks merlot from his briefcase and handed it to Walter.

Walter appeared nonplussed. He set the bottle on his desk and stared at it.

Josh continued. "It would be to Starling's advantage to become a silent partner with Vineyard Oaks. To retain their name on the labels of the wines produced there. To treat Vineyard Oaks wines as boutique wines and ship to private customers, thereby raising the price to the eighty-dollar-a-bottle range. We'd establish a niche market, Walter. It's something Vineyard Oaks has never tried."

"All right," Walter said. "Your suggestion intrigues me. I'll give you fifteen minutes to tell me more about it." He leaned back in his chair and frowned.

Josh prepared to argue his case. He reminded himself that the livelihoods of a lot of people depended on what he said. He had convinced himself that Vineyard Oaks shouldn't be sold to Starling, but now he would have to convince Walter. Which wouldn't be easy, considering the forbidding expression on the man's face.

GINA SPOTTED FRANKIE AS HE pedaled furiously past the gateposts and did a wheelie in the parking lot. He jumped off his newly painted bike, letting it fall where it landed, and stormed up the steps and through the door.

"Gina," he said, out of breath. "Is Josh coming over today?"

"I don't think so," she said. She hadn't heard from him in two days.

"Where is he?"

"He's gone to visit a friend in San Francisco, I think. Why?"

Frankie scuffed his shoe against one of the half barrels she used for storing gingerroot. He scowled. "I want to speak with him is all. I thought maybe he could talk to my dad."

Gina pushed aside the small fabric bags into which she was tying bits of lavender for sachets. She folded her hands in front of her. "Okay, Frankie, what's this about? Can I help?"

"Aw, I'm not sure anybody can. But maybe if Josh talked to Pop about my math grade he might let me play in Mr. Buscani's band. Pop really pays attention to Josh."

"Oh, math again. Frankie, your father wants you to bring that grade up."

"I've tried, honest. I did pretty good on the unit we had about learning to figure sales tax. It's those darned powers I can't get."

"Powers?"

"You know, like figuring two to the seventh power and stuff like that."

"Frankie, dear, your dad worries that playing in the band will take more time away from your studies. Show him that you can bring the math grade up, and then I'm sure Rocco won't be so concerned about your spending too much time on your music."

"I promise I'll work extra hard if he just lets me go to the practices! Can you talk to my dad, Gina? Please? If Josh can't?"

Gina sighed. "Sure. I'll try."

"When you see Josh, will you ask him?"

To see Frankie so distraught was rare. Playing in the band must mean a lot to him.

"Of course I will. I don't know when that will be."

"It better be soon. He better come back."

"He will. You'll see him at his birthday party on Sunday, remember?"

Frankie brightened slightly at the reminder. "Oh, I almost forgot. That's cool."

"Mia wants you to help with the banner. Ask her about it."

"Okay. Thanks, Gina."

"You're welcome," Gina told him, but she didn't think he should get his hopes up too high.

ON THURSDAY HER COUSIN Emily stopped by Good Thymes, ostensibly to inquire about using echinacea for a cold brought about by the chill wind that swept out of the mountains at this time of year, but when Gina had handed her back her change, Emily lingered.

"I heard Josh went to San Francisco," she said, obviously fishing for information.

"Mmm," Gina said, determined not to react. Emily was Aunt Maureen's daughter, which meant that Aunt Maureen had probably heard from Maren that Josh was away. The family grapevine was alive and thriving.

"Well, I hope he's going to be back on Sunday for his birthday party," Emily said.

"I'm sure he will be," Gina told her.

"If you haven't talked to him in a long while, how do you know?"

Gina didn't mean to sound testy, but she did anyway. "Who says I haven't talked to him?"

"Oh, I heard it around," Emily said with a vague wave of her hand toward town.

"Hasn't anyone told you that you shouldn't believe everything you hear?" Gina said, infusing her tone with a lightness that she didn't feel at the moment.

"I guess I shouldn't. Bye, Gina. See you Sunday."

Gina fumed to herself long after Emily left, and she resented that the seeds of doubt had been scattered over her plans for Josh's birthday party. She tried to reach Josh on his cell phone but hung up when he didn't answer. She'd already left a message for him, and he hadn't called her back. She wished he'd mentioned his friend Brian's last name. She'd look him up and call Josh to make sure he hadn't forgotten about the party.

Still, she was certain that Josh wouldn't forget. Even though she wished he'd call, she forced herself not to listen for the phone's ring. Instead, she made a list of items to pick up on Saturday when she went to the coast to buy the mussels.

"I'LL HAVE TO TAKE THIS UNDER advisement," Walter said in his most pontifical tone. "We've already started the ball rolling to buy Vineyard Oaks, you know."

This didn't sound good. One thing Josh had learned from playing bocce was that once a ball started rolling, it was hard to stop.

"Who's going to see that proposal next?" Josh asked.

Walter reeled off some names, but Josh realized this was only a smoke screen. He had the distinct impression that once he was out the door, Walter would toss his proposal in the round file under his desk—the wastebasket.

"If you'd let me talk to them in person," Josh said desperately. He tried hard not to sound as if he were clutching at his last straw.

"You'll be seeing one of them, I should think. Your dad."

"You didn't mention him."

"He works closely with Peter Troxler."

That was one of the names Walter had mentioned, but Josh hadn't felt that the relationship between Peter and his father was that close. Nevertheless, it was worth exploring.

On the way out of Walter's office, he asked the receptionist to notify his father that he was on the way up to his suite in the same building.

"Is there anyone else you'd like me to contact for you?" the woman asked.

Josh immediately thought of Gina, but there was no time

to talk with her now. He'd have to explain why he was in Boston, and he could think of no way to do it without discussing his mission to save Vineyard Oaks.

"No one," he said, and a bleak feeling settled over his heart. He didn't like being a continent away from Gina. He was eager to get back to her. But that would have to wait for now.

He squared his shoulders and went to plead Vineyard Oaks' case with his father.

"GAYLE CAME INTO THE BOOTERY this morning," Shelley told Gina on the phone on Friday.

"And let me guess, she mentioned that I haven't heard from Josh lately." Gina was feeding Timothy, who was meowing as he twined between her ankles. She spooned canned food into his dish, and he started to purr.

"How did you know?" Shelley sounded perplexed.

"Oh, my mother told her sister-in-law, and Aunt Gayle mentioned it to Barbara, and this morning a woman I've never seen before in my life—I think she's a friend of my second cousin twice removed—asked me if I really expected Josh to show up at the party."

"You're kidding."

Gina expelled a huge sigh. "I wish."

"Of course he'll show up. You were planning it before he left."

"He'll be there."

"Rocco said—"

"Please, Shelley, spare me from what Rocco said. It was probably something I wouldn't want to hear, like if Josh doesn't show, Rocco intends to kick him in some tender part of his anatomy."

"Can you blame him? Rocco loves you like a sister."

Gina washed off the cat food fork in the sink. "He should stop messing around in my life and look after his own."

"What does that mean?" Shelley might be on the defensive, as evidenced by her tone.

"Oh, never mind. How is it going between the two of you?"

"Great, except he won't let Frankie play in the band. We argue about it."

"I was going to talk to Rocco. I got caught up in preparations for the party and it slipped my mind. Maybe I can bring it up on Sunday."

"At the party? That might be a good time."

"All right, that's what I'll do."

"Gina, I've got to run. Tomorrow's Saturday and I'm putting out stock for our big sale."

"Bye, Shelley. I hope it's a good one."

"Thanks. I'll see you Sunday at the winery."

Gina stared at the phone for a long moment after they hung up.

"Do you suppose these people are onto something? Is Josh going to skip his own birthday party?"

Timothy only blinked at her and went to wash his paws at the window. Gina considered calling Judy Rae to ask if she'd heard when Josh would return but decided against it when she realized that it might make her seem too needy.

She missed Josh, that was all. And she was puzzled because she hadn't heard from him for five days.

"ALL RIGHT, I UNDERSTAND THAT you think it would be to Starling's advantage to keep the winery in private hands, but what's your personal involvement with these people? Gina Angelini is the girl you dumped on the TV show, so why are you hanging out with her in the Napa Valley?" Josh's father studied him over lunch at his club. Three days had passed since Josh had given Ethan Corbett a copy of the proposal he'd shown Walter.

Josh should have expected that his father would cut to the

heart of the situation in one fell swoop. "I'm crazy about her, Dad. I want you to meet her."

Ethan's eyebrows flew up into his hairline. "I'd say that I met her along with millions of viewers all over the world. She's pretty, she seems like a nice person and most of us couldn't figure out why you chose Tahoma, instead. I want to know what's between you, that's all. If anything."

"We've been seeing each other. I'd like to escalate the relationship. That doesn't have anything to do with why I think Starling should pump money into the family's winery, though. My plan makes more sense than buying the place, that's all."

"And I'm to believe that this plea has nothing to do with saving the winery for the Angelinis? Give me a break, son."

Josh fixed his father with a no-nonsense stare. "I have the utmost confidence in Fredo Angelini. He's got a good work-force, an eye for detail and determination to make the best wine in the world. All he needs is money for new equipment. After he gets that, he'll plant more vines, hire more help and ship more wine. I'm sure of it."

"We sent you out there to look the place over along with others and to give us your recommendation about where to buy. Now you're saying not to buy, to become a silent partner with these people. That would take a huge leap of faith on our part."

"You trusted me enough to send me to the Napa Valley in the first place. You can trust me now. I know the Ange-linis. My way is better. You'll see. You won't be disap-pointed."

His father took a sip of his martini and looked thoughtful. "You've never disappointed me yet, son. Can you make a presentation tomorrow to the board of directors? Several are flying in from Europe for the meeting, and it would be the ideal time."

"Tell me how long I have to persuade them and I'll be ready." He'd been agitated and worried ever since he'd given

Ethan the proposal, but Ethan was not to be rushed. Josh hadn't dared talk to Gina, and he missed her intensely. But if making a presentation to the board of directors was his only chance to argue his case, he'd take it.

"You can have two hours, maybe longer if we can bump some of our other business to next month."

"Great, Dad. I appreciate this." Despite his fatigue, he felt jubilant and optimistic for the first time since he'd talked with Walter. He pushed his chair back.

"Aren't you going to stay for lunch?"

"No, I have to work on the presentation. I'll need charts, handouts, all that sort of thing."

"You're really doing this for Gina, aren't you?"

"That's right. And for her family. They don't deserve to lose what they've built up over generations. I'll see you tomorrow." He hurried away, already configuring a flow chart in his head.

"Damn! It must be love," his father muttered so that Josh almost didn't catch the remark.

Josh turned and walked a few steps backward. "It is," he said with a grin. "And it feels great."

Ethan Corbett shook his head. "What I wouldn't give to be young again," he said, but there was a smile on his lips.

Josh headed back toward his hotel. It was Thursday afternoon, and Gina would be eating lunch at Good Thymes, perhaps dusting the shelves or puttering around the back room. He'd call her tonight after she closed the shop, check with her to make sure everything was okay.

But he didn't. Because of the different time zones, he was ready to crash and get some well-deserved rest before she closed up. And when he woke at four the next morning to resume work on his presentation, it was one o'clock in the morning in California. He wouldn't feel comfortable phoning her at that hour knowing that she had to get up early to work in her garden.

Thank goodness the driver from Vargas Aviation had given her his hastily scribbled note telling her he'd be back by Sunday.

ON SATURDAY, MAREN ARRIVED at Good Thymes to sub for Gina while she made her run to the coast for fresh mussels.

"Has Josh come back from San Francisco?" Maren asked casually as they were saying goodbye.

"No, I haven't heard from him."

"You haven't?" Maren seemed surprised.

"Not since before he left."

"Hmm," Maren said as Gina turned to leave.

On the way to her car, Gina brushed the bits of lavender off her sweater before stopping to check the water level of the birdbath. Blown against the ornate base was a scrap of paper, and thinking that it might be one of the kids' homework assignments, she bent to pick it up. When she saw the logo across the top that read Vargas Aviation, she crumpled the paper and tossed it in a nearby trash can, sure that it had nothing to do with her.

"BUT, AUNT GINA, WHAT IF Josh isn't here for his own birthday party?" Mia asked querulously. She'd been cranky all day, and Gina had regretted taking the child with her on her shopping trip to the coast. They were in Gina's apartment now, having iced the mussels down in the refrigerator, and Mia was supposed to be making name tags for the many guests that Gina had invited.

"Josh will be here," Gina repeated firmly. She'd been telling herself the same thing all day, and her patience with other people's questions was beginning to wear thin. Josh wouldn't miss this. She was positive of that.

"I made him a name tag. He'd better show up."

Gina bent over the table to inspect Mia's handiwork. "The name tags look great. Now, how about if you brush your teeth and get ready for bed? You can sleep with me in my big bed tonight.'' Usually, when Mia stayed over, she occupied the pull-out couch in the living room.

"Oh, wow! Can we watch some television together?" Mia scrambled down from her chair.

"For a little while," Gina said. Judging from past experience, Mia would fall asleep before the first commercial of any program they turned on.

Gina put the name tags in a big box and set it by the door to take to the winery when she went there tomorrow to decorate. When she got in bed beside Mia, her niece had tuned the TV to some inane sitcom and her eyes were already heavy-lidded.

"Aunt Gina, your bed smells like Josh," she murmured. "It's nice."

Gina settled back on her pillows and flicked off the TV. She sat staring into the darkness, wondering where Josh was and why she hadn't heard from him by now. She'd expected him back by today, even though they had made no plans for tonight.

Soothed by Mia's steady breathing beside her, she finally fell into an uneasy slumber where she dreamed, but not about Josh. The dream had something to do with winning a million dollars and losing it right away. In her dream, she looked for it all night, rushing from the castle at Dunsmoor to Rio Robles to Boston and points beyond, always accompanied by a host of faceless relatives who tried to help. Yet she never found the money, and when she woke up on Sunday morning, she was exhausted.

The only thing that got her out of bed for church was Mia, looking bright-eyed and excited about the day's events.

"Today's Josh's birthday. He'll be here, Aunt Gina," Mia said. "Don't worry."

"Of course I'm not worried," Gina replied briskly as she tried to cover the dark circles under her eyes with concealer.

They set off for church, and Gina braced herself for the

questions after the service. No one had seen Josh in several days, and there were bound to be some.

JOSH MADE THE TAXI DRIVER speed on the way to the private airport outside Boston where the Gulfstream jet was waiting to fly him back to California. It was six o'clock in the morning on the East Coast and he was exhausted, whipped, but he felt a sense of unparalleled elation when he considered what he'd accomplished. His machinations on behalf of the Angelinis had worked. Walter and the board of directors had resoundingly approved his plan for Starling Industries to become a silent partner in the Angelinis' winery. Vineyard Oaks would enjoy a large influx of money, enough to do anything that Fredo deemed necessary. Starling would benefit, too, by establishing a presence in the Napa Valley that could be expanded upon in the future, and they would send their Australian executives there to train before moving them on to the recent acquisition in Chile. There were no losers in this deal, only winners.

"Good morning, Mr. Corbett," said the flight attendant when he boarded the plane. "Would you care for breakfast? We have your choice of eggs Benedict or sweet potato pancakes brought in from one of the finest restaurants in town."

"I'll take the eggs," he told her wearily as he flung himself down on one of the plush padded seats.

She brought him the tray, complete with sterling silver, a snowy-white napkin and a full-blown rose in a silver vase. "I don't suppose you'd care for company while you eat," she suggested pertly.

He eyed her with trepidation. "I don't suppose I would. Thanks for the offer, but it's been a long night."

"I understand," she replied smoothly before wending her way between the row of seats to disappear behind a curtain.

Once they reached cruising altitude, the hum of the jets soothed him so that by the time he'd devoured everything on the tray, he was ready to kick off his shoes and sleep. He couldn't wait to see the expression on Gina's face when he announced to her and her family that he was singlehandedly responsible for saving the winery.

Maybe she'd be so grateful that she'd not only agree to visit Boston, but if he asked her to marry him, she'd say yes.

He couldn't think of any birthday present that he'd like better.

GINA BLENDED THE INGREDIENTS of her mussel sauce and let them simmer while she loaded twenty loaves of fresh-baked bread into the trunk of the Galaxie. Maren was putting together hors d'oeuvres and salads at the big catering kitchen, and she would bring homemade tomato pasta to cook at the winery. Uncle Aldo had personally selected the wine from his private cellar, and Aunt Dede had promised to contribute a huge birthday cake. Josh's birthday celebration had turned into a family event with everyone eager to help.

Rocco phoned as she headed out the door. "Hey, Gina. You need any help taking things to the winery? I can drive over with you. Frankie's riding his bike there early, so he won't be going with us."

"Well, sure," Gina told him. "I've already loaded the car. Are you ready?"

"I'll be right over," Rocco said.

He was there in less than five minutes. Gina, who had changed into a new silk shirt in robin's-egg blue and a pair of equally elegant pants the color of smoke, was chucking odds and ends into a picnic basket.

"Here, Rocco. You can carry this," she said.

She became aware that he was staring at her with his mouth hanging open when he didn't immediately pick up the basket.

"What's wrong?" she asked testily.

"Uh, you. I think."

This brought about a raise of her eyebrows. "What's that supposed to mean?"

"You look awful, Gina. What's going on?"

"Thanks, Rocco. I needed that." She turned her back on him and tried to remember where she'd put her largest ladle.

"You've got huge rings under your eyes and you're pale as soggy pasta. Are you sick? Or—" he narrowed his eyes for a moment "—are you and Josh having problems?"

"I can't say we are," Gina said tightly. The ladle was in a bottom drawer, she remembered suddenly. She found it and stood in time to see Rocco rolling his eyes.

"All right, tell Cousin Rocco. There's really something to the rumors I've heard, isn't there?" He folded his arms over his broad chest and waited.

"It depends what rumors you're talking about," Gina said wearily.

"The ones that say you haven't heard from Josh in a week and that he's not coming to his own birthday bash."

"He'll be there," Gina said woodenly, as if by rote.

"Who says?"

"I say."

"You really haven't heard from him?"

"Not since he left for San Francisco. I don't know what's happened."

"Did you leave a message on his cell phone?"

"A couple."

Rocco unfolded his arms, and his hands clenched at his sides. "Listen to me, Gina. If that guy hurts you again, if he upsets you in any way, I'll take care of him."

"You like him. He's your friend and Frankie's. Take the basket, Rocco. Let's go."

"To a party where the guest of honor may not even show?" Rocco muttered.

"He'll show. Stop giving me a rough time."

"Wait until you see the rough time me and the guys will give that miserable jerk if he makes any problem. Any problem whatsoever, Gina."

"He's not a jerk," Gina replied. Yet her confidence in Josh

was waning fast. Rocco picked up the basket and followed her down the stairs. He didn't speak all the way to Vineyard Oaks, and neither did she.

JOSH MANAGED TO CATCH SOME sleep during the flight to Rio Robles, and he shaved in the small lavatory on the plane before disembarking at the airport. When he got to his apartment, he realized that his birthday party had already started, but he took the time to change clothes anyway. Then he drove at breakneck speed to Vineyard Oaks.

So many cars! He recognized Gina's Galaxie parked right up close to the wine caves, and there was Maren's small coupe. The van with the Dede's Catering Service sign was parked beside it, and he spotted a red bike going hell-for-leather down the driveway, its rider pedaling head-down into the wind. The bike struck him as odd at this time, but he was intent on getting inside and seeing Gina again. He didn't know exactly how he was going to let her and the others know about the sweet deal he'd finally worked out with Starling. He'd have to trust his instincts about the proper moment to reveal the good news.

The door to the wine cave was open, and from within came the huffing of several accordions playing in concert. He paused in the doorway and took in the scene. The cave stretched back into a long tunnel lined with enormous wooden barrels stacked three high. It was cool inside, and the smell was earthy, pungent. Children were playing around the wine casks, and tables had been set up in a side room. The accordion band was arrayed along the side of the entry. Someone had strung up crepe-paper streamers in bright colors, and even from where he stood, he could see the huge birthday cake on its own table near the kitchen, which was built into the side of the tunnel.

He spotted Barbara chatting earnestly with Maren, and Rocco and some of the guys were huddled over by the gated portion where the more expensive vintages were stored. Despite the sprightly music, he sensed right away that people here were not in a strictly celebratory mood. In fact, Fredo was downright somber. He saw no sign of Gina.

Expectantly, he looked around, expecting her to appear suddenly and rush to his side, smelling pleasantly of lavender and herbs. Then perhaps she would beam her luminous smile and shyly kiss him on the cheek in front of everyone before they all trooped in to dinner.

Two women, aunts whose names he couldn't recall, stopped talking and stared. On their faces were expressions that didn't fit the occasion; in fact, they seemed disdainful. Rocco was advancing from the corner, flanked by several of the guys. He spotted Mia in a corner, her hands clasped beneath her chin and her mouth frozen into a startled O. And then he saw that even Maren was shooting daggers of disapproval at him from beside one of the wine kegs, where she had been comforting someone who looked up at that moment, her face pale and wan.

Gina.

A silence befell the wine cellar as the band stopped playing one by one in a discordance of wheezing accordions. Shelley, her mouth set in a grim line; Stacey, clinging to Barbara's side; and Frankie—but he didn't see Frankie anywhere.

Rocco's chin had a pugnacious tilt to it, and his stance when he jolted to a stop in front of Josh was threatening.

"So you finally decided to show up, did you?" Rocco's words fell into the cool air of the wine cave like heavy stones dropped from a great height.

"I couldn't help the delay. I just flew in from Boston. It's good to see you, Rocco, and everyone else." He kept his voice steady, though he couldn't avoid seeing Gina's face. It wasn't only her face that betrayed her misery, but the set of her shoulders and the dejected slope of her whole body.

"What happened—you decided to bug out of Gina's life

and then thought better of it?'' Rocco moved closer, looking even more belligerent.

"Bug out of...? No. No, Rocco, nothing like that."

"And you think you can show up a couple of hours late for your own party and we'll be glad to see you? You didn't even call to say you wouldn't be here."

He wasn't about to let Rocco get the best of him. "I had to stay in Boston. I was visiting Walter Emsing at Starling Industries." He glanced toward Fredo. "You recognize that name, Fredo."

Fredo nodded slowly. "Of course I do. I've been talking with his people almost every day."

"Then you know who he is and what he wants. Listen to me, Fredo. You don't have to sell the winery. I've found a way for you to get the money you need."

"What do you mean?" Fredo demanded, coming to stand beside Rocco. The others still had those suspicious expressions on their faces, but Josh couldn't do anything about that now. He'd rely on Fredo to do the explaining.

"I came here to work on an article about the wine industry, but I was also on a mission to check out possible wineries for one of our family businesses to acquire. When I first heard about Vineyard Oaks possibly being for sale, I picked up on it. I checked it out, saw it would be a good deal for Starling. Then I learned how your family operates this place. What it means to them. How devastating it would be if you lost Vineyard Oaks."

Gina stood, and as he watched, all the color seeped from her face. "How did you learn all that, Josh?" she said, her tone colder than ice. She advanced closer, seemingly unaware of everyone else in the room besides the two of them.

"From you," he said honestly. "You told me."

"I did. I'm sorry to say it, but I did. And now you've used the information to take this winery away from the Angelinis? After we've watered the vines with our own sweat, bathed them in our own tears, broken our own backs to make some of the best wines in the valley?'' Her tone was incredulous, her eyes full of sparks.

''No, Gina,'' he said levelly. ''Starling doesn't want to buy Vineyard Oaks. They want to participate in a silent partnership, send their executives here to learn more about the actual art of winemaking, and—well, there's a lot more to it.''

Fredo shouldered through the group of men and past Gina. ''This is true, Josh? We don't have to sell?''

''It's true. I'll set up a conference call with Walter Emsing tomorrow morning. He'll tell you what he has in mind.''

''We'll keep our jobs?'' This was one of the men with Rocco. Josh recognized him as David, the mentally challenged cousin who had never worked anywhere but in the family business.

''This is good. This is wonderful,'' Fredo said expansively. He flung his arms around Josh.

A hubbub ensued, and Josh found himself answering questions at a fast pace, doing his best to explain everything at once.

When it appeared that everyone understood, Josh was prepared to be borne away to his birthday feast. At the very least, he expected an appreciative peck on the cheek from Gina. He peered over the tops of heads, trying to locate her amid the milling group. He was gratified to see her pushing her way toward him.

He didn't expect her face to be fixed in a grim expression, her lips to be drawn into a tight line. The sea of people parted as she marched over and planted herself in front of him.

''Gina,'' he said, hoping to placate her, wanting to fix whatever was wrong. Shouldn't she be as grateful as everyone else? Shouldn't she be smiling, wishing him a happy birthday?

''How dare you?'' she said in a low tone, though he had

no doubt that everyone present could hear every word she said.

He stared at her. She was so beautiful that he wanted to sweep her into his arms and carry her off to her sweet-smelling boudoir. She was so lovely that it broke his heart to see her fury directed at him.

"You came here under false pretenses, insinuated yourself into my good graces and used Mia and Frankie to get around me when I resisted."

"That's not exactly how it happened," he told her, his eyes pleading with her not to make a big deal out of this. "I was here to research an article for Starling. The article was commissioned because of my father's association with Starling Industries, and when Walter Emsing, who is Dad's best friend, heard that I was writing the article for the company newsletter, he urged me to find out what I could. I was glad to report to Walter that Vineyard Oaks could be bought cheaply, but—"

"Nothing is ever cheap," Gina said. "Least of all me."

"One of the reasons I wanted to come here was to find you, Gina. I never thought you were cheap. You're the finest woman I've ever met—kind, clever, witty, smart."

"I'm certainly smart enough to know when I've been used. I left financial information lying around my house, confidential things that you could have read."

It was as if all the other people in the wine cave melted away, leaving the two of them alone together. His heart ached with the love he felt for her, that he had always felt for her. "I didn't look at anything that was private. I never meant to use you," he said heavily. "I know it may appear that way, but that wasn't ever my purpose."

"Oh, I disagree, Josh. I'm sure that's exactly what you had in mind."

"Doesn't it mean anything to you that I've found a way to save Vineyard Oaks for your family?"

"Not when your motive was something else entirely. It's all about trust, Josh. I was learning to trust you again, and now I can't."

He couldn't believe it when she turned her back on him and walked away.

"Gina," he began, but she whirled on him, two spots of color high on her cheekbones.

"Spare me. Get out of my life, Josh. Once and for all." She ripped the amber heart necklace from her neck and threw it at him. Josh caught it, stood staring down at it. The heart dimmed, receded, felt cold in his hand.

"Rocco?" he said. "Can't you talk to her?"

He thought he saw a softening of Rocco's expression, but perhaps he was mistaken. Rocco pointed at the door. "You heard what she said. You'd better leave."

Fredo was the only one who showed a positive reaction. "Come on, son. I'll walk you out, and you can tell me more about that conference call."

Josh and the older man moved down the row of silent Angelinis, who fell away before them. Josh's head was whirling with the unjustness of it all; he didn't think most of them understood that he had pulled a rabbit out of a hat on their behalf. He had performed magic.

When they emerged into the waning sunlight, Fredo cleared his throat. "Look, Josh, give it time. I'll explain to the family."

"And Gina?" He stuffed the amber heart deep into his pocket.

Fredo's eyes were kind, and he clapped Josh on the shoulder. "There's no use reasoning with her when she's in this mood. As for the future, who knows? Rocco and the boys seem to agree with her that you took unfair advantage. I ask myself, did you really? I answer no. I judge you by the results of your actions. All ends well if you have done what you say. My talk with Walter Emsing tomorrow will be most enlightening, I'm sure.''

They had reached the BMW, and Josh tried to take heart from Fredo's counsel. He preferred not to reveal all of Starling's plans for Vineyard Oaks, but he wanted to put the man's mind at ease. ''Walter will have suggestions about expanding the tasting room so as to bring in more tourists. He liked my idea of adding a gift shop. That way the winery will benefit from the sales. He thought that tours of the wine caves would bring people in. He suggested expanding crush to include paying guests, which would also be a good public relations tool.''

''All these things mean more employment,'' Fredo said. ''We haven't been able to do them before because we needed the money for operating expenses.''

''I know, Fredo. Now you'll have the money you need.'' By this time, they had spent fifteen minutes or so talking, and Josh wanted to get away. To go back to his apartment and lick his wounds in private. ''Fredo, about that conference call—be in your office at ten o'clock tomorrow morning. Walter will call, and I'll be on the line with you. After we've outlined the plan, I'll hang up, and you and Walter can attend to the details.''

''Good, Josh. Thank you again.''

Josh hesitated. ''Fredo, I haven't figured out what to do about Gina. If she won't talk with me, I can't convince her that I never had any ulterior motive as far as she is concerned.''

Fredo peered up at him. ''Is it serious between you, then?''

''Yes, Fredo. I was going to ask her to marry me tonight.''

''Marriage is a serious step.''

''That's why I want to marry Gina. She's the only woman in the world for me.''

Fredo studied him for a long moment. ''I see. You love her.''

"Yes. I love her."

"Perhaps it will work out, son."

"I hope so," Josh said fervently. He got into the car and started the engine.

"Oh, by the way, happy birthday," Fredo said as he backed out of his parking place.

Happy birthday? thought Josh. So far, this had turned out to be one of the unhappiest birthdays in his whole life.

Chapter Fifteen

Josh felt himself descending into a blue funk as he drove away from Vineyard Oaks. The scene in the wine cave had been surreal; all those people gathered to wish him well, and Rocco's surliness, and Gina's contempt. It wasn't what he'd expected, to say the least.

Twilight was descending rapidly, as it did in the valley. He wondered briefly if Judy Rae had returned from her daughter's in San Diego. He didn't want to see her now. He didn't want to see anyone.

As he rocketed around the curve near the water tower, he saw the shiny red bicycle that he recognized as Frankie's propped against a telephone pole, and he recalled seeing one like it racing toward the highway when he'd arrived at the winery. Something wasn't right about this bike being in this place at this time, and he eased his foot off the accelerator. Frankie hadn't been at the wine cave, and that alone was enough to set off alarms in his head.

Josh slammed the car to a stop on the shoulder of the road, scanning the rolling landscape for any sign of the boy. Nothing seemed amiss, and he considered driving away. But then a flutter of white caught his eye, and he looked up to see that it was a piece of fabric or paper hanging from the railing that edged the narrow metal catwalk circling the water tower overhead.

His heart swooped down to his toes and back up again
when he recognized the figure beside the white thing. The
figure was so high up that he couldn't distinguish any features, but he knew who it was, all right. Frankie.

He scrambled out of his car and began to run toward the
tower.

 AFTER JOSH AND FREDO LEFT the wine cave, Gina let her
mother lead her to the back of the kitchen, where she could
sit on a small stool and recover from the confrontation with
Josh. She would cry later, maybe even hate herself. But now
she was still angry, still horrified at how Josh had used her.

"I did the right thing. I know I did." Gina accepted the
cool towel that her mother handed her and blotted her face
with it.

"That's for you to decide," Maren said crisply. "If it were
me, I'd be inclined to wait and see."

"Don't you understand, Mother? It's not what he did for
the winery or our family. It's that he reentered my life under
false pretenses. Rocco thinks he dishonored me. I agree."

"Honor, dishonor, what of it? In Josh's mind he was helping. I'd think about that if I were you." Maren's ancestry
was Norwegian, not Italian. She didn't always agree with the
Angelinis' concept of honor.

Gina slammed the damp towel onto the counter and stood.
"All I want to think about is getting this party over with.
Let's eat." Although she knew full well that she couldn't eat
a bite. She was too shaky to eat anything. It felt as if there
was a huge gaping hole where her stomach should be, and in
her heart, she felt only pain. As for her soul, it would go on
weeping long after this day was finally over.

WHAT THE HELL WAS THAT KID doing up there?
Josh put his hands up to his mouth so that his words
wouldn't be whipped away in the wind. "Frankie! What's
going on?"

Frankie didn't answer. The white material flipped over, and Josh saw that it was printed with the words Happy Birthday, Josh. This barely had time to register before the wind caught the banner and Frankie lost his grip on it. It floated for a moment, crackled as it was whipped around by the wind, then plummeted to the ground a good distance away from where Josh was standing. Josh could only imagine with horror what would happen if Frankie fell; his chances of survival wouldn't be high.

"Frankie!" Josh yelled, moving closer. "Can you hear me?"

Frankie gripped the railing, freezing at the sound of Josh's voice. He looked scared to death.

"Frankie, don't move. Do you understand? Don't move!"

Frankie nodded, almost imperceptibly. He still clung to the railing, and Josh's heart almost stopped when Frankie sank to his knees.

"I said don't move!" Josh shouted. He had reached the ladder leading upward; his foot was on the first rung.

"I think I'm going to be sick," Frankie said.

Frankie, Josh remembered, got sick when he had to deal with heights. "That's okay, just don't let go of the railing," Josh told him.

As Josh began his climb, he was marginally aware of a minivan full of Girl Scouts stopping and the girls piling out of the vehicle. "I'll call for help," cried their leader, but Josh wasn't going to wait. He didn't trust Frankie, didn't know what the boy might do.

He reached the place where the first ladder ended and stopped for a moment to catch his breath before moving on to the second ladder. Frankie was now sitting on the catwalk above, and he'd let go of the railing.

"Grab hold of the railing," Josh hollered, and he started up the second ladder, climbing as fast as he could.

"No, I don't hate him," Gina said.

"Hate is a corrosive emotion," Maren said diplomatically. "I can't imagine hating anyone."

"My feelings about Josh are complicated," Gina said. "I suppose it will take a while to sort them out."

"You don't want to ruin your chances with him," Maren said.

"Oh, don't I? *He* ruined our chances of being together. *He* knew that trust was the main issue for me, that it wasn't easy for me to trust *him* after he booted me out of his life the first time—"

"Isn't that a little harsh, Gina? It was only a game."

"It started out that way. It became much more."

"Ah, Gina, maybe you have hit upon a key," Maren said.

Gina stared at her. "What are you talking about, Mother?"

"When Josh arrived in the valley, he may have been here for one reason—to investigate possible properties for Starling to buy. I think he changed, Gina. I believe that when he saw you again, when you began to trust him, his reason for coming here didn't seem as important anymore."

"You—you honestly believe that?" She had always trusted Maren's judgment, and over the years, her mother's advice had been right on target.

"Yes, Gina, I do. I believe you're on the wrong track here. And perhaps you'd better decide if you really want to send Josh away. I saw the love in his eyes tonight. It was unmistakable. Believe me, a man doesn't look at a woman that way unless he's crazy about her."

Gina was taken aback by this statement, but before she had a chance to reply, Mia came running into the room. "Aunt Gina, I've been looking all over for you. Aunt Liz's phone rang and it was her friend Sandy. She said that Frankie's up on the water tower and Josh is climbing up the ladder to get him. She said—"

"What?"

"Josh is going up to get him. Sandy was bringing her Girl

Scout troop back from a field trip and saw. She's there right now."

Gina ran into Barbara right outside the kitchen. "Is it true what Mia says?"

Barbara's forehead was knotted with worry. "I'm afraid so. Whatever has gotten into that Frankie?"

"Does Rocco know?"

"He and Shelley just left for the water tower."

Adrenaline kicked Gina into motion, that and a gut-wrenching fear. "I'm going, too," she said, running for the door. Numbness had replaced the pain in her heart, and her blood felt frozen in her veins.

"Can I go?" Mia wailed in her wake, but others shushed her.

Whatever had gotten into Frankie, indeed. Gina was willing to bet that it had something to do with his not being allowed to play in the accordion band. When Frankie acted out, it tended to be in a big way. This time, he had decided to do something really dangerous.

JOSH STARTED TO TALK soothingly to Frankie as soon as he was within talking distance.

"Easy, son," he said, taking the rungs a bit slower so as not to startle him. "I'll be there in a minute."

"I—I'm scared, Josh."

"I know. That's okay. Just relax."

"It's getting dark."

"We can climb down. Don't worry."

"I don't want to go down."

Josh reached for the edge of the catwalk, steadied himself before he pulled himself up on the platform beside Frankie. For the first time, he looked below. He didn't like heights much himself, and from this altitude everything was so tiny. Small minivan, small people surrounding it, another small car, a red-and-white Galaxie? Gina.

Josh couldn't afford to think about that now. He needed to

concentrate on Frankie, figure out how to get him down from here.

"I can't go down the ladder," Frankie said.

"You sure can. We don't have to go right away, though. We can sit here and talk for a while."

"The accordion band was playing without me, and I didn't like being there if I couldn't play. Mia made me hang the birthday banner on one of the wine casks, and it looked dumb. I figured I'd hang the banner up here on the water tower so you'd see it when you drove toward the winery. I figured you'd be here, Josh, no matter what they all said. Then, when I got up here, I dropped the tape. And the wind was stronger than I expected."

"I know. Are you warm enough?"

Frankie sniffed, and Josh realized that he'd been crying. "I'm warm," Frankie said.

"Anytime you decide you're not, you tell me. I'll give you my jacket."

"Okay."

"Let's talk about what we can do."

"You mean about getting down?"

"Right." Casually, Josh slid an arm around Frankie's shoulders. He didn't want to scare him even more, but he thought he needed to have a grip on the boy in case he did something stupid.

"I told you I can't get down. My dad's going to kill me."

"No, he won't. He'll be glad you got down safely."

"Are you going to get me down, Josh?"

"You're going to get yourself down. I'm going to help."

Frankie sniffed and seemed to consider this. "I'm not so sure it will work. I still feel sick."

Josh cast about for something to take Frankie's mind off his nausea. "You know, Frankie, I've been thinking about that mind reading you did at Mom's that night."

Frankie seemed surprised. "You have?"

"I certainly have. You knew I was thinking of an elephant

from Denmark. There was no way you could have known that.''

A smile crept over Frankie's woebegone features. "If you promise not to tell anyone, I could maybe fill you in on how I did it.''

"I might want to tell someone," Josh said.

"Well, you could tell a couple of people. I wasn't really reading your mind. A kid at school taught me how to do the trick one day at recess.''

Josh had suspected it was a trick; he hadn't put too much faith in the mind-reading process. "I'd like to learn how," he said.

Frankie relaxed slightly. "In the first place, the way it works is that no matter what numbers you choose and multiply and everything, the number you get at the end can only be four.''

"No kidding! That's cool.''

"Yeah, it's set up that way. Of course, if you're the one doing the trick, you've got to figure out a few things as the person comes up with the numbers so you can change what you say next when they tell you if it's a one- or two-digit number.''

"Hmm," Josh said.

"So I always know you're going to end up with the number four, and that has to be assigned a letter value, if you remember.''

"Yes, number one equals the letter *A,* and number two equals *B,* and so on. And you're telling me that because you know it's always going to be the number four, the person will always assign the letter *D?*''

"Uh-huh. Then most people think of Denmark when I tell them to think of a country that starts with the letter *D.*''

"I can't think of any other country that starts with that letter offhand," Josh said.

"Well, maybe Djibouti, but most people don't think of that

one. Then I told you to think of the second letter of the country's name.''

''Which, since I was thinking of Denmark, was *E*.''

''And then I told you to think of the name of a mammal that begins with the letter *E*. If there's a mammal other than an elephant that begins with *E*, I don't know what it is and I guess nobody else does, either. Then, of course, elephants are gray. The trick's never failed.''

Josh let out a long, low whistle. ''But, Frankie, that's not really a trick. It's mathematical. You said you have to figure the arithmetic out as you go along.''

''Yeah, kind of. It's not as hard as figuring out two to the seventh power, though.'' Frankie looked dejected.

''I'm going to tell your father exactly how you do that trick. He'll realize that you're not exactly a slouch in the mathematics department.''

''I never thought about it that way,'' Frankie said, brightening.

''I'll talk to him. You're a smart boy, Frankie. Hey, you know, I'm pretty good at math. I'd be glad to tutor you once in a while.''

''Would you? Oh, I'd like that!''

''Sure.''

They sat for a while longer. ''I'm feeling better now, Josh,'' Frankie said. Josh tightened his arm around him. He considered what he might do to get the boy down, and the horrible consequences if he didn't.

He made a conscious decision not to think about Gina until this was all over.

GINA BROKE AWAY FROM the huddle with Rocco, Shelley, Maren and Uncle Fredo to cast a worried glance up at the two huddled on the narrow catwalk far above the ground. Josh had given his jacket to Frankie. They seemed to be talking, but they were too high up for anyone to hear what they were saying. She was overwhelmed with fear that either or both of them might tumble to their deaths.

And if that happened, she would never have a chance to speak with Josh about his true intentions when he came to Rio Robles. She didn't know how she would be able to live with the heartache of having rejected him before hearing him explain.

"I've called the rescue squad," someone told Rocco. "They're coming from about forty miles away."

"They'll send a paramedic up with rigging to bring them both down," someone else said.

Rocco shouted this news to Josh and Frankie, who seemed to confer. "It's getting cold up here," Josh shouted back. "Frankie wants to climb down soon."

"Wait for the rescue team," Rocco called. "It won't be long."

"I don't want to wait, Pop. I might get sick again." Frankie was standing now, hanging on to Josh with one hand and the railing with the other.

Josh and Frankie had another conversation, then moved slowly toward the ladder. Everyone stood spellbound as Josh had a few more quiet words with Frankie.

"Maybe they should come down under their own steam," Rocco said. "I don't like the way the wind's picking up."

As Josh backed up to the ladder and placed his feet on the first rung, Gina pressed her fist to her lips, and beside her, she heard Shelley praying. Rocco reached for Gina's hand and gripped it.

"What are they doing?" asked one of the Girl Scouts.

"Shh," said another. "It's going to be all right."

Was it? Gina was not so sure.

EVEN THOUGH JOSH'S FIRST instinct was to wait for the rescue squad, he was aware that hypothermia was a definite danger now that the sun had sunk below the mountain crests in the west. By this time, too, Frankie seemed more confident of his ability to descend.

"You know, Frankie, my sister had a cat," Josh told the boy. "One time Fluffy ran up a tree in our backyard and was scared to come back down until we talked to her gently. Then Fluffy got herself down and went in the house for a big feast of salmon."

"It will take more than salmon to make me want to get down," Frankie said with a bit of his old spirit. "Maybe a Rocky Road sundae."

"You'll get that sundae, I promise," Josh told him. "And I'll talk to Rocco about tutoring you, like I said. If together we can bring your math grade up, I'm sure he'll let you play in the band."

Frankie squeezed Josh's hand. "Let's go, Josh. I'm ready."

Josh coached Frankie, warned him about descending too fast, cautioned him to hold on tightly to the ladder with both hands. He stayed close behind Frankie and kept him within the cage of his own arms as they slowly, rung by rung, began to climb down.

Down, down and down... Josh's legs ached with the strain of the descent, and he didn't dare reveal to Frankie how frightened he was that something would go wrong. Instead, he kept up an encouraging line of patter so that Frankie wouldn't panic.

And Frankie performed well, he'd have to say that for the kid. Now, if they could only reach the ground safely. At the moment, however, their chances seemed good.

"THEY'RE DOWN!"
Shelley said this as the rescue squad vehicles spun around the corner flashing their red-and-blue lights. Rocco set off at a run to reach the two, whose feet had just touched the ground. Josh had caught Frankie up in a big bear hug, holding

him tight. Rocco joined them, embracing both as if he would
never let them go.

All around, people were rejoicing. The Girl Scouts were
cheering. The rescue-squad people were applauding.

Gina hung back when everyone ran up to surround Josh
and Frankie. Surely Josh would never want to set eyes upon
her again after what she had said to him earlier.

Or would he?

If what Maren said was true, she owed Josh a chance to
explain, but not with everyone else around. She turned away
from the knot of people at the base of the water tower and
headed toward the shadows of the eucalyptus grove near the
road.

IT WAS TOO MUCH HOOPLA for Josh. After turning a tearful
Frankie over to his grateful father, and after several people
had thanked him for saving the boy's life, Josh stayed in the
background. When he heard that someone had called the local
television station and that a reporter was to arrive shortly with
a news crew in tow, he melted into the crowd and hurried
back to his car. The rawness in his heart had not abated; his
sense of loss was a cold hard lump in his throat.

The shadows of the eucalyptus grove where he'd left the
BMW were dark, and the car was unlocked. Wearily, he
opened the door and slid in, thinking to get away as quickly
as possible. A moment passed before he realized that someone was sitting in the passenger seat, and it startled him so
much that he dropped the keys on the floor.

"Josh," Gina said quietly.

Slowly, he straightened after picking up the keys. Her face
was shadowed, but he could tell that she was no longer angry.

"I saw your car drive up," he told her.

"I was there through most of it. You handled Frankie very
well."

"He was scared when he realized how high up he was,

that's all. He became nauseated looking down. He has trouble with heights. You told me that.''

"I don't understand what made him go up there."

Josh managed a dry chuckle. "He wanted to hang the birthday banner there so I'd see it when I drove past."

"He and Mia strung it across one of the wine barrels in the cave earlier."

"He figured that since I hadn't arrived yet, he had time to climb up the water tower and put it there, instead. Also, he was bummed out over not being in the accordion band. He didn't want to listen to them if he couldn't play with them, and he wanted out."

"Crazy kid," Gina said. "He's going to get some talking to from Rocco."

"And a Rocky Road sundae from me. I promised."

"Crazy kid, crazy guy."

Silence grew between them, a barrier. "I—I thought we needed to talk," Gina said.

"Gina—"

"What did you want to say to me earlier?" she asked.

He paused and inhaled a deep breath. "That I love you. That I would never hurt you. That almost from the first, I had misgivings about reporting to Starling Industries that Vineyard Oaks was in trouble."

"You love me?"

"So much that I would have moved heaven and earth to save your family's winery. As it was, I only had to convince the Starling CEO and the board of directors of my father's organization. It was only slightly less difficult."

She reached for his hand. "I apologize, Josh. I should have listened to you back there, I shouldn't have been so angry. At the time, all I could think was that you had betrayed me, that you'd wormed your way into my life for your own purposes. I didn't know," she began, and her voice broke.

"That I love you?"

She shook her head mutely, her eyes filling with tears.

He reached for her, drew her into his arms. Her head rested on his shoulder, comfortable and comforting.

"Another thing I didn't know," she murmured.

"What's that?"

"That I love you, Josh. When I saw you up on the tower with Frankie, I was terrified that you'd fall. I knew in those moments that I didn't want to live without you. Couldn't live without you."

He kissed her then. He had felt the same way when he was up there.

When his lips released hers, Gina moved away. "So when do you want to go to Boston?" she asked tremulously, her gaze locked on his face.

He brushed the tears from her face, kissed her cheeks. "You mean it? You'll go?"

"I have an idea that Boston's a nice place to visit, but I wouldn't want to live there," she said wryly.

Fresh in Josh's mind was the rain that had drenched him on his last visit, the gray skies, the cold. "That's more or less the way I feel about my hometown at present."

"You mean you'd consider moving elsewhere?" Her eyes had gone soft and gentle in the dim light.

"I most certainly would," he told her.

"Then," she said with the slightest suggestion of laughter, "perhaps we should go someplace where we can discuss this in private. I have quite a lot of my famous mussels and fettucine left over." Despite her light tone, she was shivering from the cold. She wasn't wearing a jacket.

He gathered her back into his arms, warming her with his body, and kissed her with great tenderness. "My place or yours?" he murmured close to her ear.

"Anywhere you like," she said. "Anywhere at all."

WHEN GINA AWOKE THE NEXT morning, her head was nestled in the hollow of Josh's shoulder and his face was buried in her hair. She remembered last night, the pure passion of their encounter, the pent-up emotion of their mating. Once inside Josh's apartment, she had very deliberately run her hands down his body from his shoulders to his waist to what lay below. She'd played the vixen, the enticer, the tease, until his eyes had flashed with the heat of desire, and then she had surrendered. In the following moments, they had really and truly become one. One person, one love, one life…together. And she knew that it would be like that again and again, every time they made love. Because that was the way she wanted it to be, no matter what.

Josh awoke and kissed her temple. "Good morning, Gina," he said.

She tucked herself in closer to his chest so that she could listen to his heart. It was beating firm and steady. "It *is* a good morning," she replied. "Oh, Josh, I love you so much."

"Words I've wanted to hear for so long," he said quietly, his voice a deep rumble vibrating beneath her cheek. "Words I was afraid I never would hear."

She cupped a hand around his face. "I wanted to tell you back at Dunsmoor. I was afraid, spooked by all the cameras rolling, worried about what it could mean."

"What does it mean?" he asked, turning so that he could look at her.

"Everything," she said in a low tone. "I want to be with you, even if I have to leave my family."

"Gina, I wouldn't make you do that. I love your family. I love *you*."

"You didn't look like you loved Rocco much yesterday when you were talking at the party." The scene was imprinted on her mind, and she regretted the part she'd played in it.

"It'll be okay between Rocco and me."

"Especially because of what you did for Frankie."

"Even if that hadn't happened, Rocco and I would be able to reach an understanding. Once he finds out that I want to marry you, he'll come around. I'm thinking of asking him to be best man.'' Josh disengaged himself and propped himself on his elbow so that he was gazing down at her.

''You—you're asking me to marry you?''

''I've loved you since you first walked down that long staircase at Dunsmoor Castle, Gina Angelini. Consider this a formal request for your hand in marriage. Will you marry me, my love?'' He smiled, kissed the tip of her nose, kissed her earlobe, kissed her chin.

''Yes, Joshua James Corbett the Third,'' Gina said, her heart expanding to take it all in. ''I will definitely marry you.''

Josh smiled. ''Good, because I want to spend the rest of my life with you. And your family, of course. Rocco, and Mia, and the Tonys, and Donna....''

She was laughing by this time.

''Now that it's settled,'' he said, ''what do you say we call someone? I'd like everyone in town to know we're engaged. Who shall it be? Your aunt Dede, or Uncle Fredo, or Rocco? I know I can count on whoever it is to spread the word, and by the time we emerge from this apartment, people will be lining up in the driveway to congratulate me on winning the heart of the most wonderful woman in the world.''

''I want to call my mother,'' Gina said. ''Without a doubt.'' She couldn't wait to tell Maren that her advice had been right on target.

''Fine, and then we'll phone my parents. They'll love you as much as I do. We'll go for a visit as soon as you can get away.''

''That'll be in a week or two. Did you really mean it when you said you didn't want me to leave my family?''

''I belong here in Rio Robles now, too, Gina. I want to live among Angelinis, celebrate holidays with Angelinis and raise a few little Angelinis of our own.''

''They'll be Corbetts.''

''Strictly speaking, yes. That's okay. There are lots of

members of your family who have different last names. But once an Angelini, always an Angelini. Correct?''

"Absolutely," she said. "I want to name our first child Joshua James Corbett the Fourth. Is that all right with you?"

"Whatever. What if it's a girl?"

"Her name will be Maren. After my mother. What's your mom's name?"

"Elizabeth."

"Maren Elizabeth Corbett."

Josh grinned. "I like it. No one could be a better mother-in-law than your mother is going to be."

"She's crazy about you. I need a phone." Gina sat up, bringing the sheet along with her.

Josh yanked the sheet away again. "Not so fast, dearest love. There are a few little things I'd rather do first."

Gina grabbed unsuccessfully for the sheet, and he caught her hand and drew her down on top of him. "Like what?" she murmured, knowing only too well what he had in mind.

"Like this," he said, demonstrating. "And this."

AFTERWARD, THEY SLEPT FOR a time, waking only when they heard someone hammering outside the window.

"What in the world?" Gina said sleepily.

"I'll see what it is," Josh said, getting out of bed. He pulled aside the heavy damask curtain. "Well, I'll be," he said. "Someone's hammering a For Sale sign into the grass of the front yard. Judy Rae must have decided to sell."

Gina reached for one of Josh's T-shirts and slid it over her head as she rushed to the window.

"She's mentioned going to live with her daughter several times," Josh said, pulling her close. "I'll bet that's what she's going to do. How would you like to live in this house, Gina? You and me and Timothy and maybe one of Frankie's puppies?"

"Timothy makes you sneeze, so he might have to live at the shop."

"Hey, the two of you are a package deal! I'll take allergy pills. They really work."

"This is my dream house," Gina said, recalling how many times she'd imagined living here. "It's the place where I always wanted to live."

"I'll make arrangements right away. Any other wishes you'd like me to fulfill?"

Gina's heart was overflowing with happiness. Overcome by emotion, she shook her head. She couldn't stop the tears of joy that threatened to spill down her cheeks.

Josh held up the amber heart necklace, which gleamed with golden promise in the light from the early-morning sunbeams pouring in the window. He slipped the chain over her head.

"You'll want this back," he said. "At least until I can buy you a ring."

"Oh, Josh, is this really and truly happening?"

"I hope so, or I'm going to be one disappointed guy." He laughed. "Now, weren't you going to make a phone call?" He handed her the phone.

Gina perched on the edge of an overstuffed armchair and dialed Maren's number. "Mother, you won't believe this," she began, and Josh went to get dressed.

Which was a good thing, because before Gina was even off the phone, the first in a long parade of relatives arrived to offer congratulations. And advice. And even an offer to cater their wedding reception.

Josh wasn't surprised. Why would he be? The quick-spreading news of their engagement was just another example—to be sure, a loving and heartwarming example—that the Angelini family grapevine, like the family winery, was alive and well.

When everyone had gone, when they were blissfully and completely alone again, Josh took Gina in his arms.

"Remember the *Mr. Moneybags* show, when everyone was leaving Dunsmoor Castle?" he asked.

She slid her arms up around his neck, gazing deep into his

eyes. "You looked at me as I got into the limo that was taking me to the airport."

"I'd just received a check for a million dollars," he began, but she put a finger across his lips to silence him.

"You and Tahoma," she said.

"Yes. We'd both received checks for a million dollars. But my eyes locked with yours before you disappeared into the car, and I knew that I'd made a terrible mistake."

"Even then?" she asked.

"Even then. I had a million dollars in my pocket, but I felt poor in all the ways that really count."

"What ways?" she murmured, kissing his neck, kissing his cheek, kissing ever so briefly his lips.

"I didn't have love. I didn't have you."

"So why didn't you come looking for me long before you did? Why did you wait two whole years? Two very long years?"

"I didn't know if you'd want me after I sent you away," he said seriously.

"I didn't think I did. Then you came along and swept me off my feet."

"And met your family, and became part of it."

"Will you ever get good at bocce?" she asked before kissing him again, longer this time.

"There's something else I'm really good at," he said, taking her hand and leading her toward the bed. "I'm going to show you what it is."

She pulled him down on top of her and gazed up at him. "Didn't you give me a demonstration of your abilities last night?"

"Yes, but there's more. In fact, there might be a few tricks you can show me."

"There might be," she agreed. "I can read minds, did you know that?" He had told her about Frankie's mind-reading trick.

"What am I thinking right now?"

"That you want me to do this, and this, and this," she said, smiling up at him.

And he did.

*Mrs. Gino Salvatore Angelini
requests the honor of your presence
at the marriage of her daughter
Gina Maren
to
Mr. Joshua James Corbett III
on Saturday, the fifth of March
Two thousand and five
at two o'clock in the afternoon
St. Vito Catholic Church
1963 Main Street
Rio Robles, California
Reception immediately following the ceremony
Vineyard Oaks Winery*

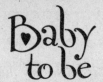
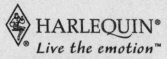

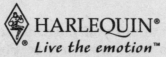